# OMAND'S CREEK

## DON MACDONALD

Cordova
Publishing Company

Cover design by Nick Venables
Author photo by Dario Ayala

Published by the Cordova Publishing Company
cordovapublishing@gmail.com

Please visit **donmacdonald.ca** to learn more and stay in touch.

ISBN: 978-1-7773629-0-4

Legal deposit - Bibliothèque et Archives nationales du Québec, 2020

First published in Canada November 2020

For Catherine, Julia, Alex and Barbara with love

# ONE

Michael Shelter climbed over the uneven terrain, eyes scanning the ground step by step. The embankment was steep, and the tall grass had been flattened into a pathway by something heavy. No shoe prints were visible — the ground was hard after ten days without rain.

He had been warned by a uniformed officer of what to expect, but the first glimpse of plastic and tape sent Shelter's heartbeat soaring and constricted his breathing. He stopped and pointed to it for his partner, Gabriel Traverse, before moving forward again.

Shelter lifted his Ray-Bans and bent at the waist to peer through the clear plastic tarp. He squinted to make out what he could of the body, laid face down as if somehow washed up by the creek. He closed his eyes and took a deep breath, struggling to bring himself under control from the surge of adrenaline. He sensed Traverse watching from a few metres away.

"You okay there?" Traverse asked.

Shelter straightened and gave a quick shake of the head without turning to face his partner. Traverse advanced, and together they studied the body in silence. Shelter flashed on the moment he had first seen Monica Spence's body sheathed in plastic a month earlier. He felt his jaw tighten as he thought about the grim visit to the girl's mother and returning home exhausted late that night, checking on his own teenage daughter sleeping safely in her room. He let his breath out in a long exhalation.

"Wrapped up just like Monica," Traverse said.

Shelter slapped at a mosquito drawing blood from his neck and turned to face Traverse. "Think I can't see that?" he demanded. Then in a calmer voice, "Sorry. You're right."

Traverse shrugged. "Let's see where it takes us."

Shelter squatted to examine the body again. She had shoulder-length black hair and copper-coloured skin. A red smear ran from her hairline to between her shoulder blades. Blue duct tape was wrapped tightly around the plastic at the shoulders, waist and ankles.

He looked up toward the banks of the narrow creek, lush with shrubs and scrubby trees in the early summer heat — a tiny piece of wilderness preserved in the midst of the city. "Ident is going to need to get a canopy up for the rain."

"What rain?" asked Traverse, looking up at the vast prairie sky.

"It'll be pouring by noon."

With a nod, he signalled to Traverse to climb back to the parking lot of Jay's, a low-rise, stucco steakhouse built above the creek in the fifties. In the restaurant parking lot, the major crimes truck had arrived. Officers were pulling on white overalls, booties and blue gloves. One officer had already begun taking pictures of the north end of the restaurant. Shelter saw the Ident unit sergeant give an exasperated shake of his head when he saw him and Traverse emerge from the bushes and duck under the yellow tape. Shelter knew they should have waited until the scene was secured before approaching the body, but curiosity had gotten the better of him.

He led Traverse to their unmarked Ford Crown Victoria sedan. He started the ignition and got the air-conditioning going. Outdoor crime scenes were the worst. Evidence lay exposed to the elements, vulnerable to contamination and the setting was detached from the context of day-to-day life a house provides. The wildness of the creek bank would make this one particularly bad. He'd had similar thoughts examining Monica Spence's plastic-encased corpse. She'd been pushed inside a culvert on a stretch of gravel road just inside the city limits, where a couple of small farms hung on, waiting to be bought out by suburban developers. The location on the east side of town was dozens of kilometres from Omand's Creek.

"Here they come," Traverse said, nodding toward an SUV that had just arrived on Portage Avenue. The driver opened the rear door and pulled out a tripod and TV camera. He began setting up his gear just outside the yellow tape. More media would be there in a few minutes. Shelter looked south toward a little park on the other side of the eight lanes of traffic of Portage Avenue. In the distance, he could see a small patch of forest where Omand's Creek broadened before emptying into the muddy, slow-moving Assiniboine River. He couldn't believe it was already early July, half of 2015 was already gone. The last weeks had passed in a blur.

He drummed his pad with his pen. "The guy's on Portage, looking for a place to dump the body. He pulls off, drives to the back of Jay's, opens the trunk and drags her down there."

"Or he comes down the back lane," Traverse said, pointing north.

"He's lucky to find a quiet place, or he's looked the spot over before he brought her here."

"Either way, we're a long way from where Monica was found."

A tap on Shelter's window startled him. It was his boss, Inspector Neil MacIsaac. His white dress shirt was tight across his beer gut under his tie and blue blazer. MacIsaac, bald and in his late forties, kept himself in a state of high anxiety and passed it along to his subordinates like an airborne virus.

"My guess is an Indigenous female," Shelter told MacIsaac after he and Traverse had exited the car. "She's naked." He paused a beat. "And wrapped in plastic secured with blue duct tape."

MacIsaac shut his eyes, bowed his head and touched his forehead with his fingertips. "Who found her?"

Traverse pointed to a woman who looked to be in her sixties seated in the back of a cruiser, clutching a panting Corgi. "She walks her dog every morning and sometimes lets him off the leash to chase squirrels by the creek. When the dog wouldn't come back to her, she went over to investigate and spotted the body. The command centre got the call at 8:29 a.m. The first cruiser arrived at 8:45."

MacIsaac surveyed the growing crowd of reporters and cameras. It would be on the national news at noon — another Indigenous woman killed in Winnipeg, more fodder for the media that put the city down as Canada's capital of racism.

No doubt, much would be made of the body being discovered below Jay's, one of the city's oldest and toniest restaurants. Shelter considered the place outrageously overpriced. Still, it was packed every day for business lunches, birthday celebrations and gossip sessions between matrons from the well-heeled neighbourhoods south of the Assiniboine. Winnipeg, dead centre in the middle of Canada, was built on plains scraped flat by retreating glaciers after the last Ice Age. The city was the butt of jokes for its clouds of hungry mosquitos in the summer and Siberian deep-freeze in the winter. But there was money here — old, discreet money from the grain trade, railways and the insurance business, the kind of money that likes low lighting, red banquettes and rib-eye steaks.

"What about witnesses?" MacIsaac asked.

"There's that apartment block," Shelter said, pointing to a building to his left. "But the view is obscured by trees. Nothing directly across, just the railway embankment. But, you know, we'll start canvassing the apartments. There are also those houses," he said, nodding toward a line of garages backing onto the parking lot.

MacIsaac nodded. "I've already had the chief on the phone. Let's not fuck this up."

Shelter glanced at Gabriel Traverse, slouched in the passenger seat with his hands folded on his stomach. They were heading downtown, five kilometres in a straight-line west on Portage Avenue. Shelter wished he'd kept in the kind of shape Traverse was in, but between work and caring for his daughter, trips to the gym and a healthy diet had gone out the window. Raised on a reserve on the west side of Lake Winnipeg, Traverse was in his mid-30s with jet-black hair that was shaved at the sides and spiked with gel on top. He wore a checked short-sleeve shirt and Levi's. Shelter wondered why his partner wasn't running through the details of the crime scene as he normally would at this point. He was silent, brooding. They'd been going day and night on the Monica Spence case, working dead-end leads until they'd slowly dwindled to nothing. In the last week, the grind had been made worse by the heat and humidity. Shelter had noticed Traverse's jokes taking on a nasty edge, and he slipped into silences more often.

"What's up?" Shelter asked.

"Nothing. I'm just sick of it."

"MacIsaac? Don't let him get to you."

"Nah, the whole thing. That woman."

Shelter looked at his partner. "You're tired. We all are." Shelter understood Traverse's frustration. He felt overwhelmed by it at times himself. So many Indigenous women murdered, their bodies found in a rundown apartment, on a riverbank or in some vacant lot. And each time it would start again: the media, the heartbroken family, the accusations they didn't work Indigenous cases as hard as white ones. What would it take to stop the cycle?

He steered the car into a parking garage beside a grim bunker known as the Public Safety Building, where chunks of the crumbling limestone façade routinely fell off, making it one of the most dangerous addresses in the city.

He tossed his briefcase on his desk in the squad room on the second floor and called the sergeant in charge of the crime scene. After a brief conversation, he hung up the phone and turned to Traverse. "Nothing so far from the scene. Until we get something from the medical examiner, I want to concentrate on seeing if there's any video, especially from buses on Portage." All city buses had video cameras pointed toward the street in front of them. "Let's see if there's a shot of a vehicle turning into that lot after Jay's closed."

Turning back to his desk, Shelter felt a knot of anxiety grow in his stomach. The murders seemed to be connected, and that suggested they might be dealing with a killer who was preying on Indigenous women, someone who would strike again. He knew, now more than ever, his every move would be under a microscope by higher-ups in the department, the media and Indigenous groups. Traverse was naturally self-assured, confident in his abilities and decisions. Shelter wasn't built like that. A doubt about how he'd handled some detail would sometimes bring him out of a deep sleep. Then he would lie awake, replaying his actions during the previous day and thinking about what the morning would bring. His wife, Christa, would reassure him that all the worrying and obsessing over details was what made him a good cop. "Gordy Taylor believes in you, Mike. And he's the chief of police," she'd said during a particularly difficult case when he was pulling sixteen-hour shifts. But she wasn't there to support him anymore — cancer had taken her the year before.

Now, he felt fear eating at his gut and realized it wasn't about how the bosses or the media were going to react. What if he'd missed something, made some mistake in the Spence investigation, and another young woman had paid for it with her life?

# TWO

Shelter and Traverse watched as Jonathan Frayne stooped over the woman's body and positioned a square of clear tape over her abdomen. He smoothed it onto the skin with his fingertips and pulled it away. He squinted at the sticky side of the tape and then placed it in a plastic folder before laying another square over a breast.

Earlier, he had cut the duct tape and gingerly opened the plastic shroud. He laid the surgical scissors on a tray, and they were taken away by a male assistant who moved silently and unacknowledged. Once Frayne rolled the body off the plastic, he'd examined both sides of the tarp closely.

Frayne looked at the two detectives standing outside the circle of light illuminating the examining table. "No bugs that I can see. No leaves or such. A black streak of something on the outside here." He pointed one gloved finger at the tarp. "Rubbed on a spare tire in a trunk, maybe, eh? Wrapped indoors, most likely. We'll see what we can find out about the floor she was laid on."

In his sixties, tall, with long, delicate fingers and a shiny bald head, Frayne had a habit of bending to bring his face close to the body, as if he were reading a book without his glasses. Despite his discomfort, Shelter found himself caught up in the cool professional ritual of examining, evidence collecting and recording. He took in every detail, even when the cutting began and Traverse's eyes went to the floor.

Shelter realized he'd already made a judgement the dead woman was a hooker who'd been killed by a john and dumped at Omand's

Creek. Sex workers made easy targets for sick, violent men, and the poverty stalking the Indigenous community led many girls and young women into the trade. Here, the scenario was even more likely, given the similarities to the Monica Spence murder. She'd been a prostitute in the West End. Shelter knew Traverse would have made the same calculation, even though it remained unspoken between them.

Still, the woman in front of him didn't match Shelter's idea of a streetwalker. There were no tattoos, needle marks or bruises that he could see. Her black hair was cropped shoulder-length and layered, an expensive styling job. The features were even. Frayne used a thumb and forefinger to open one of her eyes to reveal pinpoint bleeding in the whites. Her neck was encircled by an angry chocolate-coloured band where she'd been strangled.

When the autopsy was over — the woman's orifices swabbed, her pubic hair combed and plucked, her nails scraped and clipped and her stomach opened and the contents weighed and bagged for analysis — Frayne lowered his mask and spoke to the police officers as a professor would to students. There was a trace of a British accent.

"Quite a well-nourished young woman. She appears to be Indigenous, in her late twenties. The teeth are nice and even. I believe she wore braces to make them that way. And they've been very well taken care of. Hardly a trace of plaque."

He lightly touched the band of discoloured skin encircling her neck. With his left hand, he reached for a large magnifying glass from among his instruments.

"You see the ligature mark is even, and the angle does not rise at the back of the head in a tear-drop shape, as it would if she'd been hanged or strangled from behind by someone taller than her."

Frayne gently turned her head to the side. He indicated a deep gash near the crown of the head. "This is interesting. Here we have a small, depressed skull fracture of the type typically made by a hammer blow."

"Jason, if you please, we'll just turn the body on its side for the detectives to look at something." Frayne and the assistant rolled the body so that Shelter and Traverse could see her back.

"We have bruising here," Frayne said, pointing to a place between her shoulder blades. "I'm wondering if he might have put a knee there for extra leverage. The windpipe has been crushed. I would say it's likely this fellow hit her first from behind and then wrapped something around her neck — something quite wide, a belt perhaps — and pulled on it until she was dead."

"You know it was a man?" Shelter asked.

"No, of course not. A manner of speaking."

"Signs of sexual assault?"

"We'll have to wait for lab results, but not that I could see."

"Time of death?"

"A rather imprecise science, as you know, Detective. It's especially difficult when you have people driving bodies around in the back of cars. But last night some time, I'd say."

Frayne covered the body with a sheet, switched off the overhead light, and circled the table to stand in front of the detectives.

"We were obviously struck by the similarities with the Spence homicide," Shelter said. "The wrapping and the use of blue duct tape. Are we dealing with the same offender?"

"It would be quite a coincidence if we weren't, yeah?" Frayne said, the corners of his lips turning up in a slight, ironic smile. "We'll know more when the materials have been analyzed. But there are some significant differences."

"Like what?" Traverse asked.

"In Spence's case, there were scratches, cuts and bruises on her face, neck and hands. And second, she was throttled. In other words, there'd been a struggle, and her assailant used his hands to strangle her. And as you recall, we found fibres, pebbles and concrete chips and dust on the body. In the case of this woman, we don't see any signs of a struggle, and whoever killed her went to quite a lot of trouble to wash the body. We didn't see that kind of care with Spence."

Frayne removed his gloves with a snap and set them on a tray. He looked from Shelter to Traverse. "But it doesn't mean it's not the same person. Perhaps he's got a taste for it? Refining his technique."

When the detectives stepped outside, a storm had come and gone. The rain had cooled the city, and it was bathed in late afternoon sunshine. As Traverse waited for Shelter to pop the door lock on his side of the Crown Vic, he checked his messages. "We're still nowhere on identifying her," he said. "Ident came up empty on her fingerprints, and there's nothing from missing persons."

Driving away from the Health Sciences Centre, Shelter remembered the day Monica Spence was found. He'd gone with Traverse to a little bungalow on Langside Street, where her mother lived alone. He remembered it was a cool day, and Rose Spence wept quietly as Shelter told her what the police had found. When she'd put on her coat and was ready to leave for the morgue, she'd asked Shelter if he had children.

"A daughter. She's fifteen."

Rose Spence had taken one of his hands in both of hers. "I hope you never lose her."

Back at the office, Shelter retreated to his desk to make a call to his father-in-law's house in Gimli, an hour north of the city on the west side of Lake Winnipeg. As he dialled, Shelter thought of his daughter, her blond hair blowing in the cockpit of her grandfather's fishing boat. He was a commercial fisherman, and this was the third summer Kelsey had been helping him.

Joan and Sig Arnason had been a rock of support when Christa fell ill, and Shelter was trying to juggle visits to the hospital and hold down his job. There just wasn't time for Kelsey. They'd kept her in

Gimli during the summer months, bringing her down often to see Christa until it was over. And then Joan had come to Winnipeg to stay with them through the autumn and the dark, frigid months of the winter, helping him get Kelsey through the school year. He knew he couldn't ask her to do that again this year. How was he going to handle the needs of a fifteen-year-old by himself?

As always, his mother-in-law answered the telephone. Shelter knew it was her habit in the summer to go through sliding doors onto the deck while talking and look out over the vast, grey lake.

"Hello, Mike. How are you?"

"Not so bad, Joan."

"Sig and Kelsey are out fishing." She had a gravelly, low-pitched voice, even though she'd given up cigarettes years before.

Shelter pictured his father-in-law with his full head of white hair, his gloved hands gripping the steering wheel, Kelsey stationed beside him in the Plexiglas shelter at the rear of the boat. He was looking forward to getting out of the city and seeing her.

"I thought they might have stayed in today," he said. "It's been stormy down here. I hope they haven't gone too far."

"They'll be back soon."

Joan Arnason was keeping the tone light. Lake Winnipeg was shallow, like a saucer. Storms could whip up waves high enough to easily capsize a small boat.

"There can't be much fish this late in the season."

"No, less and less." Joan paused. "I wanted to talk to you about something. Kelsey has been asking about staying with us when school starts in the fall."

Shelter was shocked. Even though he'd been worried about taking care of her alone when she returned to the city in late August, he'd never considered the possibility she'd stay in Gimli. Where would she go to school? What about her friends in the city? And, more important: why didn't she want to be with him?

"We were surprised too," Joan said in response to the silence at the other end of the line.

"When did she come out with this?"

"The other day. We said we'd have to talk it over with you."

Shelter was reeling. Kelsey was going into grade ten, a critical time in her education. Shelter shook his head at the thought of her going to a small, rural high school far from her friends. "What's the high school like up there?"

"It has a good reputation," Joan said. "But let's not talk about the details now. I just wanted to warn you."

"I'll be there tomorrow. I'll talk to her then."

"Try not to worry."

He ended the call and sighed. Kelsey preferred to stay with two old people and go to a strange high school? He couldn't fathom it. Shelter had come to expect Kelsey to be cold and distant to him; it had been that way since Christa died. But he couldn't accept her moving away from him. He would need Joan's help in talking sense to her. He'd always had a warm relationship with his mother-in-law, whose caring nature made up for Sig Arnason's distant, aloof personality. Shelter had grown even closer to her over the months when Christa was in treatment and afterward.

Christa had collapsed one night in the kitchen, cleaning up after dinner, her muscles twitching and contracting. She'd even stopped breathing for a few terrifying seconds. Kneeling beside her, Shelter had been at a loss to know what to do. He could only hold her hand as Kelsey looked on in horror. When Christa came to, she was confused and suffering from a terrible headache. She'd wanted to go to bed, but the ambulance was already on its way. A brain scan the next day found a malignant tumour, and the cancer had already spread to other organs. Shelter had told her he should have made her go to the hospital when she'd complained of blurred vision and headaches, but Christa shook her head and hugged him. "It's nobody's fault, Mike." She was dead within a year.

Shelter stared out the window at rush-hour traffic flowing south on Main Street toward the intersection with Portage Avenue as he refocused his mind on the investigation. He needed to go over every detail of the Spence investigation, looking to fit them together with this latest murder to establish a connection or rule it out.

He realized Detective Jennifer Kane was calling to him from her desk. "The officer working the front desk says there's a woman who wants to talk to someone about the woman at Omand's Creek."

Shelter took the stairs down to the main floor and followed a long hall to a narrow rectangle of a room, where a uniformed officer sat behind Plexiglas. Beyond, three people sat in a public waiting area. Two Indigenous men were off to the side and, almost directly in front of the officer's station, sat an elderly white woman. She wore a pair of dark-framed, rectangular glasses. Her silver hair was cropped close to her small head. Her knees were drawn tightly together and her feet pulled under the steel chair.

"It's her," the duty officer said with a nod to the woman who sat clutching an umbrella across her lap. With just a small turn of the head, the woman could have watched Shelter and the officer talking, but she kept her eyes fixed on a spot on the wall in front of her.

"Her name's Violet Rempel," the officer said. "She says she might know your victim. She wants to talk to someone investigating it."

"What's the connection?" Shelter asked.

"No idea. She wouldn't say anything else. I tried. Believe me."

The lock on the door to the waiting area gave way with a loud click. "Ms. Rempel? I'm Detective Sergeant Michael Shelter. Will you come with me, please?"

Her dress was green, with a design of tiny white daisies. The neckline was high, and the hem ran below her knees. In the windowless interview room, Violet Rempel took a seat and placed her handbag and umbrella on the floor beside her.

"Now, Ms. Rempel, you told my colleague you know something about the woman who was found this morning?"

"Yes. I saw the news at noon, and right away I got ready to come up to Winnipeg."

"Come to Winnipeg?"

"My husband and I live in Steinbach."

Shelter knew the prosperous farming centre of Steinbach well. About sixty kilometres southeast of Winnipeg, it had been settled, beginning in the late 1800s, by successive waves of Mennonites, conservative Anabaptists who spoke the Plautdietsch or Low German dialect and been much persecuted in Europe and Russia.

"You drove in from Steinbach this afternoon?"

"It's about Crystal. She called me. She was very upset."

Shelter interrupted her. "Crystal? I'm sorry. I don't understand. What does this have to do with the woman at Omand's Creek?"

"She may be my daughter."

# THREE

Violet Rempel muffled a dry cough with her hand, reached for her handbag, undid the golden clasp, and rummaged until she found a handkerchief.

"Why do you think the woman we found is your daughter?" Shelter asked.

"Crystal telephoned me two days ago. She was very upset over the death of her birth mother. It was a terrible thing. She killed herself here in Winnipeg."

"Crystal is adopted?"

"Yes. We couldn't have children, and it was quite easy to adopt a Native child in those days."

"Ms. Rempel, could you tell me about this telephone call?"

"Crystal was very upset. She couldn't speak in a normal way, and she wouldn't answer my questions. She was crying, and she asked me something in Low German. We taught it to her when she was very young, but she doesn't use it anymore, not for years. She said, 'Help Nicki if anything happens to me.'"

"Who's Nicki?"

"Crystal's half-sister. We didn't raise her — Crystal's birth mother did. But Crystal feels a responsibility for her."

Shelter said, "And you heard on the radio about the woman we found?"

"Yes. I made something for dinner and called our neighbour to come be with my husband. He's not well."

"Crystal has been in trouble in Winnipeg?"

"Oh my goodness, no," she said. "Crystal finished second in her class at the law school at the University of Manitoba. There was an article about her in the *Free Press*."

Shelter was shocked. She wasn't at all who he thought she was. "Do you have a picture of her?"

She opened her purse and produced a large brown envelope. The image was in a cheap black frame. It had been taken in bright sunshine on what looked to be the back deck of a house. The young woman had been caught in a moment of high spirits. Her head was tilted back, and she was laughing about something, with her wide mouth open to show a set of perfectly even teeth. She was dressed in a pink T-shirt and cut-off jeans. Her black hair was cropped at the shoulders. Shelter had no doubt it was the same woman he'd seen on Jonathan Frayne's autopsy table that afternoon. He was careful to keep his face impassive as he examined the photo. But when he looked up, Rempel had closed her eyes and bowed her head. She raised a hand to her lips and said softly, "Oh dear."

"How old is Crystal, Ms. Rempel?"

She turned her head so that her chin touched her left shoulder and opened her eyes. "It's her. Isn't it?"

Shelter exhaled slowly. "Ms. Rempel, I'm sorry to inform you that your daughter may indeed be dead. We will need you to come to the Health Sciences Centre."

"To identify the body."

"Yes, ma'am. I'm sorry. Would you like to call your husband?"

"No. Thank you. His mind is gone."

Violet Rempel asked to use the bathroom after identifying her daughter's body. Shelter and Traverse waited for her, leaning against a wall as nurses and orderlies bustled up and down the corridor. Traverse turned his head and almost in a whisper said, "So, a lawyer."

Shelter glanced at his partner and gave a quick nod. He left unsaid how wrong they'd been in suspecting she was a prostitute.

Violet Rempel approached them, ready to be driven back to the station. She hadn't cried during the identification or the interview afterward. She sat with her hands folded and answered in that high-pitched voice, studying the face of Shelter or Traverse when one or the other asked something.

"You say Crystal was upset over the death of her birth mother," Shelter said. "She killed herself? When was this?"

"Quite recently, I think. Crystal had become close to her, but we weren't, of course. We would hear things from time to time from Crystal. It had been so many years of the drinking and drugs. We were just waiting for the day, really."

As the old woman spoke, a picture came to Shelter's mind of her in the first row of a church choir, singing hymns in a quavering soprano. "What was her birth mother's name?"

"Anne Alexander," she said. After a moment, she began again unprompted. "We were happy until Crystal started school. The other children were awful. You know how they can be? I'm sorry. What is your name again?"

"Detective Sergeant Michael Shelter, ma'am. Yes. I have a daughter. Children can be very cruel."

"Oh my, yes. Any little difference, especially the girls. And the school wouldn't do anything about it in those days. Not really. I tried, but it was always 'Kids will be kids.' And the parents were no better, filling the children's heads with all kinds of ideas about Natives." She looked down at her folded hands and added in a quieter tone, "We couldn't have known it would be like that for us, for her. We just wanted a baby."

As Shelter took notes, he thought about the girl growing up in the small Mennonite town. He searched his mind but couldn't think of a First Nations community in that part of southern Manitoba. She would have been alone. The old woman had gone silent. She ran a hand over the material of her dress to smooth a wrinkle that wasn't there. When she looked up, Shelter saw her eyes were light blue behind the lenses of her glasses. Although her skin was smooth, she was older than he'd first thought.

"We didn't know Anne until she contacted us when Crystal was still a little girl. She'd found out who we were somehow and started calling us — wanting Crystal back." Shelter wondered how Anne Alexander could have discovered who had adopted her baby. He put it down to a bureaucratic screw-up of some kind.

"She even showed up on our doorstep once with her Nicki in tow," Violet Rempel said. "She was crying and screaming. But we knew Crystal was better off with us."

"How did you know?" Traverse asked. "Maybe she needed to know her sister and birth mother." It was delivered in an even tone, but the challenge was unmistakable.

The woman reacted as if the statement was absurd. Her eyes narrowed, and for the first time Shelter heard steel in her voice.

"Just look at how she turned out."

It was close to nine by the time they'd finished interviewing Rempel. Crystal had been twenty-nine years old. She'd worked at an Indigenous centre called Anishinaabe Awakening in the city's North End. Her boyfriend, a man named Moses Kent, worked there too.

Rempel didn't know much about Kent. She'd given them Crystal's cellphone number and her address in the city centre near the legislature buildings. She also knew Nicki worked in the bar at the City Hotel.

The streets were quiet for a Friday night. Only a few other cars cruised downtown. As he steered the car across the midtown bridge, Shelter glanced down at the Assiniboine in the moonlight, gauging how much the clay-coloured water had gone down since the spring crest. The name *Winnipeg* came from the Cree word for murky water. The city had grown up around the confluence of the Assiniboine and Red rivers, a meeting place for Indigenous people for thousands of years. Now it was the bridges that were the essential transportation links in the city.

He glanced over at Traverse, who was playing with his phone. "What'd you make of that old lady?"

"The kid gets scooped and dropped into an alien place, cut off from her people, and this lady won't even let her mom see her."

"You don't know how it went down. The girl wouldn't have ended up there if she didn't need a home."

Traverse shrugged and looked at Shelter for the first time. "Question is what kind of home. They wanted a kid, and it was easy to get this one. That's what she said. Did they give one minute's thought to what it means to take a child away from her family, away from her community? I doubt it."

Traverse looked down at his phone and finished punching in what Shelter assumed would be his wife's number.

Shelter had seen so many Indigenous kids horribly abused and left to roam the streets untethered from any authority. It was hard for him to imagine how Crystal wouldn't be better off in a farming community with a middle-class family. But he knew so many of the Indigenous adoptions into white families from that period had gone horribly wrong — kids running away, falling into addiction, crime, mental illness and suicide. It was why they'd put a stop to it.

As Shelter drove, he listened to Traverse update his wife on his day. He was always texting or calling Janice. They'd been together since high school and now had three children, all under seven. They lived just outside the perimeter highway south of the city on a small piece of land, where they raised horses. Shelter knew the demands of the children, erratic hours at work and responsibility of keeping up the farm all weighed on Traverse, but his relationship with Janice seemed to keep him grounded.

Shelter and Christa hadn't had the same kind of relationship. He'd call her only if he was going to be working late. He didn't want her worrying any more than she already was. He was even more circumspect after he was shot by a teenager eight years earlier when he was still in uniform. He was covering the rear of a house in the Garden City neighbourhood, where an elderly couple had been taken hostage in a home invasion. The teenager came flying out the back door firing a .22-calibre rifle. Shelter took a round in the shoulder before his partner shot the kid dead on the deck. Shelter had been off work and in rehab for three months after the shooting. Christa took it as a blessing in disguise, having him home for that time. Afterward, he'd always said things were going smoothly, even when he'd just come off a job where he'd drawn his gun and broken down a door to make an arrest.

Traverse finished his call. "Monica Spence was raped and strangled with bare hands, wrapped up and dumped in a hurry. We know she was a hooker. Then you've got Crystal, a lawyer. Someone knocks her on the head from behind, puts a belt around her neck, and takes the time to wash the corpse."

"Maybe it's like Frayne said. He's getting better at what he's doing. The M.O. is just too similar to be an accident."

"If he picks up Crystal off the street, why would he take her indoors and spend time washing the body?"

Shelter shrugged. "Who knows? Each one is different. But we've got to get this guy off the street."

The City Hotel had been built in the fifties, with three storeys of rooms above the bar, restaurant and reception desk on the main floor. Shelter found a spot by the back fence of the parking lot. A rectangular sign over the bar's aluminum back door advertised cold beer. It was missing a shard of plastic from one corner where someone had probably thrown a beer bottle. A woman with a bloated face sat disoriented with her back to the grey cement wall beside a green dumpster. Shelter held the door open while he and Traverse considered the woman. She was bleeding from a cut over one eye. "You okay there?" Traverse asked. "That's enough partying for one night, eh? You got a friend to take care of you?"

"Go fuck yourself, man."

"Okay, then. You have a good one."

A hand-lettered sign on the door announced it was karaoke night, and the place was packed. Shelter was hit by the clamour of the crowd and sour odour of beer. Everyone at this end of the bar was standing. They formed a wide circle around two pool tables. In the centre stood a man wearing a nylon warm-up suit, two heavy gold chains around his neck and a Winnipeg Jets cap. He held a pool cue in both hands and was advancing on a thin man in jeans and a golf shirt.

Shelter said, "Ah, for Christ's sake. Here we go."

The man in the warm-up suit turned the cue half a revolution, gripping the thin end like a baseball bat. The other man took two steps backward and knocked over a table with his butt, sending glasses and beer bottles flying onto the carpet. The crowd edged forward and were now tightly packed, shouting, laughing and taunting the thin man. At the other end of the bar, a man at the karaoke machine was belting out a loud, off-key version of Rihanna's "Shut Up and Drive."

A woman called out, "Fuck him up, Rory."

Rory was short and stocky, and his neck and hands were covered in tattoos. He lunged and swung the pool cue in one motion, striking the other man's left hip with a crack. He went down hard and rolled toward the pool tables just as a second blow aimed at his head landed on the floor. The pool cue snapped in Rory's hands. A baseball cap had popped off the thin man's head, exposing ginger hair around a bald spot. He jumped up and tried to leap over a chair but caught a knee and went down hard. Rory kicked him hard in the gut.

"He's going to kill that guy," Shelter said. Traverse was already on his cellphone, calling for backup.

"Police!" Shelter shouted. He broke through the line of spectators. "Hey. Police. That's enough."

Rory, sweating and breathing hard, swung around and charged. He dropped a shoulder and crashed into Shelter, knocking him down and landing on top of him in a heap. Traverse jumped on Rory's back, put him in a headlock, and twisted hard. "Let go, now!"

Shelter managed to scramble out from under the young man and delivered a short, vicious punch to his left cheek. Together the detectives pinned him to the floor. They were all panting from the exertion. "Get off me," Rory roared and bucked. Shelter and Traverse rode him back to the filthy carpet. Shelter gave him a quick blow to the ribs with a knee that made him squeal in pain. Traverse looked into Shelter's eyes and gave him a disapproving shake of the head. Two uniformed officers shoved their way through the crowd and handcuffed the young man. The white guy had disappeared.

The uniforms each took an arm and pulled Rory up on to his knees and then to his feet. His warm-up jacket was ripped, revealing more tattoos on his chest. A drunken woman sitting at a table with her boyfriend called out, "Hey, that's police brutality." But her heart wasn't in it. A couple of patrons had already righted the table that was knocked down and put the beer bottles and glasses back on it.

Rory grinned at Shelter, who stood at least a head taller than him. He had a gold incisor, and blood was streaming from his nose. Shelter signalled with a shift of his eyes and a nod for the uniforms to escort Rory out of the bar. When they were gone, he led Traverse to a corner, where they could talk without being overheard.

"Not much of a goal-line stand there, partner. That dude ran you over," Traverse said in his usual deadpan delivery.

"Go fuck yourself," Shelter said with a smile. "You ever seen that guy before?"

"Yeah, of course," Traverse said. "Rory Sinclair, a.k.a. The Chief. Him and his crew have a rap album out. Native gangsta rap. Guns, hoes, drugs and fuck the police. Problem is Rory really is a gangster. He got popped for gun possession and dealing coke a year or so back. He beat it, but his buddy is doing a three-year bit in Stony Mountain."

"Good to know. Now, where's Nicki?" The bar was a long, stainless-steel counter where the waiters placed their rectangular trays and punched their orders into a screen. A large middle-aged woman was working hard behind the bar, setting up drinks. She opened doors set into the wall, pulling beer bottles from racks and lining them up on the bar. Then she positioned a glass under the draft tap and left it open, expertly pouring one after another, not missing a drop.

Behind the bartender, a large door swung open. A young woman emerged from the walk-in fridge and slammed the door shut with her foot. She was tall and slim, with her hair pulled into a high ponytail. Her jeans clung to her legs, and she had on a loose V-neck T-shirt and Nike running shoes. Everything from her hair to her clothes to her shoes was black. She picked up a tray from a shelf beside a glass washer and took her place at the bar beside a short waiter with a Fu Manchu moustache who kept up a constant conversation with the bartender as he loaded bottles, glasses of draft and a couple of shots onto his tray.

She said something to the Fu Manchu man and gave him a quick hip-check. He looked at her with a frown and then shook his head and broke into a smile. He gave her a push on the shoulder with an index finger. *Nicki*, Shelter thought.

# FOUR

Shelter held the door to the hotel restaurant for Nicki. She was almost as tall as Traverse, at least five foot nine, with broad shoulders. A waitress was wiping down surfaces and getting ready to close for the night. Nicki called out to her, "Hey, Deb." She led Shelter and Traverse through the empty restaurant to a corner booth.

Nicki looked from one detective to the other. "Okay, what's up? If this is about Rory, forget it. I don't know nothing about that guy except he's a dick and doesn't tip for shit."

"You weren't around for the fight," Shelter said.

"The waiters get off the floor. Fights are for the bouncer," Nicki said. Her voice was husky, low-pitched. "Of course, the bouncer was nowhere to be found. But that's not our problem."

Her skin was glowing and her dark almond eyes were blurry. She had a buzz on.

"What goes on in the cooler?"

"We chug-a-lug beer and talk to the vendor guy," she said, giving Shelter a quick, aggressive nod. "If we're lucky, we can get three bottles down before they come and get us. Now, what do you guys want? I gotta get back."

"Is Crystal Rempel your sister?" Traverse asked.

Nicki's eyes grew wide. She drew back in her chair and crossed her arms tight across her chest, looking at Shelter and then back to Traverse. "What about Crystal?"

"Is she your sister?" Traverse asked. Shelter sensed how much his partner dreaded what was to come.

"My half sister."

In a slow, formal way, Traverse said, "Nicki, we're very sorry to tell you we found Crystal Rempel's body this morning. We're treating it as a homicide."

After a beat, she whispered, "Oh, no," not taking her eyes off Traverse. "No. No!" And then silence.

Nicki chewed her lower lip, her skin flushed and brow furrowed. One large tear escaped and ran past her lips to her chin and then fell off. She lowered her head, cupped her face with her hands and sobbed.

After a time, she grabbed a wad of napkins from the dispenser and wiped her face. Her eyes were surrounded by smudged make-up.

"How?" she asked, not looking at the detectives but at the same spot on the wall.

"That's what we want to talk to you about," Shelter said.

"Where did you find her?"

"Omand's Creek, near Portage Avenue."

She looked at her hands. After a moment, she snapped her head up and glared at Shelter. "What the fuck. That's near the shopping mall, right? How was she killed?"

"We can't tell you that right now, Nicki," Traverse said, "because of the investigation."

"She was my big sister, for Christ's sake. Why can't you tell me?"

"It's the way we do it," Traverse said in a low, calm voice. "We need to keep the details quiet for now."

She gave a violent shake of her head.

"It's important we find who did this as quickly as possible," Shelter said. "The more time passes, the harder it gets. We need to ask you some questions."

"The harder it gets?" she snapped. "They're killing Indian girls all the time in this town, and you guys never catch anyone." She looked down at her hands on the tabletop again. "Let me guess, you've got Crystal down as a hooker. Well, she wasn't like that, okay?"

"We know she wasn't, Nicki," Shelter said.

"How do you know?" she demanded. "Wait. How do you even know it's Crystal?"

"Her mother identified her."

"Her mother? Our mother is dead."

"Mrs. Rempel."

"Oh my God, that bitch!"

Shelter glanced at Traverse. "Why do you say that?"

"Because she kept Crystal away from us. Crystal didn't even know about us until she was eight. She found a letter from our mom hidden in that woman's dresser." Nicki was staring at a spot between the two detectives. Her voice was soft now. "Mom begged her to give Crystal back. But she wouldn't even let us visit." Her lips trembled. "Mom even got someone to drive us to their house in the country. But that lady kept Crystal inside and wouldn't open the door. My mom stood on the porch screaming and begging for Crystal until the police came and took us away."

"Have you met Mrs. Rempel since then?" Shelter asked.

"Once, a few years ago. She came to Crystal's place but barely looked at me. She'd only talk to Crystal. Asking her all sorts of questions and ordering her around, even though Crystal was in university by then."

Nicki was crying again. "My mom had problems, okay? But she tried."

She wiped her eyes. Shelter asked, "When was the last time you spoke to Crystal?"

"Last night in the bar. She came by for a drink."

"What time was that?"

"About nine, I guess. I don't remember exactly."

"Was she with anyone?"

"No, she was sitting alone in my section. We were talking when I had a minute. She was texting and on her phone."

"What were you talking about?"

"She told me she'd broken up with her boyfriend."

"Who's her boyfriend?"

"Moses. Moses Kent. They work together in the North End. Legal advice and stuff like that. She said they'd had a fight and it was over."

"Did she say what the fight was about?"

"Not really. It was about their work. The way he was handling the organization."

"But she sounded upset?" Traverse asked.

"She'd been upset since my mom died. That's why I was surprised to see her."

"Surprised? Why?" Shelter asked.

"She just disappeared after my mom's funeral. I hadn't seen or heard from her for days. I was calling and texting her. But nothing."

"Where was she?"

"She wouldn't tell me. She said she had things to do."

"Do you know of anyone who would want to hurt Crystal? Enemies?"

"Enemies? People fucking loved her, man."

"What time did she leave?"

"Around ten thirty, I guess." She shook her head. "I've got to get out of here."

Shelter nodded. "But I need you to look at a picture before you go." He opened a file folder and brought out a picture of Monica Spence. "Did you ever see this girl with Crystal?"

"I've seen that picture in the paper. But I've never seen her in person. Why?"

"Did Crystal ever talk about Monica Spence?"

Her eyes opened wide in surprise. "You think the same guy killed Crystal?"

Shelter shook his head. "We're just checking." He glanced at Traverse and nodded to signal an end to the interview. Shelter took her phone number and address. "We'll be in touch," he said. "Nicki, we're very sorry."

She wiped her eyes and stood to leave. "When I find the motherfucker, I'm going to kill him."

"No, you're not," Traverse said. "You're going to leave it to us."

"You guys aren't going to do shit."

"Stay out of it."

"Don't tell me what to do. No one tells me what to do." She had a hand on a hip and glared at Traverse with her chin out.

Something occurred to Shelter that he hoped would defuse the situation. "What kind of car did Crystal drive?"

She turned toward Shelter with the same fierce expression. It took her a second to refocus her thoughts on the question. And when she answered, it was in a quieter voice. "It's small and blue. I'm not good on cars."

"Could we go out to the parking lot for a sec?"

She found the car by the light of a single high streetlight. It was an old Toyota Corolla parked two spots away from the detectives' Crown Vic.

"This is it." After a beat, she said, "This is where she could have been taken."

Ignoring the comment, Shelter glanced inside the car before turning to Nicki. "Thank you for this. It's important." He paused. "You need a ride home?"

"Nah, I got my bike." She left without another word.

The two detectives headed back into the bar. Traverse knew the bartender from his days in uniform. Shelter watched from near the door as he drew her away from the bar and told her about Nicki's sister. The bartender touched two fingers to her lips. Traverse put a hand on her shoulder and bent his head close to her ear. They whispered for a few moments.

Traverse returned to stand beside Shelter, and the two detectives surveyed the bar. "She saw Crystal come in, but it was busy and she sat on the other side of the pool tables, out of her line of sight."

He added, "That woman's got a big love on for Nicki. She talked to me like she was her mom. I would say she's scared for her, the way she was talking."

"Scared? Why?"

"I don't know. It was a feeling I got."

"I don't know what Nicki's doing, working in a dump like this," Shelter said.

"Come on, Mike. You think it's easy to find a job out here? She's doing okay."

Shelter thought about that. "Someone picked up Crystal here last night. We'll have to talk to everyone in the bar. Let's find out if they've got video cameras and get the car towed."

Shelter lived in the tree-lined Wolseley neighbourhood. Just before Kelsey was born, he and Christa had bought a big clapboard house a couple blocks up from the river. On Sundays in the summer, the city closed both Wolseley Avenue and Wellington Crescent on the other side of the river to cars. Christa, Kelsey and he would pedal their bikes all the way to the little pedestrian bridge over Omand's Creek and another longer one hugging the railway bridge over the Assiniboine. The route brought them to Wellington Crescent, with its mansions and central boulevard. From there, they'd make their way to his mother's house on Oak Street for Sunday dinner.

Shelter's father had clawed his way to regional vice president for a big Toronto insurance company before he keeled over in his office from a heart attack at sixty-five. His grandfather had prospered in insurance, and there was an unspoken expectation Shelter would follow them into the business or something similar — a lawyer, actuary or accountant. But Shelter knew from the time he was in junior high school he didn't want to be stuck in an office job like his father, stressed out from nine to five in a glassed-in tomb with weekends at the golf course or the Bison Club. It was his father's friend, Gordy Taylor, who first sparked in him the idea of going into the police service. Taylor and his father had been fraternity brothers at university, and every fall they went up to Riverton with some cronies to shoot ducks and get drunk in motel rooms. Taylor was an expert shot, and he also liked to hunt deer and moose, but Shelter's father wasn't into big game. "All the blood and guts," he'd say. "Cleaning a duck is as much as I can stomach."

Taylor was an inspector in the police department back then, a man who'd already seen a lifetime of action on Winnipeg's streets and up north on First Nations reserves as an RCMP officer before that. Now, he was chief of police. When Shelter announced after finishing his arts degree that he wanted to go into the department, his father and grandfather had teamed up to try to talk him out of it over dessert one Sunday night. But it was no use. His mind was made up, and there was nothing they could do to change it. So he wrote traffic tickets in a uniform while his friends were studying for a law degree, MBA or PhD. Taylor took an interest in his progress and mentored him in his early years. He'd taken Shelter to lunch every couple of months to give him advice and worked behind the scenes to move him up the ranks.

Traverse dropped Shelter off near midnight. Letting himself into the dark, silent house, he was greeted by Norman, a fat grey-and-white cat, who rubbed against his legs and purred an urgent demand for food. Shelter still wasn't used to the idea that Christa wasn't upstairs sleeping, that her warm body wouldn't be there beside him when he crawled into bed, dead tired on a night like this.

He foraged in the fridge, but there wasn't much. He ate a chunk of cheese with some crackers and washed it down with a glass of

Cabernet Sauvignon left over from the night before. Almost asleep on his feet, he dragged himself up the stairs to the big bedroom on the second floor, barely managing to brush his teeth and strip down to his underwear before exhaustion dragged him down to the depths.

# FIVE

Shelter woke up in the damp, cool basement where he'd taken refuge in the middle of the night. He refused to invest in air conditioning for the few weeks of the year that heat and humidity blanketed the city. But when those weeks came, the master bedroom on the second floor was stifling.

His ribs ached, and his right hip was stiff from Rory Sinclair's tackle. He hobbled to the kitchen and fed the purring, insistent cat, made coffee and toast, and retrieved the newspaper from the front stairs. He took a step back into the gloom of the enclosed porch and kicked the door closed. The main headline read: *Police Fear Serial Killer Stalking City.* It ran across the top of a photo shot at long distance of Crystal Rempel's body being rolled to the medical examiner's truck the morning before. A smaller photo was set into the main image. It showed Shelter and Traverse conferring with MacIsaac at the scene and gave their names in the caption below the shot. Another inset photo was of Monica Spence. Under the photos, a secondary headline read: *Woman found strangled at Omand's Creek.*

"Je-sus," Shelter whispered.

He scanned the story and saw that the reporter didn't have much beyond what the department had released: Crystal Lynn Rempel's name, her age and where she was found. Whoever leaked details of the investigation at least had the sense not to describe how she'd been strangled or how the body had been wrapped. Still, the story linked the murders of the two Indigenous women and said the police were worried about more to come. Shelter went over in his mind who in the homicide unit would have talked to the reporter. But it could have been any one of dozens of people in the police department who'd even heard gossip about the Rempel killing.

The regular team meeting was at 8:00 a.m. Shelter still had ten minutes before he had to leave the house. He called his father-in-law's house in Gimli. He knew the household would be awake and preparing for the day's fishing.

Kelsey answered on the second ring.

"Good morning, Kel."

"Hey." There was no warmth in her greeting.

"Sorry I didn't call last night. I'm working on a case, and things went late. Fishing today?"

"Fishing everyday. It's like milking cows."

Shelter could hear his father-in-law in his daughter's fifteen-year-old voice. He'd heard that line at least a dozen times over the years. Commercial fishing on Lake Winnipeg was done with gill nets. The nets were set one day and had to be emptied the next, or else the fish went bad.

"We're going out in a little while," Kelsey said. "The season closes on Monday."

"Grandma told me you want to stay up there when the summer ends."

"Yup. I'm staying."

Shelter felt his pulse quicken, annoyed she was presenting it to him as a fait accompli with no possibility of discussion, but he knew this wasn't the time to get into it with her.

"Let's talk about it tonight. Tell your grandma and grandpa I'll hopefully be there around six. If there's a change of plans, I'll call."

"Yeah, okay." The line went dead.

The six homicide detectives rolled their chairs into a circle. Shelter nodded to Traverse and took his seat moments before Inspector

Neil MacIsaac entered the room with a copy of the newspaper in his hand. He was perspiring heavily, even though air conditioning had the office at a comfortable temperature for everyone else.

He held up the front page. "Whoever did this is jeopardizing two murder investigations," said MacIsaac, glowering at one detective after another. "The chief takes this very fucking seriously. There will be no mercy when we find out who it was." He turned on his heel and stalked out of the room.

Shelter waited while MacIsaac's words sank in. "Okay. Let's get started," he said. "We have preliminary autopsy results, but nothing yet from the crime lab. As you know, the victim is Crystal Lynn Rempel, aged twenty-nine, residing at twelve Edmonton Street, suite fourteen. She graduated from law school three years ago and was working at a North End activist organization called Anishinaabe Awakening. Her ex-boyfriend, Moses Kent, is the executive director. She was killed at an unknown location, washed, wrapped in a plastic tarp and driven to Jay's parking lot. Blow to the head, likely a hammer. Cause of death: strangulation, possibly with a belt. Time of death: sometime late Thursday or early Friday." Shelter looked at his notebook. "As of now, she was last seen in the bar of the City Hotel on Thursday night. Gabe and I talked to her half sister, Nicki Alexander. She's a barmaid there and says Crystal came in at about nine and was sitting alone, texting and talking on her phone. She left around ten thirty. As of now, we've got no witnesses or video after that."

He glanced at his notebook. "We found Crystal's car in the parking lot, so it looks like she was picked up. Two other notable things. According to Nicki, Crystal had disappeared for a few days before she showed up at the bar. And she'd recently broken up with Moses Kent."

"What do we know about the boyfriend?" asked Jennifer Kane, knowing where obvious suspicion would fall.

"His father, Daniel, was the grand chief of the southern Manitoba chiefs in the early nineties. Moses graduated from U. of M. law school the same year as Crystal and got his call to the bar. He's twenty-eight."

Shelter turned to Himmat Sharma. "What else we got?"

Sharma looked more like an accountant than a police officer in his pressed, button-down shirt, striped tie and thick glasses. He was a dogged detective, but his true passion was the Winnipeg Jets. His family had immigrated from India when he was a little boy, and he'd taken to hockey with even more passion than his Canadian schoolmates. Now, he followed the Jets obsessively, even through the summer doldrums, listening to sports talk radio and speculating with other fans in the office on trades and minor league players who could make the difference next season.

"We canvassed the apartment block and nearby houses," Sharma said. "Nothing. Jay's doesn't have a camera on the parking lot."

"What have we got from her cellphone records?"

"They're coming in this morning. I spent most of the day looking at video from buses going up and down Portage Avenue. Still haven't found a car pulling into that lot."

Shelter nodded and picked up his notebook. "Okay, let's keep at it. Gabe and I will see what Moses has to say for himself."

It wasn't hard to track down Moses Kent. A Google search turned up a long list of entries, including his blog, a Twitter feed, Facebook page and a professional profile on LinkedIn.

According to its website, Anishinaabe Awakening "defended the rights of the seventy-five thousand Indigenous people living in Winnipeg." Shelter opened a *Winnipeg Free Press* article. A photo showed Kent and Crystal Rempel leading a march of a few hundred people down Memorial Boulevard. The marchers carried a long banner that said in crimson letters: *Justice and respect — Now!* Shelter scanned Kent's blog. He wrote often on subjects such as treaty rights, the huge number of First Nations children taken into care and the need for a commission of inquiry into the more than one thousand Indigenous women who had gone missing or been murdered over the last thirty years in Canada, many of them in Manitoba.

Shelter found a phone number for Anishinaabe Awakening.

"Been waiting for your call," Kent said after Shelter had introduced himself.

"Mr. Kent, we need to meet with you to discuss Crystal. Can you come downtown and see us?"

"I'd prefer to meet at my office, if that's alright with you." The tone was courteous. Kent gave an address on Selkirk Avenue, the North End's main drag, and said he'd be there at 11:00 a.m.

Shelter steered the car onto Main Street with Traverse in the passenger seat, sipping on a cup of coffee. They drove through a crumbling underpass beneath the Canadian Pacific railway's main line and emerged in the North End. They passed skid row hotels, pawnshops and vacant lots.

"You know this guy?" Shelter asked Traverse.

Traverse turned his head slowly toward his partner. "Like, personally? You think we all know each other?"

Shelter smiled. "You fully caffeinated yet?"

"Not even close, my friend."

After a moment, Shelter said, "I'm heading up to Gimli later on to see Kelsey."

Traverse nodded but remained silent. Shelter thought he detected disapproval. "I'll be back early tomorrow. You can hold the fort till then."

"You don't need my permission to go see your daughter." Shelter glanced at his partner but decided to let it go. Traverse's silence had said it all. It was crucial hours in the investigation, but he needed to sort out what was going to happen to Kelsey in the fall.

Shelter's cellphone rang just as he turned onto Selkirk Avenue. The call was from Sergeant Richard Slawsky, the officer in charge of the Ident unit. Shelter pulled to the curb to take the call. "We're at Crystal Rempel's apartment on Edmonton Street," Slawsky said. "Someone beat us here. The place has been ransacked. Drawers dumped and clothes pulled out of closets."

"What do the doors look like?"

"No forced entry. There's an outdoor staircase that leads from a parking lot to the back door. It was unlocked. Looks like our visitor had a key."

"And was anxious to find something," Shelter said, glancing over to Traverse and giving him a nod.

"You got it."

"I'll get some uniforms over there to canvass the area."

The building housing Anishinaabe Awakening looked to have been a pharmacy or a small department store at one time. It had large display windows on either side of a glass door. Kent was seated at a battered desk positioned for a receptionist. When he stood to shake hands, Shelter saw he was tall, dressed in jeans and a navy-blue golf shirt. He wore his hair in a long plait, and Shelter caught a subtle whiff of aftershave. Kent's handshake was firm, and he kept steady eye contact through the introductions.

Along the walls on either side of the building, dividers had been set up to create offices. He led them to the back of the building, where he had the only enclosed office. When they were seated, Shelter told Kent they were investigating the murder of Crystal Rempel and asked him how long they'd known each other and what their relationship was. As he replied, Shelter studied him closely for signs of nervousness.

"We met in law school and started going out something like four years ago. We lived together for almost a year."

His voice was even and his breathing shallow and steady. No sign either way of whether they were dealing with a distraught ex-boyfriend or a brutal killer.

"When was the last time you saw her?"

"I hadn't seen her in a couple of weeks, at least. We weren't together anymore. I took my stuff and moved out, and that was it."

"Out of the Edmonton Street apartment?" Traverse asked.

When Kent nodded, Shelter followed up. "And why did you break up?"

"Once I've told you I hadn't seen her in two weeks, I'm not sure why that's relevant."

"We'll decide what's relevant," Traverse said. "Why did you break up?"

"And if I said it's none of your damn business. What would you say then?"

"We'd say you had something to hide."

After a pause, Kent said, "What community you from, Detective Traverse?" He said it with a smile, but his eyes were serious.

"We're talking about Crystal Rempel. Not my background."

"It's all about our background, brother."

"Why did you break up with Crystal?" Shelter asked.

"She was committed to the work we do in this office, providing legal advice to people and fighting to change what's wrong with the system. We also do organizing to celebrate all the good that's happening here. Help people reconnect to their identity and share their gifts with the world. That's why it was so hard when Crystal started to change."

"Change how?" Traverse asked.

"She just became really angry about everything — the gangbangers, dealers, pimps. She pulled back from me, and not just me — everybody around her. She didn't want to see me anymore, and I couldn't get her to talk." He paused and shook his head. "And on top of it all, her mother commits suicide."

"When was that?"

"Recently. Anne was living in a shitty apartment block, and Crystal had to get the caretaker to open the door. She was in the bathtub in cold red water. Slashed her wrists."

Shelter nodded and waited before asking, "But she was already upset before that happened. Why? Was it connected to some event? What did she tell you?"

"Not a lot. That's why it was so hard to understand. Something was bothering her, but she wouldn't share it with me."

Shelter was again struck by what seemed to be a lack of emotion in Kent's demeanour. People grieved in different ways, and it wasn't unusual for men especially to shut down emotionally in the face of such a loss. Or perhaps it was the mask he'd chosen to put on for this conversation.

"Where were you on Thursday night?"

Kent chuckled. "Always the boyfriend, right?"

"You're a lawyer, Moses. You know we need to eliminate you from our investigation."

"I was at home watching the football game on TV. The Bombers lost to Saskatchewan, and then I went to bed. I was interviewing somebody for a job the next morning, and I wanted to be fresh."

"Were you with anyone?"

"No. I live alone now."

"Do you have any ideas about who could have done this to Crystal?" Shelter asked. "Did she have enemies?"

"If you don't fight, nothing is going to change in this world, and that causes friction, okay? But if you want a name of someone who would kill Crystal, I can't help you."

"Her adoptive mother, Violet Rempel, said something or someone was scaring her. Do you know anything about that?"

Kent shook his head.

"Why wouldn't she have come to us if she was worried about her safety?"

Kent shook his head again and let out a harsh laugh. "No offence, but she didn't have a great opinion of the Winnipeg police. She would have wanted to handle it herself. That was her nature."

Shelter considered this. "Did Crystal know Monica Spence?"

"Not any more than what's been in the media, as far as I know."

They got up to leave. "If we need to talk to you again?" Traverse asked.

"Tomorrow, you can find me at city hall. We're going to march on the place."

"What march?"

"To honour Crystal and Monica and all the other girls and women we've lost. And to put this city on notice that we want justice and change, and we're going to get it."

# SIX

Shelter had his sunglasses on, the windows down, and the radio tuned to an FM rock station. Highway 8 cut straight north to the west side of Lake Winnipeg through farmland that slowly transitioned from fields of golden wheat and lemony canola to scrubby bush. He'd be in Gimli in an hour.

It had been two weeks since Shelter was up to see Kelsey. He knew fifteen was a difficult age, but it wasn't helping to have her so far away from him, and he didn't like the idea of her staying in Gimli when the new school year started. He feared becoming like those divorced fathers who only saw their daughter once every couple of weekends, and he knew Christa wouldn't have wanted that either. But could he take care of her with the crazy hours of this job? It wasn't just the practical considerations like feeding her and getting her to school; it was also the fights over everything from her clothes to the late hours she kept. Christa had always known how to smooth things between them, what it took to soothe hurt feelings, find a compromise. Without her, arguments flared over the slightest disagreement.

"Dammit!" he said out loud, banging a hand on the steering wheel when he realized he'd been ruminating on the problem for the whole trip. He made a conscious effort to break the loop by concentrating on the passing countryside, picking out details like a collapsing barn, waterfowl in a pond and stands of trees until he was in sight of the turn-off for Gimli.

He pulled off the highway and headed toward the little town with its familiar grid of streets hugging Lake Winnipeg. Shelter caught site of the banquet hall where he'd met Christa when he was nineteen. He'd come up from Winnipeg with a gang of his buddies for a dance, and they'd ended up in a brawl with some local boys. It didn't come to much, but his white T-shirt was ripped and smeared with blood from someone's nose. When he'd gone to the parking lot to grab a shirt from the car, he'd passed three girls standing in a circle.

"Going home so early?" one of them had called out to him. He turned around and picked her out right away. Her white-blond hair was illuminated by a streetlight, and she wore a halter top, tight jeans and sandals. He'd turned and sauntered back. He kept his eyes on her and said, "I just got to change my shirt. I'll be back. You'll be around?"

Her friends giggled and hooted, but Christa ignored them. "Yeah, I'll protect you from those idiots." Shelter had laughed and nodded. He noticed her glance down to where his ripped shirt exposed half of his chest. "Okay, sounds like a deal." She was still standing there with a friend when he came back from the car.

They danced together all night and afterward walked to the beach, where they kissed under a dome of stars. They were together through the summer: the Winnipeg Folk Festival, a canoe trip and lots of nights in his apartment in Winnipeg. When it was time to go back to university, she moved in with him.

Gimli's main drag led to a long cement jetty in the shape of a J that created a harbour for pleasure boats and the commercial fishing fleet. To the left was the long municipal beach where he'd taken Christa all those years before. He made a turn on the last street before the lake and drove to the northern edge of town. Pulling into the dirt driveway of his in-laws' white bungalow, he tooted his horn. It was just after 6:00 p.m., and the sun was still high — the long days were one of the best things about the early summer.

When she was a little girl, Kelsey used to run to the car when he arrived. Those days were over. She waited inside the screen door and had to be shooed forward by her grandmother.

"Hello, Kel." Shelter put his arms around her and gave her a kiss that landed on her forehead near her hairline. She squirmed away, not answering.

Joan Arnason watched from the front porch. "Wash up, Mike. Dinner's almost ready."

Shelter noted that Kelsey's jeans were cut off high, and her strappy tank top revealed a jogging bra. He thought it was inappropriate but let it go. You had to pick your battles. "What's for dinner?"

"Steaks are on the barbeque," Joan replied over her shoulder.

"I knew it," Shelter said with a smile.

"And those tiny potatoes," Joan said. "Oh, and peas — they're so sweet, I had to save you some from Kelsey. She eats them like candy in front of the TV."

Shelter made his way through the kitchen, slid back the screen door, and stepped out onto the large deck. Growing up, he'd spent his summers at Lake of the Woods, two and a half hours east of Winnipeg. He would always prefer its granite cliffs, wind-swept pine trees, islands and channels. But he'd come to appreciate Lake Winnipeg's own beauty, its expanse, stretching to the horizon, fine white sand beaches and its wildness when whipped up by a storm. Now, with the early evening sun glinting off the water, the lake was calm.

Sigudur Arnason was standing at the rail, looking over the water with his back to him. He turned and nodded. "Mike," he said. He made no move to shake hands and instead went to the barbeque. He held a bottle of Molson Canadian.

"How's it going?"

"It's going. You want a beer?"

Without waiting for an answer, Arnason hobbled to the screen door and was soon back with a bottle for Shelter and a fresh one for himself. At seventy-two, Arnason was compact and strong, although he'd lost much of his once impressive muscle mass with age. He had a bad hip from years of fishing on the lake but refused to consider a replacement.

From his name to his blue eyes and right down to his work as a commercial fisherman, Sig Arnason was every millimetre a descendant of the first Icelandic pioneers who settled this side of Lake Winnipeg in 1875. They called the territory New Iceland, but during the first harsh winter they had to rely on the generosity of Indigenous people for food, advice and even clothing to help them survive the snow, ice and frigid temperatures. At the time, the province of Manitoba didn't extend as far north as the colony, and the Icelandic settlers adopted their own constitution, laws and system of representational government until it was folded into the newly enlarged province of Manitoba in the 1880s. Manitoba became home to the largest Icelandic population outside of Iceland, but it wasn't until Shelter first started dating Christa that he realized he'd grown up surrounded by families whose names ended with "son," the descendants of those settlers.

"How's the fishing?" Shelter asked.

"Not so bad. Monday's the last day of the season," Sig said, absent-mindedly picking at a callous on a hand made rough and scarred by a lifetime of spreading nets, pulling fish into the boat and wielding a filleting knife in the wooden shack that stood near the waterline.

"I hope Kelsey's not too much trouble," Shelter said, glancing over at this daughter seated in a lawn chair, her eyes on her iPhone.

"She's a good worker, like her mother." Sig didn't look at Shelter but instead opened the top of the gas barbeque. Arnason waved away a cloud of smoke rising from the grill and set about flipping three T-bone steaks. Shelter and the old man had stood side by side in a hospice room for the terminally ill and watched Christa slip away, but it hadn't drawn them any closer. Shelter never understood why his father-in-law had taken a dislike to him, and the old man wasn't the type to share his feelings. Still, the distance between them was made up for by their common love for Kelsey and by Shelter's warm relationship with Joan Arnason. Besides helping each other through those terrible days in the hospital and after, he and Joan had also been allies in trying to get Sig off the lake once and for all. He was still strong, but his memory was starting to play tricks on him.

Kelsey was working her phone, sending a text to one of her friends. "Hey, can you put that thing away and join the conversation?" Shelter said. The girl wrinkled her nose, drew her lips into a scowl, and continued tapping the phone. Shelter tilted his head back and looked to the sky.

Joan Arnason appeared on the deck with a drink. "The peas are done. You almost ready, Sig?" She sat down at her place at the glass patio table that had already been set for dinner. "I know this is your line of work, Mike. But if I were a detective, I would suspect our Kelsey has a boyfriend."

"I do not, Grandma!" Kelsey shot back.

Shelter raised an eyebrow and looked at his daughter. "Who's this?"

"I don't have a boyfriend, okay?"

Joan Arnason smiled and turned to Shelter. "I read in the paper about those two Indian girls. What's going on in that city?"

"Life," Shelter said. He sighed and shook his head. "It's nice to make it up here for a few hours." The sun was softening, and a warm breeze was blowing off the lake.

"Okay. Let's eat," Sig Arnason said from the barbeque.

After Joan had cleared the dinner dishes, Kelsey retreated to the living room. Shelter took the opportunity to talk to his in-laws about keeping Kelsey in Gimli for the school year. "I'm not comfortable with it."

Sig wrapped a hand around his beer bottle and gave a shrug. "She's the one who asked."

"I miss her, and I think it's best if she comes back to Winnipeg." Shelter said nothing about his doubts about the quality of education she'd get at the high school in town compared to what Winnipeg had to offer. He'd been an indifferent student himself, much less diligent than Kelsey. If he were honest, he couldn't be sure his thinking didn't reflect prejudices about rural life or the reality of limited resources in a small town. Either way, he knew it would be offensive to his in-laws.

Just at that moment, Kelsey appeared at the screen door. She'd been eavesdropping on the conversation from the kitchen.

"What's your problem?" she demanded. "I'm staying."

"Kelsey, don't speak to your father like that," Joan said.

"I'm not going back to the city," she shouted.

"That's enough," Shelter said, his voice rising.

"You're never even at home," she said through the screen. "What does it matter if I'm there or not?"

"That's not fair to me or your grandparents. You're coming home at the end of the summer, and that's it."

Silence, and then tears began rolling down Kelsey's cheeks. She ran to her bedroom, slamming the door.

It took Shelter a moment to recover from the shock. He got to his feet and marched down the short hall that led to the bedrooms. Somewhere deep in his brain, he knew he should back off until they'd both cooled down, but he was being pushed forward by something stronger.

He knocked on her door. "We need to talk."

"No, go away. I hate you."

"Open this door right now."

"No!"

"Mike." It was Joan. She'd put a hand on his shoulder and was speaking in a calm, soothing tone. "Come sit down. You can talk later."

The next morning, Shelter came awake with a jerk. He looked to his right and saw the digital clock glowing 6:00 a.m. on the bedside table. His cellphone was buzzing in the pocket of his pants on a chair. He fished it out. It was Inspector Neil MacIsaac.

"Where are you?" MacIsaac asked without preamble.

"What's up?"

"There was a shooting on Higgins last night."

"Yeah, okay." Shelter pictured in his mind the city's skid row just off Main Street.

"One of our guys shot a Native man just after two in the morning," MacIsaac said. "In the back."

"Oh, shit."

"Yup. The guy is in critical condition. We've got that march today, so the powers that be are, ah, let's say, upset. They want all hands on deck. So, you need to get downtown ASAP."

Shelter ended the call and rolled out of bed. He pulled on his shorts and tiptoed to the bathroom, where he quietly brushed his teeth and shaved. When he came down the hall, Sig Arnason was sitting at the kitchen table with a mug of coffee in front of him. "There's trouble in the city. I've got to get back to town."

"Okay."

"Listen, about the fall. Give me a chance to think about it."

"You're the boss."

"Say goodbye to Kelsey for me and tell her I'll call tonight."

# SEVEN

The highway was deserted, and Shelter drove fast, going over the exchange with Kelsey and wondering what to do about it. When he hit Winnipeg, he stopped for breakfast at Tim Hortons. As he gobbled it down, his cellphone rang.

He was surprised to see the name on the display was Gordy Taylor, the chief of police.

"I want to talk to you about the murders of these Native girls."

Shelter was momentarily at a loss for words. "No problem," he said. "What did you want to know?"

"Meet me outside the church a little after eleven."

After showering and changing, Shelter arrived downtown just before eight and only had time to open his computer to look at an emailed update from MacIsaac before it was time for the team meeting.

"As you know," he started, "we had a shooting last night involving a constable and an Indigenous man. Name of Jason John Courchene. He's out of surgery and in critical condition."

"What's the cop's name?" asked Ian Sim. He was short and overweight, with a mullet hairdo. Shelter suspected his hair was cut by his wife, and behind his back Traverse referred to the style as a Tennessee Waterfall. Sim's attitudes were just as outdated as his haircut, and he had a knack for avoiding work. He was a constant source of irritation to Shelter and the rest of the team, but they were stuck with him.

"They're not releasing—" Shelter said before he was cut off by

Himmat Sharma.

"Dustin Crowley. He's got two years in," Sharma said. "Sorry Mike, the news is out."

Shelter knew Crowley faced an inquiry and months of harsh publicity and stress, even if the shooting was ruled justified. The toll had ended careers. He also knew the shooting would inflame the march that afternoon.

"The march route will be closed to traffic from 2:00 p.m. to 7:00 p.m. That means the east end of Selkirk and Main Street to City Hall will be closed. With this shooting and the Rempel homicide, we're expecting a large turnout. I want our eyes on the crowd," Shelter said, looking at each detective individually. "Moses Kent is organizing the march. Let's see who he shows up with."

Shelter opened a beige legal folder. "Now, on the investigations. With the publicity about the Rempel homicide, we've been getting lots of calls from the public — not just about that case, but about Monica Spence."

Checking out tips, even if they turned out to be rumours, baseless suspicions or deluded fantasies, was better than having nothing to go on at all. Before she was killed, Spence had been doing out-calls — visiting men at their homes or in hotel rooms — and some street-walking in the West End. It was all to service a raging cocaine habit. She was sleeping in multiple locations, crashing at crack houses or on the couches of people she met on the street. Her wild lifestyle had made it hard to pin down her movements or associations. What made it worse was she was underage and on the run from a group home, so she was even less likely to stay in touch with relatives and friends.

And then there was the frequently anonymous nature of prostitution. In a typical homicide, the victim and perpetrator know each other, and the crime takes place in a home or some other location where they have a shared history. A prostitute would often never have met her killer before. Two people came together for an encounter on one night that ended in murder. In the Spence case, the autopsy had produced little evidence. They'd also come up empty on video of her the night she was killed, and her cellphone had never been found.

"We've got more information on Crystal Rempel from the medical examiner," Shelter said. "No evidence of sex before her death. There was some alcohol in her system, but well below the limit and no drugs." He paused. "Her apartment was in a shambles. It looks like someone was very hot to find something there." The officers exchanged looks. "Ident thinks entry was through a back door on a fire escape, but we've got no witnesses."

He picked up another piece of paper and glanced at Ian Sim. "Records of Rempel's cellphone conversations indicate she'd stopped using the phone two days before her death. The question is why and what phone was she using that night at the bar. She could have borrowed one or got herself a prepaid."

He turned to Sim. "You want to fill us in on the calls she made before she stopped using the phone?"

"They were mostly to and from who you'd expect," Sim said. "Her sister, her mom in Steinbach and some friends I tracked down. Nothing of interest there. But there were three calls to a number on the Lone Pine reserve belonging to someone named Joseph Bear. I tried that number a bunch of times, but they're not calling back. No surprise there," he added with a smirk.

Traverse turned on him with a frown. "What's that supposed to mean?"

The smile dropped off Sim's face. "Nothing. I'll keep trying."

An awkward silence descended on the room. The implication of Sim's comment was clear to everyone in the room. A few decades earlier, he would have been more explicit in putting the failure to return the calls down to "Indian time."

Shelter watched Sim, letting him soak in his embarrassment, before lowering his eyes to the file on the table in front of him. He moved his finger down a sheet of paper.

"Crystal's people were from Lone Pine, right?" Shelter said, looking at Traverse. He paused. "The break-up with Moses Kent, her disappearance for those days, the sudden end to using her cellphone. Why?"

He turned to Jennifer Kane. "What did we get from her car?"

"Not much so far," Kane said, flipping the pages in a notebook and gnawing the inside of her lip in concentration. Kane was tall, with shoulder-length hair with blond highlights. Even on a casual day like this one, she dressed with style. Her sky-blue blouse was fitted, and her jeans rode low on her hips, held with a wide black belt with a large square buckle.

Shelter had come up in the department with Kane, and he was closer to her than anyone else at work, except Traverse. She was married with two young kids, and they often shared both laughs and their problems over lunch or a drink to the point where Christa had once asked him if he was going out with his girlfriend again. That's when Shelter had told her Jennifer Kane was married to a woman named Sherry.

Kane looked up from her notebook. "There was some fresh mud on her driver-side floor mat. It's still in the lab, but the techs think it may not be from this area."

"So maybe a trip up to the rez?"

Kane shrugged. "We'll see." She reached into a file box on the floor beside her. "They also found this when they popped the trunk." She held up a photocopy of the cover of a CD. It had a photo of an Indigenous rapper wearing a snapback Winnipeg Jets cap and heavy gold chains around his neck.

"That's Rory Sinclair," Traverse said. Shelter's head jerked in surprise. He'd been so focused on breaking up the brawl at the bar, he hadn't even stopped to consider Sinclair might have known Crystal Rempel. It was a mistake.

Back at his desk, Shelter pulled up Sinclair's file and court record on the computer. He was twenty-seven years old, older than he'd looked at the bar. Before the cocaine trafficking bust he'd beaten two years earlier, there'd been many other scrapes with the law: a break-and-enter, a charge for possession of marijuana and an aggravated assault on a seventeen-year-old girl for which he'd received two years' probation. For the bar fight the night before, he'd been charged with assaulting a police officer and released on bail. Shelter made a note to take a closer look at the assault on the teenager. There was also a notation from the street gang unit in his file. Sinclair had been seen associating with members of the Manitoba Tribe gang.

Shelter drove to River Heights and waited on the boulevard in front of the brick church his great-grandfather had helped build. Shelter had spent many hours there as a kid, between Sunday school, youth group meetings in the basement and accompanying his parents to services. By the time he was twelve, his mother had given up on fighting to get him out of bed, and he'd been back only for the occasional Christmas and Easter service.

A little after eleven, Shelter spotted Gordy Taylor and his wife among the members of the congregation exiting the church. Many of the men were dressed in short-sleeve summer shirts, but the chief of police was old-school. He had on a navy-blue suit and tie over a white shirt. His wife was decked out in a sky-blue sleeveless silk dress and a formal sun hat with a broad white brim and a broach set in the side. Taylor was a bull of a man, over six feet with broad shoulders, a thick neck and a barrel chest, despite being in his sixties. He wore big old-fashioned rectangular eyeglasses that touched his cheeks, and his bald head only had a few wisps of grey brushed over the top. He met Shelter's eyes and nodded as he descended the stairs to the sidewalk, his wife holding his arm.

"Good morning, Mike," Taylor said, extending his hand.

Janet Taylor nodded and smiled but remained silent as Shelter shook her hand. They had a cordial relationship, but Shelter's family had been closer to Taylor's first wife. Shelter's mother was close friends with her and reacted with fury to the news that Taylor was leaving her for a younger woman. "He's a nasty one. She'll find that out before long and be sorry she met him." Shelter had been surprised by the vehemence of the comment. Taylor could be curt, but he'd never seen a cruel side to his personality. Shelter put his mother's reaction down to anger for her friend, who now faced starting her life over after a divorce.

"Would you excuse us, dear?" Taylor said. "I want a word with Michael."

Shelter and Taylor watched as she strolled a little way down the block into the shade of a giant elm tree. She took a cellphone from her miniature purse, pushed a button and nestled it to her ear. Taylor turned to Shelter. "We have a luncheon." Then, after a moment, "You heard what happened last night?"

"Yes."

"You going to this protest downtown?"

Shelter nodded.

"Good." Taylor was toying with his car key. When he looked up, Shelter felt his chest constrict at the intensity of his gaze.

"Where are we with these Indian girls?"

"We have a few leads but nothing solid," Shelter replied. He wasn't surprised to hear the chief refer to the victims as "Indians." The word was now widely considered a slur, and the police chief would be roasted if he used it in public. But Shelter had heard him use it many times and chalked it up to his age. Many years before, Shelter had resisted dropping the word from his own vocabulary. He'd been put off by words like First Nation and Aboriginal as sops to political correctness. But he'd come to see the racist overtones of the word, its association with a dark, shameful period of the country's history. Now he regarded its use — except by the most out-of-touch in the older generation — as a put-down, a sign of disdain for the aspirations of Indigenous people. He doubted the chief would ever come to the same realization.

"What leads?" Taylor asked.

"We're looking at the boyfriend and another guy, a rapper with a pretty long sheet. He hangs out at the same bar as Crystal Rempel. Her sister works there too."

"Name?"

"Rory Sinclair."

Taylor nodded. A drop of sweat ran from his temple to his jowl before he flicked it away. "The same guy did both, yeah?"

"It looks that way, although we've got some significant forensic inconsistencies."

"How about the boyfriend?"

"Ex-boyfriend. Moses Kent. He's a possibility, but I can't see a link with Monica Spence. I think we should focus on Sinclair for now."

Taylor grunted in disgust. "The Indian groups and the media are screaming. The mayor's panicking." He glared at Shelter for a long moment before his expression softened. "Listen," he said. "I know you're working your tail off on this. Keep at it, step by step, like we've always talked about. I wouldn't want anyone else on it but you."

Taylor was retiring at the end of the month, and Shelter suspected he was worried about the killings putting a stain on a forty-year career. He felt a deep need not to let him down.

Taylor put a hand on his shoulder and spoke in a low, confidential voice.

"We were thinking of you. It's coming up to a year since you lost Christa. I want you and Kelsey to come over to the house for dinner soon, yeah?"

"Just let me know when, and we'll be there."

Taylor nodded and turned to join his wife. They got into his black Chrysler 300 and drove away.

# EIGHT

Shelter could feel the sun burning through his shirt, and his back, neck and scalp were wet with sweat. Lifting his sunglasses, he brought a pair of binoculars to his eyes. In the distance, a line of marchers shimmered in the heat haze coming off the cement. A large hand-painted banner carried by the lead marchers read *Justice for Crystal, Monica and Jason* — the man who'd been shot the night before.

Packed solid in the four southbound lanes of Main Street, the marchers were led by a line of women who Shelter assumed were family and friends of the two murdered women and Jason Courchene. In the lead group were also several leaders in tribal headdress, carrying long staffs adorned with feathers. The breeze brought the sound of drums and rhythmic chanting from traditional singers. Shelter spotted Nicki among the lead group. She wore a New York Yankees baseball cap, a plain black T-shirt and black jeans cut off at the knee.

Shelter lowered the binoculars and turned to Traverse. "Looks like hundreds of them." The two officers stood on the roof of a low building with a good view of Main Street. With traffic stopped, the area in front of them had been transformed into a broad public square. Steel dividers were set up along sidewalks on both sides of the wide avenue. These were to corral the marchers and keep them away from city buildings on this side and the Concert Hall and the Pantages Theatre on the other. Dozens of uniformed constables were positioned around the site. A police helicopter buzzed overhead, and the media was out in force.

Finally, the march reached city hall, and the people quickly filled both sides of Main Street and grew steadily more tightly packed. The chiefs and other leaders, along with Nicki, Monica Spence's mother, and members of Jason Courchene's family, climbed the low steps in front of city hall and stood in a semi-circle. Shelter scanned the crowd. There was a mix of all ages and included many non-Indigenous people who'd come out to show their support. For such a large number, they were surprisingly quiet. Someone blew a whistle, another honked a vuvuzela and some teenage girls gave occasional whoops. But mostly there was a low rumble as the people talked and waited for something to happen.

A loud bang shook the street, followed by a gasp, screams and finally a sustained cheer washed across the crowd. Shelter recovered from a flinch and caught sight of a trail of smoke wafting over the crowd. He followed it into the sky. Someone had fired a flare, and it burned as a bright, fluorescent ember high above the marchers. The sun glinted off hundreds of pairs of sunglasses as every head tilted skyward to watch it burn and drift in the wind.

Shelter looked to his right and saw the sergeant in charge of the crowd control unit talking with his inspector. Shelter knew both of them — good men.

Moses Kent stepped forward from the semi-circle of leaders to a microphone stand. "*Boozhoo! Miigwech!* Welcome, and thank you for coming." The crowd applauded and whistled. "We honour the memory of Crystal Rempel and Monica Spence." The words boomed out from two large bullhorns that had been set up on the steps. "We pray for the full recovery of our brother, Jason Courchene. And we honour the families who have suffered so much."

He swept his eyes from one side of the huge gathering to the other. "We are here today on Treaty One territory, yes, to talk about what happened to our sisters and brother, but also to talk about why it happened. Why Crystal, Monica, and twelve hundred other

Indigenous women have been murdered or disappeared in this country. Why Jason Courchene, unarmed and alone, was gunned down on a dark street like others before him. They are not statistics. They are not numbers. They are our brother and sisters, our children and grandchildren. They were loved and are loved."

The crowd let out what to Shelter sounded like a collective sigh and pushed closer toward the stairs where Kent spoke. He dropped his voice. "It is a sad day. Monica and Crystal have been taken from their families, taken from all of us. Jason is fighting for his life. What message does it send? Is the message it's okay to kill our young people? Well, we say it's not okay!" The crowd applauded, and a circle of drummers at the side of the stairs banged out their approval.

"Our young people are precious. Every single person in this province, this country, has a responsibility to say we will not accept this any longer. We all have the responsibility to find justice for Monica, Crystal and Jason and all the other victims and their families."

Kent raised his voice again, and it echoed off the buildings across Main Street. "Why do these situations happen over and over again? How many deaths will it take before there is change?" He paused. "We will not stop asking questions and demanding answers. We ask everyone to stand with us, not only to change the system to prevent what happened to Jason, but also bring justice for Monica and Crystal and closure for their families. Someone out there knows who killed those young women, and it's their responsibility to step forward and tell what they know." The crowd was solemn, and the applause in response to Kent's words died away quickly. "Again, *miigwech* to you all for coming. Let this just be the beginning of a new day of action."

Kent gave way at the microphone to a woman. As the new speaker began, Shelter scanned the march leaders for Nicki. To his surprise, he caught sight of her striding down the stairs and into the crowd. Shelter looked ahead of her to see where she was heading. For the first time, he spotted Rory Sinclair. He called to Traverse and pointed. "Nicki's going after Sinclair."

Sinclair was six or seven rows back from the front of the crowd, laughing with a friend. Nicki pushed her way through to him and gave him a hard shove in the chest. When Sinclair recovered from his surprise, he barked something at her. She didn't back down. She was up in his face, yelling at him.

People in the immediate vicinity of the confrontation had turned to see what was going on. Nicki was jabbing a finger into Sinclair's shoulder. He backed away, trying to move off. Nicki circled, blocking his way. He gave her a hard slap, sending her stumbling backward. She fell and landed hard on her side. People around them backed away in shock and began shouting at Sinclair.

Shelter looked to nearby cops. None had reacted to the slap, perhaps not wanting to wade into the tightly packed crowd. He raced down a set of stairs and through an emergency exit that led onto the sidewalk. By the time he reached Nicki, she'd regained her feet but was doubled over and had a hand on her cheek. A young woman had an arm around her and was whispering something in her ear. Sinclair was nowhere to be seen. Shelter placed a hand on Nicki's shoulder. "You okay?"

She straightened up and gave a hard shrug. "Get the fuck off me, man," she shouted.

Shelter stepped back, and Nicki glared at him. He became aware of the curious onlookers in a circle around them. Together, Nicki and her friend moved away as the people in front of them opened a path to let them get to the edge of the crowd. Shelter returned to stand beside Traverse but kept his eye on Nicki as she first spoke to the woman and then eventually rejoined the leaders of the march.

When the speeches were over and the crowd began to break up, Shelter snaked through the dispersing people until he reached

Nicki, who was chatting with a group of women.

He got her attention and signalled to her. "I need to talk to you," he said when she'd detached herself from the circle of friends.

"So talk."

"Not here. Come for a coffee."

She glanced back at her friends, who were watching their conversation with undisguised curiosity. "I'm with my friends."

"It's important. It won't take long."

Nicki followed a half step behind Shelter the two blocks to the Peking Garden. As he held the door open for her, Shelter was hit by a blast of cold air, and once inside he felt dizzy in the gloom of the restaurant. He pointed Nicki toward a booth and went to the men's room, where he doused his face with handfuls of cold water. After drying his face, he raked his hair with his fingers, tucked in his shirt, and hitched up his pants.

Nicki was waiting for him, her sunglasses over her eyes. The Peking Garden had been a popular spot back in the sixties and seventies, with its Art Deco dining room and waiters in jade-coloured tunics. But the decor, uniforms and menu hadn't changed in fifty years, and the restaurant was dying a protracted death. Arthur Yee approached the table and laid a starched white tablecloth over yellow Formica. There were two other parties eating lunch at tables around the dining room, but Shelter's was the only one with a tablecloth.

Back in the seventies, Yee had given up his waiter job at the Garden to open a little restaurant on Main Street near the train station. Shelter's father had championed the restaurant, taking his insurance cronies there for lunches and his mother for dinners with other couples. His father had even found an entry-level underwriting job for Yee's eldest son, who was now a vice president with the Royal Bank in Toronto. The restaurant had failed after a couple of years, and Arthur was forced back into the green jacket of a Peking Garden waiter, but he'd never forgotten the support he'd received from Shelter's father over the years.

Nicki and Shelter sat in silence as Arthur laid down glasses of water and a stainless-steel teapot with jasmine brewing.

"What you want to eat?"

"I'm good with water for now," Shelter said. "Nicki?"

Nicki shook her head. "I'm taking off."

Yee retreated, and Shelter studied Nicki. "You okay?"

She scanned the room slowly rather than meet his gaze.

"That was a helluva scene back there," he said. "It was good to hear Moses ask for people to come forward with information about Monica and Crystal."

"You guys need all the help you can get."

Shelter picked up his ice water and drained the glass, the cubes clinking against his teeth. He put the glass down with a bang.

Nicki jumped.

"All of this is a distraction, as far as I'm concerned. The longer it takes to find who killed Crystal, the worse our chances get. That's just statistics."

"I'm not a kid, so don't talk to me like one."

"There's someone out there hoping, praying, believing a little more every day he's getting away with it."

Nicki bowed her head and toyed with a thick bracelet on her left arm, just one of the pieces of silver she was wearing — rings, bangles and a chain peeking out from her T-shirt. Shelter observed her: straight black hair, thick eyebrows and full lips. He detected light eye make-up and noticed her black T-shirt was new and fitted perfectly in the shoulders. The sleeves were rolled once, showing strong arms. He found himself wondering whether she was involved with someone before quickly pushing the thought from his mind, alarmed by the attraction he felt in that moment.

Quietly, he said, "It's a beautiful bracelet."

She let go of it and looked him in the eyes. "It's Mike, right? What do you want from me, Mike?"

Shelter was surprised she'd remembered his name. "It seems like you know Rory Sinclair after all."

"Of course I know him. Everyone knows him."

"So why lie the other night? You said all you knew about him was he's a crappy tipper."

Nicki gave a shrug and a quick frown. "Rory's not the kind of guy you run around talking to the cops about."

"Okay. Let's go back to the beginning. How do you know him?"

"We were in high school together. He's a year older than me."

"And Crystal?"

"She met him through me. When she first came in from the country, she was going to university and hanging out with her white friends. Then she started seeing Moses."

"What about Crystal and you?"

Again, their eyes met. Now it was Nicki who was studying his face. Shelter sensed she was making a judgment about whether she could trust him. She let her eyes slide to the right.

"It's complicated, you know? We were sisters, but we didn't know each other. Something inside her wanted to connect back to who she was, who we are. She started to go and see my mom, trying to help her get straight and such. Good luck with that, eh?" She began playing with her bracelet again. "She would come see me at the bar, and that's when she met Rory."

"So, she was into the night life?"

"She'd have a drink, but her work was her passion, and reconnecting to our culture and spirituality, especially after she started going to see our grandmother on the rez."

"But she was hanging out with Rory at the bar?"

"No. She couldn't stand him," she said, shaking her head. "He tried coming on to her. But she just laughed it off. Little Big Man — that's what she called him. He hated that." Nicki took a sip of water.

"You went after Rory pretty good today. What's that about?"

She started playing with chopsticks on the table. He waited. Finally, she said in a low voice, "He had a big fight with Crystal."

Shelter frowned in surprise. "When?"

"The week before..."

"She was killed. What kind of a fight?"

"It started in the bar — them arguing. She had a finger in his face and was yelling at him."

"About what?"

"I don't know. I was working the far section, but I could see Crystal was really pissed off. By the time I got over there, she'd left."

"Why didn't you tell us about this the first time we talked to you?"

Nicki met his look. "I was in shock. I didn't remember it until yesterday morning."

Shelter considered this. He thought it was more likely that in her world you don't help the police. You take care of your own problems.

"Moses told us she'd been upset for a while, but she wouldn't say what was bothering her. Is that what the fight was about?"

"I don't know. She hadn't been herself, that's for sure. I asked her what was going on, but she wouldn't tell me. Said it was nothing for me to worry about."

"So what about today?"

Nicki seemed to gather herself. "I've been looking for Rory."

Shelter put his teacup down. "You've been looking for him?"

"I want to know what that fight was about. What he knows about Crystal."

Shelter glanced around the restaurant as he digested this information. In this section, only one other table in a far corner was occupied. An elderly couple were eating their soup. In a little while, the Sunday night crowd would come in, but not many at this time of year. One of the reasons he liked this place was you'd never bump into someone you knew. He brought his eyes back to Nicki and moved forward in his seat. "And at the march?"

"I asked him what happened to her. He told me to back off, and then there was just so much noise and shit going on."

"It looked like you said a lot more than that."

"I guess you could say I was accusing him."

Shelter was silent for a moment. "Was Rory in the bar the night Crystal was killed?"

"I'm pretty sure he didn't come in."

"But Crystal was there. It could have been Rory she was texting."

Nicki shrugged and then nodded.

"Where do think he'll be now?"

"I have no idea. I went over to his store yesterday. But his crew said they hadn't seen him."

"His store?"

She rolled her eyes in a silent comment on how clueless the police were. "He runs a little place downtown where they sell hip-hop stuff. T-shirts, baseball caps, shit like that. He runs his record company from upstairs."

Shelter made a mental note. "Where else were you looking for him?"

"Just around. A couple of different bars and the pool hall he likes, the Double Deuce on Sargent."

Shelter's mind went to the cue in Rory's hands when he first saw him in the bar. He knew the Double Deuce from his time in the robbery squad and before that when he was young and shooting pool himself. It was a hangout for thieves, drug dealers and other assorted hoods.

"How about Moses in all this?" he asked.

"Nah, he's solid." Nicki pushed her chair back, stood up in one motion and slid her iPhone into a back pocket of her cut-offs.

"Just stay away from Rory, okay? Put my number in your phone."

Her eyes narrowed. "Last time I say it. Don't fucking tell me what to do. Ever."

Shelter shook his head and scrawled the number on a napkin.

She stuffed it into her back pocket and was gone.

# NINE

The next morning, Shelter arrived at the office to find the team of detectives hunkered down at their desks reading newspaper accounts of the march and the musings of a *Free Press* columnist. He laid the blame for the shooting of Jason Courchene and the failure to catch a killer stalking the city's Indigenous women on incompetence and a culture of racism in the police department.

In the lunchroom, Shelter had just got his coffee from the machine when Jennifer Kane entered the room with her mug. "Hey, how's it going?"

Shelter clicked his tongue against his teeth and shook his head. "Kelsey's driving me nuts."

"Okay." Kane pronounced the word slowly. "What's going on?"

"She wants to stay up in Gimli for the school year."

Kane nodded as she thought about it. "You were worried about taking care of her in the fall. This could be a solution, no?"

"I guess, but she doesn't want anything to do with me. It's like I'm to blame for Christa."

She touched his forearm. "It's still really soon for both of you. Give it time and see what happens."

Shelter's head was bowed and his lips pursed. "I got to go," he said, looking up at her.

They headed for the door together. Kane stopped him just before they entered the squad room. "Let me know if you want to go for a drink and talk about it."

"I will. I need to talk to somebody."

Shelter and Traverse stood on the sidewalk outside a brick, three-storey walk-up at the south end of downtown. Crystal Rempel's apartment on the second floor had been thoroughly gone over by the Ident unit, but the detectives wanted a look for themselves. The parking lot beside the building was full of cars belonging to provincial civil servants who worked at the legislature building one street behind. The building had flowers planted in boxes on either side of the entrance. Shelter pushed a button marked *Caretaker* on the intercom panel.

The man who buzzed them in was a senior citizen named Ronnie. He was waiting for them at the door of his basement apartment, still in pyjamas and housecoat, the white fringe of hair around his bald head uncombed. Under one thin arm, he clutched a vicious-looking Pomeranian that kept up an incessant chorus of barks, yips and growls.

"Stop that, Casey! I said stop it," Ronnie told the dog after Shelter and Traverse had shown him their identification. "We've had so many police in here. It's terrible for our tenants."

"Could you put your dog in the apartment and step out, please?" Traverse said.

Ronnie retreated into the apartment, and the door swung closed. Casey's muffled barking was punctuated by a thumping noise. Traverse smiled at Shelter. "He's head-butting the door. That thing's scary, man."

Shelter was smiling, too. He glanced down the hall. It was gloomy, with no carpeting and only a couple of other doors.

Ronnie's door opened a crack, and the old man squeezed out of the apartment sideways. "Stay, Casey. Daddy has to go out now."

When the door was closed, Shelter asked, "How was Crystal Rempel as a tenant?"

"I told the police this already."

"Then you won't mind cooperating again."

"She kept to herself. It's not our business what the tenants do in the privacy of their own suite. But some of them have parties and don't think about the noise."

Ronnie led them upstairs. "We're not prejudiced here," he said with a glance over his shoulder as he climbed. "But we are very careful about who we accept as tenants. You have to be these days. But she had nice references."

"Did she have many visitors?" Shelter asked when they'd arrived at the door to the apartment.

"We're not snooping around the suites. But she did have some Indian visitors, as I told the other officers," the caretaker said before catching himself. "If you'll excuse the expression."

"Men or women?

"Both."

"Any of them stand out?"

The caretaker shrugged. "She was a nice girl from what I could see — a lawyer, but you already know that." The more the caretaker spoke, the more it became clear he was enjoying his five minutes of fame and all the details had been gone over not only with the police but also in multiple gossip sessions. "The other officers said they'd bring pictures for me to look at. To try to identify the visitors."

They were standing outside a door sealed with yellow tape. Traverse took out a pen knife, cut the tape and unlocked the door. Ronnie peered into the apartment. "It's a beautiful suite." He took a step forward, but Shelter moved to block him.

"Thanks for your help. Someone will be by to show you those pictures. We'll take it from here."

Before the well-to-do had moved out to the suburbs decades before, this apartment block had been a fashionable address. It had high ceilings, crown moulding and blond hardwood floors. The large living room had a manufactured oriental rug with an intricate pattern in red, gold and black. A flat-screen TV had been set up across from a beige couch between two windows that looked out over the street. A good sound system sat on a table.

The Ident team had already gone over the apartment, photographing and fingerprinting. When they were done, they'd carted away Crystal's clothing, papers and anything else that might produce evidence for analysis. When they were finished, they'd replace the drawers and hangers in the closets. There was no visible evidence of the late-night visit that had left the apartment in a mess.

"What are we looking for?" Traverse asked.

"I'm not sure. I wanted to get a better fix on Crystal," Shelter said, noticing Traverse was studying a framed print over the mantle. It was a large drawing depicting a scene from long ago. In the foreground, a group of Indigenous people wrapped in blankets sat on the ground in a semi-circle. In front of them, three men on hard chairs faced white men, who were standing, two in military uniform and two in suits with hats. Women dressed in the billowing gowns of the era looked on in the background.

"I've seen it before," Traverse said. "It's the signing of Treaty One at Lower Fort Garry in 1871 — the Stone Fort Treaty."

Examining the print, Shelter realized how little he knew about the history it depicted. Eighteen seventy-one was a year after the province of Manitoba was founded and four years after the creation of Canada. Settlers were beginning to pour in from the east. Three decades later, his great-grandfather had arrived from England with his three sisters to start a new life.

The picture had triggered something in Traverse. "We agreed to share the territory in peace," he said, nodding toward the image. "We never gave up anything."

Glancing over, Shelter could see tension around his partner's eyes.

"We never saw ourselves as owners of this land. So how could we give it up, sell it or surrender it?" Traverse looked down, lost in thought. When he spoke again, the words had a harder edge. "Share. Not be controlled, abused and disrespected."

Shelter was taken aback. He'd never heard Traverse talk like this, but he couldn't disagree. Cultures and ways of life thousands of years old had been uprooted by the desire of European migrants to make a new beginning for themselves. Through the Indian Act, every aspect of the Indigenous peoples' lives had been controlled by the state, including ripping children as young as five and six from their homes and sending them away to residential schools. There the government, and the churches that ran the schools, tried to take the Indian out of the child, assimilate them into the white mainstream. Successive generations were separated from their parents and communities, prevented from speaking their language and often physically and sexually abused. Shelter and Traverse saw the consequences on the streets of Winnipeg every day, but they'd left in silence their feelings about the horrors they witnessed together — the poverty, violence, abuse and suicides.

Traverse turned to Shelter. "Mike, I'm thinking about leaving the service."

Shelter was shocked. "Why?"

"The job. It doesn't get any better. I can't remember why I got into this work."

Shelter thought about it. He'd actually been feeling more hopeful than ever, mostly because of people like Traverse and the Indigenous leaders he'd seen emerging. "You got into it because you're damn good. You're exactly where you should be. There's no one who can bring what you do to this job. Take your time and think about it."

Traverse flared. "I *have* thought about it. It's all I can think about." After a moment, he calmed down and lowered his voice to almost a whisper. "I feel like I'm getting numb to the suffering. That's not who I want to be."

Shelter had grown close to Traverse over the five years they'd been partners and considered him to be one of the best, most intuitive detectives on the force. But he knew it hadn't been easy. Shelter had watched him take insensitive comments in the squad room, racist taunts from offenders and gibes from his own people, accusing him of selling out.

"What is it you want to do?"

"I'm not sure. Something different. Maybe teaching."

Shelter nodded. "When is this going to happen?"

"I don't know, but I wanted you to hear it from me first."

Shelter also understood Traverse's fear of losing his humanity in the face of so much violence and abuse. He felt it too and had to constantly guard against being consumed by cynicism and indifference.

"Is it this case?"

"It's been building for a long time." Traverse paused and looked Shelter in the eyes. "But there's one thing I'm really going to miss."

"What?"

"I won't have you to kick around anymore."

Shelter laughed. "Something tells me you'll get over it."

He'd come to rely on Traverse as a partner and as a friend. They were good together and he hated the idea of no longer being able to depend on his perspective, instincts and toughness. Instead, he would have to start from scratch with an unknown quantity in a new partner. It was one more blow after the loss of Christa and Kelsey's desire to stay in Gimli.

There was nothing to be done but get on with the job. He turned and squatted in front of the fake fireplace, where a square plastic heater had been positioned. Leaning forward, he pulled it out and examined it. Straightening up, he said, "Where would you hide something in here if you wanted to make sure it wouldn't be found?"

"I guess that would depend on how big it is," Traverse said. "You thinking about her cellphone?"

Shelter shrugged. "If Crystal was as scared as her mother says she was, maybe she hid something in here."

"Doesn't hurt to have a look."

They split up to search the apartment. Shelter entered Crystal's bedroom. He touched a collection of rings, necklaces and a miniature dream catcher in a dish on top of her chest of drawers. He examined her framed law school degree before moving to the wall closest to the windows, where he took out his Swiss army knife and squatted to unscrew the cover of an electrical outlet — nothing. He checked the closet, peering at the ceiling and knocking to try to find hiding places.

Crystal's photos had been taken away by the Ident team, and Shelter had already looked them over at the office. They'd helped him trace the arc of her life, from her childhood and adolescence with her white family and friends to later snapshots taken on various occasions with university friends, Nicki, Moses and an older woman Shelter assumed to be Crystal and Nicki's birth mother, Anne Alexander. He'd closely examined one photo, a badly lit shot of Crystal sitting beside a very old woman on an ancient couch in what looked to be a cabin. She held the old woman's hand, and Shelter assumed this was her grandmother on the Lone Pine reserve.

When he emerged from the bedroom, Shelter found Traverse on his knees in the bathroom, where he'd unscrewed a trap door hiding the bath plumbing. After another fifteen minutes searching the kitchen and a screened-in back porch, they gave up.

"I'm just going to give a card to Ronnie," Shelter said as he resealed the apartment with police department tape.

In the basement, the caretaker's dog went crazy again when he knocked. The caretaker opened the door a crack, allowing him to thread his card through the gap. "By the way, did Crystal have a locker or a storage cage down here?"

"We don't have lockers for the tenants."

"Where do these doors lead?" Shelter asked, pointing down the hall.

"One is the laundry room, and the other is for the hot water tank and electrical panels."

"The laundry room," Traverse said.

Shelter realized there were no washer and dryer in Crystal's apartment. "Can we have a look?"

The laundry room had a bare cement floor. A folding table was built into a wall, and a coin-operated washing machine and dryer were wedged into a corner. Shelter squatted to check under the table while Traverse examined the machines. He edged the washing machine away from the wall before giving a hard jerk to turn it around.

The Ziploc bag was taped into a space between the drum and the steel side of the washing machine. Traverse put on a pair of gloves and gingerly removed it.

Inside was an iPhone wrapped in a sheet of paper, held in place by a rubber band. He pulled off the rubber band and placed the phone and paper on the top of the washing machine. The sheet had been torn from a notebook. A few words and numbers were scrawled on it. *Agassiz Holdings* was underlined. Below were the digits 01-06933 and on a third line 1.5M.

"Agassiz Holdings — so, a company?" Shelter asked. "The only Agassiz I know is the ski hill."

"The numbers aren't right for a bank account. Maybe it's in the States."

Shelter picked up the bag and turned it over, examining the cellphone and piece of paper. "This is what our guy was looking for upstairs."

Traverse nodded. "What he killed Crystal for."

# TEN

Shelter and Traverse set out to find Rory Sinclair. They got no answer at his apartment in a swanky high-rise near Osborne Village, and the door was locked at the tiny store just off Portage Avenue where Sinclair sold hip-hop clothing and accessories. The words *Urban Impressions* had been painted on the glass door, and underneath in smaller lettering, *A Division of Chief Records*.

The Double Deuce was the next stop. The detectives descended a flight of stairs and entered the sprawling pool hall. The ceiling was low, and most of the illumination came from the lights suspended over a half dozen snooker tables on one side of the room and twice as many smaller pool tables on the other. The place was nearly empty.

On a flat-screen TV affixed to a wall in the snack bar area, Mayor Sam Klein and police Chief Gordy Taylor were on the muted screen, holding a press conference on the Jason Courchene shooting and the protest march.

"There's Freddy," Traverse said.

Shelter followed his gaze to the far corner of the pool hall, where a man with his back to them was pulling on a cream-coloured suit jacket. "Freddy!" Shelter called. Fast Freddy Boyle flinched at the sound of Shelter's voice but recovered quickly. Looking over his shoulder, he greeted them with a broad smile. Shelter could tell from his reaction that Boyle had spied them coming into the pool hall and had hoped to make a discreet exit.

"Hey, how you doing, Mike?" He nodded to Traverse. "Gabe."

Boyle was as slender as a teenager, even though he was in his late fifties. His suit was well pressed and his navy-blue tie tightly knotted with a matching handkerchief in the breast pocket. His black, wavy hair was shiny with gel. Shelter suspected the clothes came from the Salvation Army store, but he wore them well.

"You're not leaving so soon, are you, Fred?" Shelter asked. "How about a game?"

Boyle had been hustling pool around town all his adult life. "A hard way to make an easy living," he liked to say. These days, it was harder than ever. Instead of going out to the pool hall or the racetrack to bet a couple of hundred, guys sat in their basement playing online poker in their underwear. It didn't help that Boyle was known by every bar regular in town and was too old now for the barnstorming trips he used to take to the States, hitting joints from Fargo all the way to Chicago.

Still, he was able to eke out a living, taking in a hundred bucks in an evening from tourists or businessmen out on the town. Every once in a while, he'd still hit it big — a thousand or more — if his opponents were drunk, cocky or rich enough to bet some serious coin.

"Sorry. You gentlemen will have to excuse me," he said with a chuckle after shaking hands with the two detectives. "I'm late for a little appointment."

Shelter had known Boyle since he was in his late teens and looking for excitement in rough bars downtown and in the North End. One Saturday afternoon, Shelter had lost twenty dollars shooting pool with a guy. Boyle took pity on him and offered to give him lessons for two bucks a game. Shelter got good enough over the next month to briefly consider a career in hustling himself. Now, Boyle was an occasional source of street intelligence.

"You know this guy, Rory Sinclair?" Shelter asked. "Apparently he hangs out here."

Boyle was leaning against the snooker table with one ankle

crossed over the other. On hearing Sinclair's name, he pushed off the table with his hands. "Can't help you."

"Can't or won't?"

Boyle sighed. "A guy like that figures out I'm talking to the cops, and I get hurt. I got a family to feed, man."

"What do you know about him?"

Boyle's eyes swept the pool hall. "What can I say? He's a heavy guy, judging by the company he keeps. But you know that already."

"What kind of company?"

"You know, gangbangers. He's got a regular crew, and then you see other guys come in to see him. He uses this place like a damn office."

"Which gang?" Traverse asked.

"How would I know? I'm too old for that shit. I gotta go."

Shelter reached into the inside breast pocket of his jacket and pulled out pictures of Crystal Rempel and Monica Spence taken from their Facebook pages. He laid them on the dark wood of the snooker table rail. "You ever see him with these girls?"

"No, I have not seen him with those girls. I'll tell you one thing, and then I'm gone. Rory's been in here a lot with a new friend. They're shooting pool and talking a couple times a week."

"What kinda new friend?"

"Some sort of an Indian politician from a reserve north of the city. He's always got a big roll on him and a diamond pinkie ring. I won five hundred bucks off him and he just laughed it off."

"What's his name?"

"Charlie. That's all I know." Boyle unscrewed his pool cue and put the two pieces in a black leather carrying case. He clicked the clasps shut. "Have a great day." He made his way through the tables to the young woman who was doing double duty at the bar and cash register. After a couple of words, he was out the door.

Shelter was about to ask Traverse what he thought about what

Boyle had said when his partner gave a sharp nod in the direction of the entrance. Rory Sinclair was collecting a set of pool balls at the front desk. He was accompanied by two other Indigenous men and an Asian woman in her early twenties. Shelter quickly turned toward Traverse so they were in profile to the group choosing a pool table at the far end of the room.

Sinclair was dressed in a black T-shirt, black jeans and his Winnipeg Jets cap. The second man was well over six feet and heavy-set. Also extensively tattooed, he wore jeans and a leather vest over a white T-shirt. The third man was older, in his mid-forties and obese. He was in casual business attire, a pair of dress slacks with a blue oxford cloth shirt open at the collar to show a gold chain. Sinclair and the taller man wore their hair shaved tight to the scalp, but the businessman's braided hair reached halfway down his back.

"The big guy is Darren Thompson, Rory's bodyguard," Traverse said. The detectives had first seen Thompson during the bar brawl at the City Hotel. The intelligence file on Sinclair identified Thompson as an associate with a lengthy record of weapons and assault convictions. He'd done a couple of stints in Headingly jail and broke into the big leagues when an attempted murder rap landed him in Stony Mountain for four years.

"And the other guy?" Shelter said as he and Traverse took seats on a bench running along the wall. "Maybe it's the new friend Freddy was telling us about."

Sinclair broke the pool balls with a crack, all the while chatting and laughing with the older man. The Asian woman wasn't interested in the game. In her cream-coloured miniskirt, white halter top and high heels, she sat cross-legged at a high cocktail table and texted.

Thompson bent over the pool table to line up a shot that brought Shelter and Traverse into his field of vision. He stood up and spoke to Sinclair, whose head snapped in their direction.

"Let's go," Shelter said.

Without taking his eyes off the approaching detectives, Sinclair said something to the older man. He slid his cue onto the pool table and retreated to the cocktail table. Thompson took a couple of steps forward, like a tank moving to protect Sinclair's right flank.

"Hey, Rory," Shelter said with a relaxed smile. "We met the other night. Detective Sergeant Michael Shelter, and this is Detective Sergeant Gabriel Traverse."

Sinclair glowered at them. Traverse swivelled slightly so he was angled to face Thompson. "We haven't been introduced. It's Darren, right?" Shelter said. The man's eyes flickered with doubt.

"Don't answer that," Sinclair cut in. His eyes were almost hidden by the long brim of his baseball cap. "What you guys want?"

"Darren, we want a few words with your boss," Shelter said to the bodyguard. "You can join your friends."

"Damn! An Indian can't get no respect in this town," Sinclair barked, sounding as if he was straight out of Compton. "Where you get off giving a brother orders?"

Traverse smiled at Shelter and nodded his head toward Sinclair as if to say, *Can you believe the gangsta act?* Traverse turned back to Thompson. "Fuck off." Shelter kept his eyes on Rory, still smiling and waited.

Sinclair glanced at his buddy and gave an almost imperceptible nod. Thompson lumbered to the cocktail table.

"You're not an easy guy to get a hold of," Shelter said. "Where you been?"

"Been around. Come on, man. We're trying to enjoy a game here."

"How about you come downtown and answer a few questions about Crystal Rempel," Traverse said.

Sinclair dipped his head so his face disappeared behind the brim of his cap. When he raised his chin, he was smiling, the gold incisor glinting. "Am I under arrest here?"

"No. But we'd like your cooperation."

"No warrant. No dice." He turned slightly to face Shelter. "How you feeling there? I laid you out pretty good the other night, eh?"

Shelter nodded. "Hope that wasn't your best shot." Then, a little louder for the benefit of the three people watching from the cocktail table, "We know you and Crystal were involved in a pretty serious argument the night before she was killed. What was that about?"

There was a flash of anger in Rory's eyes. After a beat, he said, "I don't know who you been talking to, but there was no argument."

"Where were you on Thursday night."

"Home. With my girl."

"How about Monica Spence? Did you know her?"

"I seen her name in the paper."

Shelter was ready with another question when Sinclair piped up again.

"Shelter, right? Seen your name in the paper too. That's an unusual one you got there, dude." He added, "Was that your daughter I found on Facebook the other night? Nice-looking girl."

"What did you just say?"

Shelter closed the gap to Sinclair with a quick stride. He grabbed him by the neck and tilted his head back with a thumb under the chin. Nose to nose, he spoke in a low, angry hiss. "That's a dangerous game, buddy. I'm not sure you'll like where it takes you."

Sinclair jerked his head and pushed Shelter hard in the chest. "Get the fuck off me."

Thompson jumped off his stool and took two quick steps forward before Traverse brushed past Sinclair and stopped him with a fist in his chest. "Sit down, *now!*"

The big man backed off, and Shelter, his heart pounding, approached the cocktail table. Sinclair circled to stand behind the other three in his party. Shelter glanced at the Asian woman and then focused on the third, older man. He saw he was wearing a diamond ring on his right pinkie finger and a gold Rolex on his left wrist. He was massive. His pectoral muscles sagged like a woman's breasts. His protruding belly lay on his lap. Only the toes of his cowboy boots touched the floor, and he struggled to keep his balance on the bar stool.

"What's your name?"

The corners of the man's mouth turned up in an awkward closed-mouth smile, but he didn't answer.

"Detective Sergeant Michael Shelter of the Winnipeg Police Service. Now it's your turn."

"Charlie Osborne."

"Okay, Mr. Osborne. Can I see some identification?"

Sinclair placed an arm on his shoulder. "You don't need to show no ID."

Osborne's eyes bounced from Shelter to Sinclair and back. He remained silent. His brow was wrinkled with tension, his lips pursed. A sheen of sweat made his fleshy face look like he'd been sitting in a steam bath.

"Where do you work, Mr. Osborne?"

"I'm a councillor for the Lone Pine First Nation."

"What brings you to Winnipeg?"

"We have an office in Winnipeg. I'm down on business."

"What kind of business?"

"Lone Pine First Nation business."

Sinclair interrupted the exchange. "Okay. That's it. Let's get out of here."

Shelter got up close to him so he was looking down into his black eyes again. In a low voice, he said, "Go near my daughter and I'll make you sorry."

# ELEVEN

The car was an oven when Shelter and Traverse climbed in, and they waited in silence for the air-conditioning to kick in. In the passenger seat, Shelter closed his eyes, took a deep breath and let it out in a slow stream. He was still turning Sinclair's threat to Kelsey over in his mind.

Shelter opened his eyes and banged his fist on the dashboard. "Little fucker!"

Traverse threw the car into gear and pulled onto Sargent Avenue. Shelter leaned back in his seat and struggled to calm down. He scowled at Traverse. "The guy's looking me up online? He's worried."

"Yup."

"Crystal had something on him. Those days when she disappeared, stopped using her phone and credit cards all of the sudden, it had to be him scaring her. He knew Crystal well. It wouldn't have been hard to get her out of the bar and into a car."

Shelter was interrupted by the sound of his phone buzzing on his belt. It was Moses Kent. "There's something I want to discuss," Kent said.

"What is it?"

"I'll let you know when I see you. Can you come now?"

Traverse steered the car down Main Street with his wrist over the wheel. Shelter slouched in the passenger seat, his elbow propped on the door and his chin resting in his hand. He closed his eyes, listening to Neil Young belt out "Cinnamon Girl" on the radio.

"How you sleeping?" Traverse asked.

"You know. It's always the same. I wake up in the middle of the night and then can't get back to sleep. A ten-pound cat on my chest doesn't help, of course."

Traverse smiled. "That's the love you're feeling."

"Right. He loves what my hands can do with a can opener. Why?"

"You're not looking so hot. Get some rest." After a beat, he added, "You're not getting any younger."

Shelter looked over at his partner and rolled his eyes. But he was bone-tired, and his prospects for a good night's sleep weren't good.

At the Anishinaabe Awakening office, a young woman was working on a computer near the front door. She looked up when the detectives entered but apparently wasn't there to play receptionist. At his desk in the back of the building, Moses Kent watched them approach with his fingers steepled to his chin.

"Gentlemen." Kent spread his hands, indicating the two seats in front of his battered grey metal desk.

"What can we do for you?" Traverse asked.

Kent leaned back in his chair and looked from one officer to the other. "It's about Crystal and Monica Spence. I found out this morning they knew each other pretty well, and I wasn't sure you were aware of that." Shelter fought the urge to look over at Traverse and check his reaction. Instead, he fixed his gaze on Kent.

The young man smoothed his hair and sat up straight. "Maybe it was because Crystal was separated from her own mother and sister as a baby, but she wasn't going to turn a blind eye when kids were being hurt. We worked on it together, but really it was her fight. She found girls who were being trafficked and got them help, usually starting with a place to live and help with substance abuse. Monica was one of those girls."

Shelter remembered what Nicki had told him about Crystal working with girls to get them out of the sex trade. His mind raced over the implications.

Kent anticipated his next question. "Like I said, I just found out about it myself."

"Where did Crystal meet Monica?"

Kent hesitated and then rose from his chair. "I want you to meet someone. Let me make a call." He walked to the outer office and punched in a number on his phone. After speaking to someone briefly, he returned and stood in the doorway.

"Let's take a drive."

Shelter looked at Traverse and then glanced at his watch. It was almost 4:00 p.m.

"Where?" he asked.

"Not far. I'm driving a red Honda Civic. I'll meet you out front."

Traverse gunned the Crown Vic's engine a couple of times and pulled into traffic behind Kent's beat-up Honda. Selkirk Avenue was the North End's main commercial artery. There was a day when it was lined with delis, small department stores and an old-time movie palace. They were the businesses of Jews, Ukrainians, Poles, Germans, who landed there at the turn of the last century.

These days, it was surrounded by a huge Indigenous population, and he knew people in more prosperous parts of the city looked upon it as a dangerous stretch of urban decay. But amid the rundown houses, vacant lots and boarded-up stores, Shelter had begun to notice shoots of revitalization, and it gave him hope. There were clusters of businesses: a bakery, low-end restaurants, convenience and discount stores, and social development agencies. Despite the crime and poverty, Shelter chose to focus on the people on nearby streets who were just trying to get up every day, get their kids to school, go to work and make a better life for themselves.

He and Traverse had worked dozens of murders in the North End and downtown over the last five years, mostly drug dealer score-settling and petty domestic beefs that spiralled into violence. Almost all were cleared or well on their way to being cleared in the first forty-eight hours. Shelter could keep a cool, detached attitude to the mayhem, except when it came to the kids. He had that in common with Crystal and a lot of people working down here, including Traverse.

He glanced to his right, down McKenzie Street, and remembered a case he and Traverse had worked a year earlier. It was the dead of winter, and they'd been called out to a clapboard house with boarded-up windows. An eighteen-year-old Indigenous man had his throat slashed with a broken beer bottle as the sun came up on an all-night party in a crack shack. When Shelter and Traverse arrived at the scene, they'd found three kids, all under eight years old, sitting side by side in the back of a cruiser.

They were dressed in filthy, ripped parkas, pyjama bottoms and running shoes, despite a temperature of twenty below zero. One little boy of about four sat closest to the car window that Shelter peered through. He had a grimy face, an angry bruise on his cheek and big, dark, pleading eyes. Shelter remembered smiling and giving a little wave, but there'd been no reaction. Taking a step back from the car, he'd thought of Kelsey at that age — warm, loved, protected. What was in store for these kids? Future customers for the police? That little boy's eyes had brought Shelter out of his sleep with a jerk every night for a week. He knew a lot of people were working to make it better, but the problems ran deep. The gangs and drug trade weren't going away and neither was the poverty that fed them. He understood why Traverse was feeling beaten down. But he wouldn't give in to despair. This was the job he'd chosen, and he was hoping Traverse would come to the same conclusion.

Shelter hit the accelerator to keep up with Kent, who'd turned onto McPhillips Street, heading north. The broad avenue was packed with rush-hour traffic. Shelter went over what it meant that Crystal and Spence knew each other. As if reading his mind, Traverse said, "Wouldn't the connection with Crystal have come up in the Spence investigation if they knew each other well enough to make a difference?"

"Not necessarily," Shelter said. "They were from different worlds. If Crystal didn't want to approach us after Monica was killed, probably no one else thought much about it until Crystal got killed too."

Kent made a right onto a side street lined with tightly spaced houses. He crossed an intersection and pulled to a stop. Shelter pulled in behind him and looked over at Traverse with his lips pulled into a tight frown.

Traverse was peering through his window at a white stucco house with blue shutters. He turned to meet Shelter's gaze and shook his head. "Oh, man," he said. "Where's this heading?"

Shelter and Traverse knew the house well. In the last weeks, they'd visited it a couple of times to interview the staff and other residents. Monica Spence had run away from the house two months earlier, and a police search for her had turned up nothing. Three weeks later, her body was found in the culvert. She'd been running away from foster homes and group homes since she was twelve. By sixteen, she had a cocaine problem and her picture was turning up on escort sites.

"Monica Spence lived in this house before she was killed," Shelter said to Kent, who met them on the boulevard in front of the group home.

Kent nodded. "Crystal used to come here to work with girls in care. Mostly to take them out for coffee and just, you know, be there for them."

A pair of Indigenous teenage girls dressed in jeans and T-shirts emerged from the house and crossed the intersection, heading west. They looked carefree in the brilliant sunshine, chatting and laughing.

Kent pulled his phone from his jeans pocket and punched in

a short text. After a moment, he said, "Okay, she's ready to see us." When Kent reached the house, he went around the side and opened a wooden gate that was almost as tall as he was and ushered the two detectives into the yard.

A woman dressed in a sleeveless T-shirt and Adidas soccer shorts sat on a picnic table on a cement pad surrounded by patchy, weed-infested grass. She took a puff on a cigarette and blew smoke rings as she watched the men approach.

"Karen," Kent said, giving the woman a brief hug, and sat down beside her on the table. "Thanks for doing this."

"This is Karen Roth," he told the officers. "She's a worker here who knew Crystal and Monica. She called me this morning asking for help, and I thought it best she talk to you guys."

She was slender and wore her auburn hair in a bob with bangs that touched her eyebrows. Shelter had misjudged her age from a distance. She was at least thirty-five but dressed much younger. She exhaled a final drag from her cigarette, ground it out on the patio and dropped the butt into a Diet Coke can.

"Hello, Karen," Shelter said without warmth in his voice.

Kent looked from one to the other. "You know each other?"

"Yup," Shelter said. "We interviewed Karen a couple of weeks ago. What have you got for us?" A sense of foreboding had been building in Shelter from the moment he laid eyes on Karen. He felt tension in his gut, and the muscles in his neck and shoulders were rock-hard.

When Karen spoke, her voice was raspy. "It's about Crystal Rempel. She came by once a week to hang out with the girls. She was really good with them. Not judgmental. Just someone to talk to who wasn't in the system, you know?"

She pulled another cigarette out of her pack and lit it. "It's hard to crack the shell, but she had a knack for it. Her and I got to be friends over the months." She glanced over at Moses. "We all got to be friends."

She gathered her thoughts. "Monica was one of the girls she talked to. I don't think it was anything that special for Crystal. But for Monica it was huge. No one had ever really spent time with her like that." She took a deep drag. "That was one screwed-up girl, okay? Like, you can't imagine the abuse, starting from when she was a small kid."

Karen looked toward the sky. She seemed to gather herself and continued. "It was obviously horrible here after Monica was killed. The media was going nuts, and the investigation has been torture for the people in this house. Crystal came around after it happened, and she was as broken up about it as anyone. Sad for Monica and really pissed off."

"When was this?" Shelter asked.

"It was maybe a week or ten days after Monica's body was found. I can't be sure."

"You say she was sad about Monica, but also angry," Shelter said. "Angry about what?"

"We knew Monica had been into the sex trade. And Crystal seemed to know something about it. She asked me if a pimp was involved."

"And?"

"We knew she'd been on the street and involved in the sex trade in the past. But I didn't know anything about a pimp."

Shelter was angry. His face was hot, and the sweat on his back made his shirt cling to him. He took a moment to try to gather and calm himself, but it was a lost cause.

"You never mentioned Crystal when we talked to you about Monica, and you didn't call us after she was killed. I can't understand that, especially after all the speculation about her and Monica in the media."

"I thought you guys already knew about this," she said. Shelter raised an eyebrow. Her comment rang false, and she knew it. "Okay.

I didn't want to get involved."

Kent cut in. "Karen, maybe this is a good time to tell the officers about Pam."

"Yeah. Okay. Right," she said, recovering her train of thought. "I didn't know who to call, so I called Moses. There's a friend of Monica's, and she's scared shitless. She called me yesterday. She needs help, like protection."

"What's this girl's name?" Shelter asked.

"Let's just make it Pam, okay? Thing is, she used to work with Monica. They met here at the house, but Pam turned eighteen and got kicked out on her ass just like that. How are these kids supposed to survive, eh?" She glared at the two detectives as if they were responsible for the failings of the child welfare system. She rubbed her hands up and down her thighs vigorously. "The bottom line is that Monica didn't work alone. Pam was her partner."

"What do you mean, partner?"

"She was in the business too. They watched each other's back."

Walking back to the car, Traverse looked at Shelter and shook his head. Spence had left the group home three weeks before she was killed, and the investigation had focused on her descent into a chaotic 24/7 existence of drugs, partying and prostitution. The chaos in her life had made it difficult to piece together her last days. This was the first real breakthrough after a month of running into one brick wall after another. Shelter phoned Neil MacIsaac and briefed him on what Karen Roth had told them.

"I can't believe we didn't have this before now," MacIsaac said. The comment sent Shelter's pulse racing—he didn't need to be told it was a grievous oversight, one that Crystal Rempel probably paid for with her life. Although he didn't know what he could have done differently, Shelter felt he was to blame.

"Let's take another look at everyone working or living at that house," MacIsaac said, his words dripping with disgust. "We have a link, and there's a good chance it leads back to the group home. When are we talking to this Pam girl?"

"Karen won't give us the phone number," Shelter said. "She's going to try to set up a meeting tomorrow. The girl is going to want protection. What can we do for her?"

"Let's see what she's got. Maybe we can put her up in a hotel room for a little bit if it's good."

"We can't leave her out here twisting in the wind."

"She's got to produce. We're not running a charity here," MacIsaac said and ended the call.

Shelter tossed the phone in a cup holder and glanced at Traverse, who read his mood from the grim look on his face. Traverse pushed his sunglasses to the top of his head and looked his partner in the eyes.

"Stop right there, Mike, okay? Beating ourselves up isn't going to help."

"No one in that house mentioned Crystal. How could that be?"

"Exactly. Good question. There's no answer, so let it go. We've got something solid now, and we're going to hit it hard."

# TWELVE

Shelter heated a frozen dinner of mac and cheese in the microwave and ate it standing at the counter with a large glass of Cabernet Sauvignon. If he lay down on the couch to watch TV, he'd be out until the morning. Instead, he dialled Kelsey's cellphone and listened as it rang through to voicemail. He texted her, telling her to call him, with two exclamation marks. By the time he'd finished cleaning up the kitchen and living room, there was still no response. He tried the house in Gimli, and after exchanging a few pleasantries with his mother-in-law, he got Kelsey on the line.

"Why don't you answer when I call you?" It came out as an accusation, but he couldn't help himself. "That's why I'm paying fifty bucks a month for that phone." There was silence on the other end. "Are you there?"

"Yes. I'm here."

"So why don't you answer my calls or my texts?"

"I was busy."

Shelter struggled to control his anger. He needed to warn her about Rory Sinclair, but he realized his tone was too stern. He didn't want to alarm Kelsey unduly by telling her she'd been stalked online. Instead, he needed to be calm and reassuring, especially because there was little chance Sinclair would actually track her down.

"Listen, something happened during one of the investigations I'm working on. I don't want you to worry, but I need you to be a little more careful. Keep your eyes open on the street for anything unusual and be aware if someone you don't know tries to talk to you either outside, online or on the phone."

"What do you mean something happened? What happened?"

Her reaction sparked a wave of tenderness for his daughter. "I'm sure it's nothing," he said in a quiet voice. "But I want you to be extra aware. Make sure Grandma and Grandpa know where you're going and let me know right away if anything strange happens, okay?"

"Dad, I'm old enough to know what's going on."

"I know you are. But I can't really go into the details, Kel. It will be okay."

He tried to lighten the mood by asking about the closing of the fishing season, but Kelsey's answers consisted of *yes, no, fine, nothing* and *I don't know*. Her tone was once again frosty, rancorous. Finally, he gave up and told her he loved her, but the words came out hollow, perfunctory.

"Okay. Bye," Kelsey replied.

Shelter braced himself against the counter with splayed hands as he went over how the conversation had begun. How could he be so harsh with her? He pressed his fingers into the countertop. A memory came to him of sitting in Christa's room in the Health Sciences Centre, watching her brush Kelsey's hair slowly and whispering close to their daughter's ear, soothing her and even making her smile. He longed to be able to reach her like that.

Kelsey had been left on her own a lot between Christa's operations, radiation treatments and his crazy work schedule. Shelter should have tried to be with her more during those months. But he hid in his work instead of taking time off, and now he was paying the price. What could he do to repair the damage to their relationship? He'd have to be patient, but it was the fall that worried him. If she stayed in Gimli, they would grow even further apart. Next summer, she'd be working and there wouldn't be time for a vacation. It felt like he was on the verge of losing her from his life.

But if he was honest, there was a part of him that wanted her to stay in Gimli. He'd grown accustomed to the freedom it afforded him. It relieved him of guilt when he had to work late or slept in on the weekend rather than come up with something to do together, and the responsibility for shopping, preparing meals, washing the kitchen floor and bathroom once a week. When she wasn't there, he could fall into his sloppy bachelor ways.

He couldn't believe he'd just had that thought. Preferred not to have Kelsey with him? What was happening to him? In that moment, another memory surfaced. When Kelsey was small, he would take her on bus rides on weekend afternoons to give Christa a rest. They would set off together with no particular destination in mind, transferring downtown to ride to some unfamiliar neighbourhood. She was delighted by the motion of the bus, the passengers and passing scenery. He would take her off at a random stop near the end of the line to buy her ice cream or a bag of chips before returning home. She held his hand as they walked, and he basked in her perfect love and trust. She'd continued to hold his hand unconsciously until she was ten, long past the age when he'd expected her to stop. Now, he felt as if he could let his knees go and drop to the floor, collapse right there. His thoughts were interrupted by a beep signalling a text. He pulled it out of his pocket, hoping it was a message from Kelsey. He opened the text message app.

*It's Nicki. Need to see you tn, come to bar after 10.*

Raindrops threw up little puffs of dust in the parking lot of the City Hotel. Shelter ran to the back door as the downpour began and lightning traced a jagged white line across the sky. His head down, he almost ran into two men waiting with their cases of beer for the rain to ease up.

Inside, only a couple of tables were occupied. Shelter saw Nicki sitting on a counter that ran off the end of the bar, legs dangling. He took a seat with his back to the wall.

Glancing up, Nicki noticed him. She jumped down from the counter, circled the pool tables and slowly approached. Shelter smiled and nodded a greeting. "Got time to talk now?"

She surveyed the empty barroom. "I'm run off my feet." Then, after a beat, "Not here, I need a smoke."

She dropped her tray at the bar and had a few words with the bartender before leading Shelter outside, where they stood beneath the awning, watching rain sweep across the parking lot. She pulled out a pack of cigarettes. Shelter shook his head when she offered him one. "How you doing?" he asked.

"You catch the fucker yet?" She took a deep drag, narrowing her eyes and searching his face through the smoke.

"We're working on it."

"Yeah, I thought so." She shook her head, looking down at her black, high-top Converse sneakers. The rain drummed down on the pavement made shiny and yellow by the illumination of a streetlight. After a couple of seconds, she looked into his eyes. "Rory called me today."

"What did he want?"

"He said you guys were at the pool hall asking questions. He wanted me to talk to you."

Shelter took a moment to absorb this. "I thought you were going to say he warned you not to talk to us."

"Yeah, I was surprised too," she said. "He wants to meet you, just you. And he warned me to keep my mouth shut about it."

Shelter exhaled loudly. "What did he say exactly?"

"He said he didn't kill Crystal and he's being set up for it."

"You believe him?"

"Probably not. But he's scared."

"Set up by who?"

"I don't know. But he wants a meeting." Nicki hugged herself, looking out over the parking lot.

"All he has to do is come in."

"No. Says he won't. He's going to call you. I gave him the number."

Shelter nodded. "You asked him about who killed Crystal, right?"

"He says he doesn't know anything."

Shelter wondered what possible motive Sinclair could have for reaching out to him. The last thing a guy like him does is go to the police. If someone were trying to set him up for the murders, he'd try to handle it himself. It didn't make sense unless he was feeling cornered, searching for a last-ditch way to implicate someone else. He looked over at Nicki. Could she know more than she was telling him?

"What does he want to talk about?"

"No idea. He just wants to see you."

After a moment, Shelter asked her again, "How are you doing?"

It took her a long time to answer. She smoked her cigarette down to the filter before flicking it into a puddle. She rubbed a tear away with a finger.

"What's driving me crazy is fucking people trying to figure out what to say to me about Crystal. You end up comforting *them*." She gave a grim little laugh. "I used to think about Crystal a lot when I was bouncing around foster homes," she said, turning to look at Shelter. "At night in my room, I'd try to imagine what she was doing right at that moment in her room, you know? It was like a piece of me was missing. When she moved to Winnipeg, that piece was put back. For her too, getting to know me and my mom and where we came from. That was huge for her."

Shelter waited and resisted the urge to reach out to comfort her. Instead, he jammed his hands into his pockets. "I lost my wife last year, so I know a bit about what you're talking about."

She considered this and was about to say something but changed her mind. Shelter was aware of her body close to his, their hips almost touching as the rain enclosed them like a curtain.

"This girl, Monica Spence," Shelter said, raising his voice to be heard over the rain hammering on the canopy above their heads. "We heard today that Crystal knew her. She was one of the girls Crystal was working with at a group home in the North End."

"I knew she was helping girls. We talked about that, but like I told you, she never said anything about Monica."

"And you never saw Monica at the bar, right?"

"No."

She took a step toward the door. "Maybe it was Monica's murder that made Crystal so upset," Shelter said.

Nicki thought about that before nodding.

"So, Rory's going to call me?" Shelter asked.

"That's what he said."

"I guess I'll see you tomorrow at Crystal's memorial service?"

She pulled open the door and twisted to look at him. "Guess so but stay away from me. You're bad for my reputation."

# THIRTEEN

Transcona was laid out on a grid on the east side of the city, surrounded by railway yards, industrial zones and open prairie that would one day fill up with cookie-cutter housing developments. Shelter slowed the car to a crawl, following the house numbers on the modest bungalows built for railway workers. He found the one he was looking for and pulled to the curb.

"Ah, beautiful Transcona," Traverse said. "They've got their own micro-climate out here. Always a bit sunnier, always a bit warmer, a bit happier."

Shelter grimaced at the joke as he surveyed the little house. It was a wreck in contrast with the well-kept homes on either side. Cream-coloured paint peeled from the stucco, and a decorative shutter hung by a nail beside a picture window, shrouded by curtains. The front lawn was mostly weeds. Bits of yellowed newspaper and a potato chip bag were caught in the shrubbery beside the crumbling cement steps. Shelter thought he could smell diesel wafting from the railway yards but decided it was his imagination.

Earlier, Shelter had called Karen Roth at the group home. They'd wanted to get Pam into an interview room downtown to find out what she knew about the murder of her partner in prostitution, Monica Spence. But when Roth insisted she was too scared to leave the house, they were forced to make the long drive out to this neighbourhood.

Traverse pushed the doorbell and gave two sharp knocks on the aluminum outer door. After a few seconds, he opened it and hammered on the main door. The curtains fluttered. A dead bolt lock was thrown, and the door squeaked open as far as a chain lock would let it.

One brown eye examined Traverse through the crack. "Pam?" he said, holding up his badge. She released the lock, opened the door, and stood aside. They advanced into a tiny living room. Dusty beams of sun penetrated the room from cracks in the curtains. A sixty-inch flat-screen TV showing a daytime talk show with the sound muted provided the only other illumination.

"Sorry, I had the headphones on." Pam nodded down a hallway toward a couple of closed doors. She was a big white girl, not overweight but solidly built. Her shoulder-length hair had been bleached blond and dyed with magenta streaks.

She picked up the remote control from the coffee table, snapped off the TV, and retreated to a recliner. She was wearing sweats with the word *Juicy* printed across her butt. Pulling her legs underneath her on the chair, she seemed to be trying to make herself as small as she could, like a cat curling up for a snooze.

The detectives helped themselves to seats on the couch. Traverse thanked her for seeing them and after a pause said, "Let's start with your name."

"It's Pam. No last name."

"No, uh-uh," Traverse interjected, patient but firm. "If we're getting off on the right foot here, we've got to know who we're dealing with."

She thought about it before sighing. "It's Pam. Pamela. Pamela Daniel. Okay? Happy?"

Her face was puffy, eyes bleary. Shelter guessed she wasn't used to being out of bed before noon and wondered if she was in withdrawal. Her eyes bounced from one detective to the other. She reached for a throw cushion and held it to her chest like a shield.

"We need to talk to you about Monica Spence," Traverse said.

"We understand you were working with her, like her partner in the business."

"I'm not telling you guys one fucking thing about Monica until you promise me a safe place to stay."

"Let's just talk, and we'll see what we can do, eh? We can't help you unless you're willing to help us."

"Don't give me that shit. Not one word."

Shelter changed tacks. "Whose place is this anyway?"

"My uncle, my mom's brother. I swore I'd never come back to this neighbourhood, and here I am. I'm broke, and I gotta get out of here." She tossed the pillow aside and grabbed a pack of du Maurier cigarettes off the table. She lit one with a trembling hand.

Shelter was torn, and he knew Traverse would be feeling it too. He didn't want to make a promise to this woman he couldn't keep, especially before he knew if she had anything valuable to give them. But they had to get her talking. He decided to take a chance and sort it out with MacIsaac later.

"We can't make any promises, but we'll do our best to get you into a hotel with some police protection until this thing is resolved," he said. "That's the best we can do. We've got bosses, and they've got budgets. If you help us, we can probably move you this afternoon."

She took a deep drag from her cigarette and examined the blood-red nails on her right hand. Shelter knew she was bluffing, like a poker player taking her sweet time to save face before folding a losing hand.

"Alright, but I'm going to hold you to that. I'll go to the media. I fucking swear I will."

"Let's start with how you knew Monica," Shelter said.

"We met at the group home," she said in distracted, almost casual way.

"When did you go into care?"

"I don't know. I'm eighteen now, so five years ago, something like that. My dad's a drinker, and he beat us up — my mom, my brother and me. So, when Mom took off, my brother and I ended up in care."

"You became friends with Monica at the group home?"

She nodded. "We stayed friends when I got kicked out at eighteen. She'd had it really hard too. Lots of abuse and foster homes. But she was sweet. We got along good."

"How did you get into the business?" Traverse asked.

Pam climbed out of the recliner. Sunshine flooded into the room when she pulled back the curtain to peek out the window. She let the curtain go, turned and fixed her eyes on Traverse. Shelter sensed she trusted his partner more, for whatever reason, and he was content to let Traverse take the lead.

"It wasn't anything you haven't heard a hundred times before. He was sweet at the beginning, taking me out to the mall and buying me clothes and jewellery and shit. And the booze, of course, and blow. Before long, he's telling you he loves you and you love him, eh?"

"How old were you?" Traverse asked.

"Sixteen."

She turned so she was in profile to them. "And then it starts with a guy in a room, and, you know, 'If you love me, you'll do it.'" She examined her nails and gave a resigned shake of her head. "The hardest thing? It was me who brought Monica to him."

"Brought her to who?"

She ground out the cigarette hard into an ashtray. "Fucking Rory. Who else?"

Traverse let it sit there. "Rory Sinclair was pimping both you and Monica. That's what you're telling us?"

"That's what I'm telling you. When Monica ran away from the group home and I let her stay at my place. That's where Rory met her. We were partying, eh? She didn't want to go back to the house, and she needed the money."

She let out a heavy sigh and examined a bangle on her wrist before looking up at Traverse.

"After a while it was through that bitch girlfriend of his, the Vietnamese chick. She would set up our dates and take Rory's cut, but at the beginning he plays the boyfriend until you're so deep into the life, you can't get out. He's good at it."

Shelter remembered the Asian woman with Sinclair at the pool hall. "What's the girlfriend's name?"

"Jasmine. That's all I know."

"Okay, let's talk about the protection system you had with Monica," Traverse said.

Pam crossed the room and flopped into the recliner again. "We only did it when we were out on the street. When dates were arranged, like online, we felt safer. There were still sick fucks, but at least they know you've got their phone number if anything nasty happens."

She was starting to talk faster. "But if we were hard-up for cash, we'd work the street once in a while, you know?" She lit another cigarette. "Dumb, right? But that's what we did. I would take down the licence plates of the cars she got into, and she did the same for me."

"Looking out for each other," Traverse said.

"Yeah. If the john started doing sick shit or pulled a knife, we could tell him our friend had his licence plate, and he'd back off. That's the way it was supposed to work."

"Was Monica working the night she got killed?"

"Yeah."

"What happened?"

It took a long time before Pam answered. She had her eyes on the coffee table and brought a fist to her mouth to contain a sob. When she did speak, her throat was constricted. "She had a bad cold, and she wasn't going to go out on dates." She had to pause again to calm herself. "I was downtown at a bar, and she called me. Rory was pissed off because she didn't want to work. She owed him for some coke."

Shelter interjected. "How did she sound? Do you remember?"

"Scared shitless. You have no idea what it's like to have an asshole like that in your life, man. She was afraid he was going to beat her up again. She couldn't take that."

"So she went out on a call?"

"No, she went out on the street, the same place we always worked — on Ellice."

"If you were downtown, how do you know what she did?" Traverse asked.

"That's what Rory said. When I woke up the next morning, I saw she hadn't come home. That wasn't weird. She'd disappear for days on end, partying here and there. But I couldn't get her on the phone, and she always answered her texts. I started freaking out, but I couldn't get hold of Rory all day either. And then it was on the news that you guys found a girl's body outside the city."

"And that was Monica," Shelter said.

Pam nodded and began to sob. Shelter became aware of the sound of a clock ticking somewhere behind him in the gloomy house. He gave a slight shake of his head to Traverse. All this information she was giving them was what they'd spent weeks looking for. Pam grabbed a couple of tissues from a box on the coffee table and dried her eyes.

"What did Rory say when it came out it was Monica?" Traverse asked.

"He came over to my place, and he's playing it cool. You know — there's nothing we could do for her now. Shit like that."

"He didn't seem upset or worried?"

"He was pretending to be broken up, but he's a heartless prick," she said. "He told me to be cool, and everything would be okay.

But I just couldn't calm down. Monica was on the TV every fucking night." She paused to wipe her eyes. "What if it was Rory who did it?" Her voice went up, a hint of panic. "What if he finds out I'm talking to you guys?"

Traverse waited for her to calm down. "How was he acting in the days after Monica was found?"

"Business as usual until that lawyer lady started coming down on him. Then he started to freak."

"By lawyer lady, you mean Crystal Rempel."

"Oh, yeah," Pam said. "She found out Rory got Monica into the business, and she would not let it go. She was calling him and coming up to him in bars. Asking him what happened to Monica and threatening to go to the police."

"How did Crystal find out about Rory and Monica?" Shelter asked.

Pam lowered her eyes and went quiet.

"You told her," Traverse said.

Pam nodded. "He'll fucking kill me if he finds out."

"You called her?"

"Monica told me she was cool, and I remembered where she worked." Pam took a deep drag from her cigarette. "I was so scared. I needed to talk to somebody. We met at a coffee shop in St. Vital, a place Rory would never go. She was super smart and beautiful. I told her about Monica and him. And she starts asking me about dates we'd been on, eh? And I couldn't help myself." She paused, her eyes fixed on Traverse. "I told her about the picture."

"What picture?" Shelter said, suddenly alert.

Pam stood up and went to the back of the house. She returned and handed Traverse a photocopy of a photo. Shelter leaned over to study it at the same time.

It had been taken in a dimly lit room but was in focus. It showed four people partying in a hotel room. Rory Sinclair was seated on the king-size bed closest to the camera. He was looking over his shoulder at a man whose head was tilted back, laughing at a joke. The laughing man was Indigenous and obese, with a heavy gold chain around his neck. His name was Charlie, just Charlie — that's all Pam knew. He was holding a rolled-up bill, ready to snort a line of cocaine off the top of a chest of drawers strewn with beer cans and miniature liquor bottles.

In the background on the other side of the bed was another man, standing with his profile to the camera. His face was indistinct, but he was white, in his fifties, bald with a fringe of grey hair, glasses and a pot belly. Pam remembered his name was Bill. He had an arm wrapped tight around the shoulder of a smiling girl with shimmering black hair facing the camera. She was dressed in a clingy charcoal mini-dress and was petite beside his bulky frame. The girl was Monica Spence.

"You gave this photo to Monica?" Shelter asked.

Pam nodded.

"And Crystal?"

She nodded again before burying her face in her hands.

# FOURTEEN

Shelter leaned back in his chair and looked up at Traverse standing in the entrance to his cubicle. Shelter was listening to him talk about Rory Sinclair, but part of his mind was measuring the change in his partner. The meeting with Pam Daniel seemed to have thrown a switch in Traverse. He was back to his old self: excited, engaged, on the hunt. Shelter hoped it was the start of a new chapter, and he would decide to stay with the department.

"I don't know what Nicki is talking about. There's no way Rory is calling you," Traverse said. "We're going to have to bring him in."

"If he doesn't want to be found, he won't be," Shelter said. "He'll just jump up to the rez."

"What possible reason could he have to want to talk to you?" Traverse asked. "Don't get me wrong. You're a great conversationalist and all, but Monica, Crystal, it's pointing to him."

He was interrupted by Ian Sim's nasal voice. "He's ready for you now," Sim said, looking over the chest-high cubicle wall. Shelter led the way to Inspector Neil MacIsaac's office. On the way, Shelter realized he hadn't had a chance to grab lunch, and he felt a headache starting behind his eyes. This visit to the boss's office wasn't going to help.

"Okay, give it to me," MacIsaac said.

Shelter had his notebook out and was flipping pages. "Pamela Mary Daniel. She'll be nineteen on August 12. Arrested twice for solicitation. She says Rory Sinclair groomed her for prostitution when she was sixteen."

Shelter ran down how Pam knew Monica Spence and had introduced her to Sinclair, and how they'd worked the street together.

"And the night Monica was killed?" MacIsaac asked.

"Pam got a call from Monica. Rory was pissed off over a drug debt, and she was hitting the street alone. When she turned up dead, Rory told Pam to sit tight and ride it out."

Traverse interjected. "But she panics and decides to take it to Crystal Rempel."

Shelter glanced at Traverse. "Show him the picture."

Traverse opened a file folder and laid the image on MacIsaac's desk. "Pam took this at the Bond Hotel less than a week before Monica was killed," he said. "She comes out of the bathroom and pretends to be sending a text. Instead she takes the picture, a little habit of hers."

"Dangerous habit," MacIsaac said, shaking his head as he scanned the photo. "What am I looking at?"

"Rory brought the girls and an eight-ball of coke," Shelter said. "He stayed to party for a while." Shelter scooted forward on his seat and leaned over the desk, pointing to the large Indigenous man. "Besides Rory here, you've got Charlie Osborne." He moved his finger left to the white man in the background, his face in profile, indistinct. "She only knows this guy as Bill." He straightened and pushed himself back in his chair. "And she says there was one other man in the room."

"What do we know about him?"

"An older white guy in a suit. He didn't stay long. That's it."

"Who set up the party?"

"Pam doesn't know. Just that they were celebrating something. A business deal."

MacIsaac nodded. "Who else has the picture?"

"After Crystal was killed, Pam was so freaked out, she erased it from her phone and destroyed the SIM card."

"Why so scared?"

"Because of the way Crystal reacted to it," Shelter said. "When they met, they talked about Monica's dates — who she'd been with. Pam showed Crystal the picture, and she was very hot to get a copy."

MacIsaac took that in, lowering his eyes to the jumble of paperwork on his desk. It took a couple of seconds for him to come up with the question Shelter and Traverse were waiting for. "Did she give a copy to anyone else?"

It was Shelter who answered. "Monica Spence."

MacIsaac raised an eyebrow.

"If she was hard-up for cash, maybe she decided blackmailing someone in that room was the solution," Shelter said.

"Okay, what's our play?"

"We're looking for Rory. We've got him on pimping," Shelter said. "We're also trying to track down Charlie Osborne and find out who the other two guys in the hotel room were. Sharma and Sim are working on the hotel — who booked it, video from the parking lot and front desk."

On the way back to their desks, Shelter said to Traverse, "I want you on Charlie Osborne. We need more on him — his work, who he hangs out with." Shelter sat down at his desk and said over his shoulder, "All these guys are probably talking to each other. When we find out who everybody is, it's going to unravel...hopefully."

Shelter leaned against the car hood a couple of hundred metres from the Indigenous Friendship and Assistance Centre on the northern edge of downtown. Mourners had begun to file into the two-storey cinder-block building for Crystal Rempel's memorial.

Shelter was there on the off-chance Rory Sinclair might show up. It had been a long, frustrating two days. A search of his haunts around town had come up empty, and the RCMP on his home reserve couldn't find him either. They hadn't had any more luck bringing Charlie Osborne in for questioning about the hotel room party and the identity of Bill and the other man.

He'd considered attending the service and decided to watch from afar. Christa's funeral was still a raw memory. He had sat numb in the front pew in the little church in Gimli with Kelsey and the rest of the family. The church was packed with most of the Gimli community and friends and family up from Winnipeg. The emotion had been wrung out of Shelter over the previous three months, and with one arm around Kelsey, he listened impassively to Bible readings and Christa's musical selections, "Amazing Grace" and a cover of "Up Where We Belong." It had been a eulogy by Christa's brother that had finally cracked the shell. He talked about Christa's kindness, her joy, her capacity for love, all she had done in her short life. As he listened, Shelter choked up, and the tears flowed not only for the loss, but also for all he'd left undone in the years they had been together, for all his failings as a husband, a father, a man. He hadn't loved her hard enough, and now it was too late.

The sun was high over the friendship centre and beating down on mourners filing into Crystal Rempel's service. Shelter spotted Nicki across the street, accompanied by Moses Kent. She was wearing an elegant black dress that reached to her knees. Moses, who was in a navy-blue suit and a black tie, touched her arm as they entered the service together.

A limousine pulled up, and the premier of Manitoba and attorney general got out and nodded to the phalanx of TV cameras on the sidewalk. Only Mayor Sam Klein, who'd never seen a microphone he could resist, stopped to briefly answer reporters' questions. Shelter's attention was drawn to the thin, stooped figure of Crystal's adoptive mother, Violet Rempel. She was dressed all in black, with a large sun hat, and her arm was supported by a younger woman as she climbed the stairs and entered the building. Shelter thought about Crystal's birth mother, Anne Alexander, who'd committed suicide just before her daughter was killed. Could it have been the suicide that led Crystal to disappear in the days before she was murdered?

The service had drawn a large crowd, hundreds of people, despite it being a weekday morning. The day before, a smaller private family service had been held in Steinbach. Shelter wasn't surprised to see the politicians come out for this one. The city was on edge, and the heat wave wasn't helping, or the shooting of Jason Courchene, who was still in a coma. There was a blackout on details, but the scuttlebutt at the station was that Dustin Crowley, the young constable who had shot Courchene in the back, had straight-up panicked in a struggle. It was a huge embarrassment to Chief Gordy Taylor, the mayor and the whole city. Crowley's career was toast — that was a given. But worse for Shelter was that the shooting was feeding the media frenzy over the Spence and Rempel killings.

Shelter thought about Monica Spence's funeral a few weeks earlier at a church in the West End. He'd watched from across the street as Monica's mother and a small group of friends and family straggled into the church. The media had been there too, but no dignitaries had turned up on that day. Monica hadn't been a star in law school or the leader of an Indigenous rights group, like Crystal Rempel. Today, the politicians were putting on a show of concern for the cameras, hoping to keep a lid on the situation in the Indigenous community and limit the political damage in the wider population.

"Detective." The gruff voice made Shelter jump.

He pushed off the car and turned around to find Gordy Taylor on the sidewalk in full uniform. He was accompanied by an elderly man in a black shirt with a clerical collar. The priest had thick, rimless glasses, a sharp nose and a soft, round body that made him look like a tiny owl beside Taylor's hulking frame.

"Working hard?" Taylor asked with a smile. Shelter thought the police chief's hale and hearty tone struck a false note, given the circumstances.

"Yes, sir," Shelter said.

"Michael, come here and meet a friend of mine."

Shelter circled the car and shook hands with both men. "Michael Shelter, this is Father Ted Wright. We bumped into one another in the parking lot."

The priest's pale blue eyes studied Shelter's face. "Are you coming in for the service?"

Taylor cut in and answered for him. "He has a lot of work to do on the murders of these two Native girls. Detective Shelter is leading the investigations." Shelter noted the chief referred to the investigation in the plural, as if they weren't linked.

"Ah. Important work," the little priest said. He pulled a pressed handkerchief from his pocket and dabbed his forehead. "Most important work. To bring some relief to the families and this city."

"Ted, would you excuse us?" Taylor said. "I want to have a word with Detective Shelter. I'll see you inside."

Wright raised a hand in acknowledgment and hobbled across the street.

"Got a bad leg there," Taylor said. "I met him many, many years ago when I was a young Mountie working on the reserves. A great man, but he seems to be getting a bit foggy."

The police chief turned to Shelter. "Are we making any headway on tracking down this Sinclair guy?"

"Not yet. But we're hoping to get him soon. He can't hide forever."

Taylor took a step toward Shelter and put a hand on his shoulder. "This case is going to make or break your career," he said in a quiet, encouraging voice. The tone was familiar to Shelter from other mentoring sessions with Taylor over the years. "You've got a real chance here, Mike."

The bill on Taylor's cap was just a few inches from Shelter's forehead.

"We'll get him, sooner or later."

"Make it sooner."

Taylor crossed the street to join Wright, and they entered the friendship centre together.

Shelter returned to lean against the car, going over the exchange in his mind. He'd sensed again how anxious Taylor was about the case. The clock was ticking to his retirement.

An hour later, Shelter sat at his table in the Peking Garden and shovelled Singapore noodles into his mouth. He had a napkin tucked into his collar and his iPhone in his left hand. From an ancient set of speakers up in the corners of the dining room, Dionne Warwick was softly crooning "Walk on By" on an oldies radio station.

Shelter ate lunch alone if he could. He liked getting away from the office to this table in this dark, cool room. A place to read or just stare into space for forty-five minutes. It had also been a place for quiet, sad conversations when Christa was sick, and afterward, to make arrangements.

The image from the hotel room had been scanned and now glowed on the phone's screen. For what seemed like the thousandth time, Shelter examined every detail, bringing the phone close to his eyes. What had brought the men together in that room? What were they celebrating? Who were Bill and the other man — the one who had left the party early?

The sudden vibration of the phone in his hand made Shelter jump — a call from an unknown number. He punched the screen and put the phone to his ear. "Michael Shelter."

"It's Rory Sinclair. I hear you're looking for me."

The voice was breathy, choked, nervous.

It took a moment for Shelter to overcome his surprise. "You've got to come in, Rory."

There was silence on the other end. Arthur Yee approached the table with a pot of tea but retreated when Shelter waved him away.

"I didn't kill no fucking girls, okay?" Rory said, his voice rising.

"Okay. But you've got to come in. There's no other way."

Shelter could hear him breathing on the other end of the line.

"Nicki says you're okay. I'll come in with you. No one else."

"Where are you?"

"I'm not telling you that until you guarantee my safety."

"What are you afraid of?"

"I'm being set up, man."

"I'll meet you outside the Double Deuce at three."

"No. Not there."

"Okay. Where?"

The line went silent while Sinclair considered a meeting place. "The square at King and Bannatyne at five. Come alone. No other cops."

He meant the Old Market Square. Shelter saw it in his mind, a slice of green space carved out by intersecting streets in the city's Exchange District. It was surrounded by heritage buildings, tall brick warehouses dating from the turn of the last century, when Winnipeg was a boom town, the Chicago of the north. The square was popular with strollers in the summer, and there'd probably be a busker or two and maybe even a singer on the little stage. It would have to do.

"You come alone too," Shelter said. "I don't want to see that goon of yours."

Rory grunted.

"And, Rory, come unarmed."

# FIFTEEN

Shelter spent much of the afternoon with Neil MacIsaac and the head of the tactical unit, George Schur, discussing the operation. MacIsaac and Schur favoured staking out Market Square and taking Rory Sinclair as soon as he showed up for the meeting.

"He's a suspect in two murders. Let's do this right. Clear the square and grab him," said Schur, a veteran of fifteen years on the force. He was of Ukrainian descent, with close-cropped silver hair and a build chiselled from granite. He wanted discreet but full coverage of the square by the tactical unit, including snipers on rooftops.

"That's not necessary," Shelter said. "He's scared and wants to come in. Besides, I gave him my word that it would be just me."

In the end, it was a moot argument. MacIsaac got a call from upstairs — there was no budget to deploy the tactical team.

The decision angered Schur. "Who made the call? The chief?" he demanded.

MacIsaac shrugged. "Your guess is as good as mine. It came down from on high."

Traverse and Jennifer Kane plus four uniformed cops would keep an eye on the meeting from discreet locations. Schur would coordinate the coverage.

"And you need to wear a vest," Schur told Shelter.

Time dragged after the preparations had been made. No matter how many arrests he made or how routine the job appeared, Shelter was always keyed up. He knew the nerves were normal, like an actor getting ready to go on stage or a soldier before a battle, but it had become worse since he'd been shot when he was still in a uniform. That incident had marked him in ways that went much deeper than the angry red scar on his shoulder. He was more cautious on the job and slept less soundly.

"God, would you sit down?" Traverse called from his desk.

The comment snapped Shelter out of his thoughts. He looked over at his partner and gave him a grim smile and a shrug, as if to say *it's bigger than me.* At four forty-five, he told MacIsaac and Schur he was heading out. He felt the eyes on him as he made the short walk from the PSB to the Old Market Square. The officers monitoring the arrest were in place.

He was relieved to find fewer people in the square than he'd expected. A couple walking a baby in a stroller, a few winos, and a group of wannabe hippies. They were spread out, either using the benches ringing the square or lounging on the patch of grass at its centre.

Shelter chose a spot a few metres in from the sidewalk, where he had a good line of sight down both Market and King Streets to the south and the entire square when he turned north. He listened in his earpiece to occasional radio chatter between the cops watching the meet and fingered the microphone that ran down his sleeve and into his hand. He was sweating under a Kevlar vest and sports jacket. He'd been in the square less than five minutes when one of the uniforms reported, "Subject approaching on King Street. Accompanied by a female."

Shelter turned in the direction of King and caught sight of them right away. Sinclair standing close to Nicki, waiting to cross at the light. What was Nicki doing here?

He waited for them with his arms crossed and a frown on his face. As they approached, he examined Rory's low-slung jeans and black T-shirt — if he was carrying a weapon, it was well concealed. Even before they reached him, he jerked his head at Nicki and demanded, "What are you doing here?"

"Brought a friend — another set of eyes," Sinclair replied for her. He was distracted, his eyes darting around the square.

"I'm not your friend, asshole," Nicki said. She turned to Shelter. "He wouldn't come without me."

"You should have called me."

"It's my sister. I've got every right to be here."

Shelter turned to Rory. "Let's get you off the street. You're under arrest for living off the avails of prostitution. Do you understand?"

Sinclair was sweating, fidgety, unfocused.

"Do you understand?"

"Yes."

"You have the right to retain and instruct counsel without delay. We will provide you with the number of a lawyer referral service if you don't have your own lawyer. Anything you say can be given in court as evidence. Do you understand?"

"Yeah. Yeah. Hold it. What's going to happen to me in there?" Sinclair asked.

"What do you mean?" Shelter said, his brow wrinkling in irritation.

"You'll protect me, right?"

"Rory, you're under arrest."

"I'm being set up."

"Who's setting you up?

Before he could answer, Rory spun around. The sound of a rifle shot came a fraction of a second later. Blood sprayed Shelter's face, blinding and choking him. At first he thought he'd been shot. But as Sinclair fell, Shelter saw a piece of his skull had been blown away. The sound of the rifle blast reverberated off the buildings. Shelter stared at the body, and another shot slammed into Sinclair's chest.

A third round hit the pavement just to the left of Nicki. The shooter was targeting her now. Shelter pulled her to the ground as another bullet sent cement chips flying beside his ear.

He held her tight and rolled twice until they were under a bench. "I've got you."

People were screaming and running from the park. Shelter heard Schur's authoritative voice over the radio. "Shots fired. Who's firing?" Then, "One man down. Everyone hold your positions. Where's the shooter?"

Shelter was still holding Nicki in a bear hug. He saw officers taking cover against the surrounding buildings, their weapons raised, heads swivelling, searching the surrounding buildings.

Shelter loosened his grip on Nicki. Looking down, he saw the fronts of their shirts were covered in blood, and a piece of human tissue was stuck to his sleeve. "Are you okay? Are you hurt?"

Nicki was sobbing and shaking violently. She turned her head, and Shelter saw blood flowing from a deep gash in her cheek — something had cut her badly.

Schur called each of the officers over the radio. No one had sighted the shooter. He gave the order to advance and secure the square.

Traverse and Kane were the first to reach Shelter and Nicki. "Let's get you out of here," Traverse said, helping them up and hustling them down a side street amid the blare of approaching sirens.

At the hospital, Shelter had insisted on being in the examining room, watching Nicki's reactions closely as an ER doctor worked on her. She was glassy-eyed and uncommunicative as the doctor examined her, testing her reflexes and taking her pulse and blood pressure. He had closed the wound on her cheek and bandaged it, and she was taken to a ward to recover.

Shelter found the doctor at the nurses' station and asked about her condition. He said he thought she'd been cut by a shard of flying cement, and she was suffering from shock, not a concussion. All she needed was some rest.

After examining Shelter for injuries, the doctor had ruled him unharmed and free to go after waiting an hour under observation. By the time he was done, Shelter was sore from hitting the ground and bleary-eyed with exhaustion. He slipped off the green hospital smock and threw on a T-shirt, jeans and a pair of running shoes Traverse had collected at his house when the madness died down. Shelter stretched and massaged his left shoulder and arm. He threw back the curtain enclosing the examining room and went looking for MacIsaac and Traverse.

A nurse directed him to a tiny meeting room off the main ER, where the officers were seated at an oval table.

MacIsaac brought Shelter up to speed on the shooting. "The Ident team worked out a preliminary trajectory from Rory's wounds, and they're thinking the shooter was on the roof of the parking garage diagonal to the square. No shell casings, and we've got nothing so far on video or from a canvass of businesses and passersby." He studied Shelter's face. "What happened out there? What did Rory say to you?"

Shelter gathered his thoughts. "He was terrified."

"How so?" MacIsaac asked.

"On edge. Jumpy. After I gave him his rights, he wanted me to promise to protect him. And he repeated he was being set up."

"Who was setting him up?"

Shelter shrugged. "He didn't get a chance to say." He looked from Traverse to MacIsaac, brow wrinkled with concern. "The shooter was trying to take out Nicki too."

MacIsaac shook his head. "She's making someone nervous. We don't need another victim. Tell her to back off and leave it to us."

The corners of Shelter's mouth tightened into a rueful frown. "I've already done that. Let's just say she doesn't respond well to authority."

"She's going to have to learn, or she's going to end up dead."

After a moment, Traverse asked, "You need a ride home?"

"Nah, I'm going to look in on her. See she's settled in."

Traverse raised an eyebrow. "I'm sure she's fine."

"Yeah. Just want to make sure."

Traverse accompanied Shelter a short way down the hall to Nicki's room, where they found her asleep. Shelter watched her for a second before looking over to Traverse, who was studying him.

"You sure you don't want a ride?"

"I'm going to stay a little while."

"Okay. Your call. I'll see you at the office."

Later, Shelter observed Nicki from a high-backed padded chair in a corner of her hospital room. Her hair contrasted with the white hospital sheets. She'd been asleep for almost two hours after being given a sedative. A uniformed cop was stationed outside the room.

Her eyes fluttered open, and she looked around the room as if she didn't know where she was. When she spotted him, she nodded and gave him a bashful half smile.

"Hey," she said softly. Her eyes were bleary, dreamy and her words slurred by the sedative. "What're you doing here?" She turned her head toward the window. It was dark, and the moon was nearly full.

Shelter stood up and went to the side of the bed. He put a hand on her forearm. He was struck by how soft her skin was. "I wanted to make sure you're okay," he said. "How do you feel?"

She reached up and touched the square of gauze covering her left cheek. "I just can't believe it happened."

Shelter nodded. "You've got to be careful now."

She nodded and reached out to give his forearm a squeeze. "You too."

"I'll talk to you tomorrow. Get some rest." She closed her eyes and was asleep again. On his way out, he took a last glance at her and wondered if he'd be able to keep her safe.

# SIXTEEN

Five a.m. The kitchen table. A soft-leaded pencil. A broad sheet of paper. Three crude sketches. The first two drawings were of women's bodies wrapped in plastic and dumped — one in a culvert under a rural road, the other beside a creek near a busy avenue in the heart of the city. The third sketch showed two women and four men in a hotel room. Around the sketches and down the page were notes in Shelter's cramped scrawl.

He sat on the edge of a chair in his boxer shorts and a T-shirt, his head resting on a fist as he worked on the pad of sketching paper. His body still ached from taking Nicki down hard to the cement. A dream of blood spattering his face had awoken him and given no hope of getting back to sleep.

Who'd known the time and place of the meet with Sinclair? Nicki, for one. Maybe Jasmine, Rory's girlfriend, and Darren Thompson, the bodyguard. Who else? Who would have access to a high-powered rifle and the marksmanship skills to make the shot? Who needed to shut up Rory Sinclair and Nicki badly enough to risk shooting them in broad daylight during a police operation?

Shelter took a sip of cold coffee and stretched. He opened his laptop and pulled up the front page of the *Free Press*. Main headline: *Rapper Shot Dead in Old Market Square*. Sub-headline: *Suspect Slain While Being Arrested*. Shelter's jaw tightened as he scanned the article. The reporter had identified the victim as Rory Sinclair, and the story consisted mostly of details about his criminal record and music career, as well as quotes from witnesses at the scene of the shooting.

Shelter zeroed in on a paragraph. "Sinclair had known both Monica Jane Spence and Crystal Lynn Rempel and had been a suspect in the killings of the Indigenous women, according to a police source. His shooting has thrown the investigation into disarray."

Shelter swore under his breath — the leaker was back at it. He scanned the rest of the article. A public relations officer had maintained Sinclair was undergoing a routine arrest when shots were fired but refused to give more details. Shelter was relieved to see he and Nicki weren't named in the article.

Grey light filtered into the living room, and Shelter saw the streetlight in front of the house switch off. His mind went to Nicki and touching her arm the night before — the sensation of her skin under his hand. He rose from the table. The desire he felt for her was undeniable, but he had to push those thoughts away. She was a witness in a murder investigation and grieving for her sister. That made the power imbalance between them even wider than it already would have been and made it all the more important to keep his distance. A romantic relationship could cost him his job. He struggled to focus on the mundane tasks of feeding the cat and eating a piece of toast. He waited until 7:00 a.m. before calling Traverse.

"You see the paper?" Shelter asked.

"Uh-huh." Traverse's bass voice was sleepy, and Shelter could hear his kids fighting in the background. "How are you feeling this morning?"

"I'm going to survive," Shelter said.

"How about Nicki?"

"They kept her in for observation. She was shaken up. But she's young." Shelter paused for a beat. "We've got someone who was very desperate to keep Rory from talking to us."

"Guess Rory was right to be scared."

"Scared of who?" Shelter said in a low voice, almost to himself. "What did you find out about Charlie Osborne yesterday?"

"No record and nothing on him in CPIC," Traverse said, referring to the police database. "He's been on the band council up at Lone Pine forever, a cousin of the chief. He's the president of their economic development corporation but keeps a low profile. It's the chief, Lyle Mackay, who does the talking — and he does lots of it."

"Anyone know why he was hanging out with Rory, or who this guy Bill is?"

"Nope," Traverse said. "I found a news article about Lone Pine settling a land claim with the federal government for a huge amount of money — $21 million."

"It looks like Nicki is a target too. We need to take a closer look at who she's been talking to."

"She was talking to Rory. Maybe the killer didn't want to leave any loose ends."

Shelter heard shouting in the background — Traverse's wife berating one of his kids. "Hold on." Traverse came back on the line, sounding harassed. "I gotta go."

"See you downtown."

Rather than the usual buzz of morning chit-chat over coffee, the office was hushed but for the sound of fingers tapping on computer keys. Making his way down a corridor of cubicles, Shelter received only perfunctory nods from detectives hunkered down at their desks. He bumped into Jennifer Kane coming out of the small kitchen with a cup of coffee. She had a worried look and spoke in a whisper. "Are you okay?"

Shelter nodded and gave her a grim half smile.

"The bosses are meeting upstairs," Kane said.

"I know. I already talked to MacIsaac." He'd had a curt, unpleasant telephone conversation with his boss before leaving the house. Chief

Gordy Taylor was in a rage over the handling of the Sinclair arrest and had called a meeting of the department's top brass for 8:00 a.m. MacIsaac told Shelter he'd let him know if he was needed to answer questions.

"The good news is no civilians were shot. We dodged a bullet there," MacIsaac said without a trace of irony.

"Taylor knew how we were bringing Rory in, right?" Shelter asked.

"I assume so. It was approved right up the line. But when an arrest goes sideways this bad, well, someone's going to have to hold the bag. Just sit tight. I'll keep you posted."

MacIsaac had hung up, and Shelter was left looking at the phone in his hand. His mind was racing. More than anything, MacIsaac was a bureaucrat focused on self-preservation and career advancement. How bad was this going to get? Pulled off the case? Suspended? Fired? He'd made a series of quick calls, dishing out investigative tasks, including sending Himmat Sharma and another detective, Dave Zelinsky, out to supervise more canvassing for someone who might have seen the shooter escaping the scene. He sent Ian Sim to search for video from the area after the first sweep of the parking garage, buildings and shops had yielded nothing.

Now, Shelter could smell the aroma of Kane's freshly brewed coffee and felt her studying his face. "Is Gabe in yet?" he asked.

"He went down to the cafeteria to get some breakfast," Kane said. "What was that woman even doing there?"

"She wasn't supposed to be, but that's the way it went down." He shook his head and gave a shrug. "No meeting this morning. I'll let you know what I have for you in a couple of minutes."

Shelter stowed his briefcase and was getting his computer started when the phone rang. It was Sergeant Rick Slawsky from the Ident unit. They had a better fix on where the shots came from. It had been an eighty-seven-metre shot from the top of the parking garage to where Rory was standing. Slawsky said his people had found a bullet in the square that had gone right through Rory — a .308 calibre slug, a standard hunting bullet available from any Canadian Tire or Walmart.

"How about Rory's phone?" Shelter asked.

"It's a disposable, with three numbers on it besides yours," Slawsky said. "One is Nicki Alexander's. Another is the Lone Pine First Nation office in Winnipeg and the other belongs to someone called Tran Phuong Thao." After getting off the line, Shelter only had time to briefly glance at his email — nothing from MacIsaac. He looked up and saw Traverse approaching his desk.

"The bosses are deciding my fate upstairs," Shelter said.

Traverse tilted his head and gave his partner a quizzical look. "Come on. You handled it the best you could."

Shelter shrugged. "Let's get rolling," he said. He called across the squad room to Kane. "We need to get Pam Daniel under protection. Can you take care of that?"

He stood up. "Let's talk to Rory's girlfriend."

Rory Sinclair's apartment was in a high-rise overlooking the Assiniboine River. It was an exclusive address with a circular driveway in front. Shelter and Traverse nodded to the doorman and made their way across the lobby, where a couch upholstered in shiny gold fabric and two matching armchairs had been arranged into a waiting area. In the elevator, Shelter punched the button for the twentieth floor.

When no one answered the doorbell, Traverse knocked two times before a female voice demanded to know who was there.

"Police," Traverse said, holding his ID up to the peephole. "Open up."

The door swung open. Jasmine swore under her breath before retreating into the apartment without a word, leaving the door open.

Following her, Shelter admired the panoramic view from the floor-to-ceiling picture windows in the living room. The sun was high over the city, and from the twentieth floor the Assiniboine was a toffee-coloured strip in the foreground, with downtown skyscrapers to the right, the rail yards to the left and North End neighbourhoods in the distance.

They found Jasmine in the bedroom. She had a suitcase open on the bed and was throwing clothes into it from a chest of drawers. The detectives watched the young woman in silence from the doorway. Shelter was struck by how tiny she was, no more than five feet tall in her bare feet. She had none of the glamour girl look they'd seen at the Double Deuce. She was dressed in jeans and a fitted plaid shirt with mother-of-pearl snap buttons. Her black hair was pulled back in a ponytail, and she wore no make-up.

She ignored them, pulling out a drawer and dumping a pile of socks into the suitcase.

"We need to ask you some questions about Rory."

She finally looked up, focusing on Shelter. "You're the one who was supposed to protect him."

Shelter kept his face impassive and waited a long moment before speaking. "Who would have done this to Rory?"

"He said he could trust you and he'd be okay."

"We need your help to find out who did it."

She shook her head. "Get out!"

Shelter said in a calm voice, "Who was he so scared of?"

"I have no idea. Go away."

Shelter glanced at Traverse and decided to take another tack. "Is your name Tran Phuong Thao?"

"It's Jasmine."

"There was a call on Rory's cellphone to a Tran Phuong Thao yesterday. That's you, right?"

She nodded — a quick jerk of her head — and went back to

folding and arranging her clothes.

"What did he say to you?"

"He said he was being arrested and you were doing it. He said he could trust you. That's all."

"Did you tell anyone else he was going to the police?"

"No, of course not. Who would I tell?"

Shelter held her gaze for a second. Was she lying? Could she be the link to whoever shot Rory? "Where were you yesterday at 5:00 p.m.?"

"I was here. Alone. He told me not to go out."

"The other day, we saw you in the Double Deuce with Rory, Darren Thompson and another man, Charlie Osborne. What do you know about Charlie?"

"He's Rory's friend."

"What kind of business were they doing together?"

"How should I know? I'm not involved in Rory's business."

"Actually, we know you arranged dates for Monica Spence and collected money for Rory," Shelter said. "Other girls too, yeah? I think we need to take you downtown."

"No," she said. "What do you want to know about Charlie? There's nothing to tell. He likes the girls."

"How often?"

"A couple of times a week when he's in town."

"How about another friend of Rory's by the name of Bill?"

She pursed her lips and shook her head. "Don't know any Bill."

"How about a party at the Bond Hotel a couple of weeks ago? Rory went with Monica and another girl. What do you know about it?"

She stopped packing, a T-shirt in her hand. Shelter sensed she was deciding whether to lie — considering how much he knew.

Finally, she said, "Charlie called. They were having a party, and he wanted two girls to come over."

"And some coke."

Jasmine shrugged.

"What did Rory tell you about it afterward?" Shelter asked.

"Not much, except one guy wasn't happy about seeing the girls. Charlie had laid them on as a surprise, and the guy was pissed. He left right away."

Shelter said, "Okay, you mean there were three men there when Rory arrived?"

Jasmine nodded.

"Who was this guy — the one who left? Did Rory know him?"

"Charlie was boasting about doing business with the dude. Rory was surprised he was there. A big-shot. Somebody in the news."

"What was the name?"

"Rory didn't say, and I didn't ask."

Jasmine began packing her suitcase. She pushed down on the lid using her forearms, but it was too full. She turned, jumped and sat on it. She reached down on either side of her thighs and snapped the clasps shut. "I got to get out of here."

"What else do you know about Charlie?"

She got down off the suitcase, straightened her shirt and brushed tendrils of hair behind her ears. The nails were long and carefully manicured, with a coating of blood-red polish. "He's a gambler," she said. "He loves the casino and the horses."

"Where did Rory go yesterday?" Shelter asked.

"He knew you guys were looking for him, so he'd been on the rez hanging out with friends. He called me and told me he was coming down for a meeting. He arrived about noon, dumped his shit, made a call and left. Don't ask me where because I don't know."

"Who did he call?"

"No idea."

"What's he been saying about Monica Spence and Crystal Rempel?"

She looked down at her hands spread out on the top of the suitcase. "He couldn't calm down. He was losing it," she said. "It was bad enough after Monica was killed. The other one, Crystal, was all over him. She thought he did it, but he didn't. And then when she got killed, Rory was freaking out. He was saying someone was trying to frame him for both girls. That's when he left town."

Jasmine pulled the suitcase off the bed. It landed on the hardwood floor with a thump.

"Where you going?" Shelter asked.

"My parents' place."

"Let's have the address and phone number." Once he had them, he added, "Stay in town."

# SEVENTEEN

Shelter and Traverse cruised Portage Avenue with the windows down, warm air washing over them. In a few months, this street would be a vicious wind tunnel where commuters would huddle, waiting for buses in long, hooded parkas, their faces covered by scarves, hands encased in pillowy mitts. Low banks of hardened grey snow would form between the four lanes in each direction and a fog of exhaust would swirl around the cars waiting for the light to change. A sunny summer day was not something to be taken for granted.

The middle class had abandoned the inner city decades ago for the leafy subdivisions and malls of the south end. Shelter wondered if the latest in a long string of revitalization projects might actually succeed in breathing new life into the downtown. Mayor Sam Klein had announced a target of bringing twenty thousand new residents into the area, and the idea didn't seem so far-fetched when a group of wealthy investors had miraculously put up $400 million for a new office building, shopping and residential complex — the biggest project of its kind ever.

At a stoplight, Shelter looked over at Traverse. "The other guy in the hotel room was someone Rory recognized — that could be just about anyone," he said. "A politician, a sports star, a businessman."

"If Rory knew who he was, maybe Monica did too," Traverse said. "She could have tried to blackmail him."

"But if Monica recognized him, Pamela would have too, right?" Shelter said.

"Not necessarily, I doubt Pam spends her time watching the news," Traverse said. "And if Monica was thinking about blackmail, she'd probably keep it to herself."

Shelter considered the scenario. "Maybe she calls one or more of the guys in that hotel room and demands money. That's a pretty ballsy move for a teenager."

"She was doing a lot of drugs, so I wouldn't put it past her at all," Traverse said. "Let's say she threatens to put the picture online. She's hoping that's all she'll need to do to get money out of them."

"But they're not going to give her money until she shows the picture," Shelter said. "And Charlie Osborne is the only one you can clearly make out in it. Do they care enough about their reputations to kill a girl?"

Traverse gave a shrug. "They don't know what the photo shows, right? And maybe it's not the hookers. It's what they were talking about in that hotel room before Rory and the girls arrived. Just knowing they were together might have been enough to get her killed."

"And Crystal stumbles onto the same thing."

Back at the office, Shelter realized with a jolt that his cellphone had been on silent since before they'd interviewed Jasmine. He reached into his pants pocket, pulled it out, and saw Neil MacIsaac had tried to reach him twice and then sent a text message telling him to call back. MacIsaac picked up on the first ring.

"The chief is pissed off," he said in an agitated tone.

"I got that this morning."

"He ranted for an hour. Apparently, we're a bunch of incompetent assholes. And you're about an inch from going back into a uniform."

Shelter felt his blood pressure shoot higher. His face burned, and his vision narrowed to a tunnel. "What did you say to that?" he asked, struggling to keep control of his voice.

"I defended you, of course. But we're going to have to be more careful in the future."

There it was — MacIsaac's famous *we*. "*We* didn't almost get our ass shot off in Market Square trying to make an arrest," Shelter said. He knew MacIsaac would sacrifice him like a lamb if he felt his position was threatened. Shelter also knew it was useless to justify his actions or remind MacIsaac that the operation had been fully approved.

"Calm down. It didn't help Taylor's mood that his retirement was supposed to be announced today. They'd laid on a big press conference that got cancelled."

"When's his last day?"

"The end of the month. He went on and on about how unfair the media is and how he wasn't going to let these murders stain a forty-year career."

"Yeah, he was telling me the same thing the other day."

"You were talking to Taylor about this case?" MacIsaac said with suspicion.

"He wanted a briefing."

"When was this?"

"Last Sunday, before the protest march."

MacIsaac was silent as he digested the news. "Well, if he talks to you again, let me know, okay?"

Shelter rolled his eyes. The subtext was that the chief should have gone through MacIsaac if he wanted information on the investigation. It once again occurred to Shelter that MacIsaac might be harbouring hopes of being plucked from the ranks to become the next chief. An absurd idea, but you could never underestimate a man's capacity for self-delusion. He could see the political jockeying and jostling among the top ranks of the service was about to intensify.

"Any word on who the new chief is going to be?" he asked, his tone neutral.

"The rumour is it's going to be filled temporarily until they can do a proper search." MacIsaac paused. "What's going on?"

"We just talked to Rory's girlfriend," Shelter said. "I'll run it down for you when I see you."

He ended the call and dialled Nicki's phone. She answered on the second ring. "How you feeling?" he asked.

"I'm sore, but I'm okay."

"I need to talk to you."

"I'm not working till four."

"I'll meet you at the corner of Sherbrook and Broadway in an hour."

Shelter shielded his eyes and spotted a cyclist in the distance cutting across two lanes of traffic on a ten-speed. Nicki was wearing her Yankees cap where a helmet should have been, her black hair streaming in the wind. She skidded to a stop at the curb beside Shelter and jumped off the bike. Her skin was glowing from the ride. For once, she wasn't all in black; she had on a crimson T-shirt and pair of jeans with holes ripped at the knees.

"Hey," she said, pulling her bike up on the sidewalk and slipping her shades into her backpack.

"Nice bike," Shelter said.

"Got it out of the garbage and spent two hundred bucks to get it fixed up. It goes good now."

They were facing each other, with the bike between them. Shelter scanned the intersection before refocusing on her face and the bandage covering most of her right cheek. She stood with a hand on a jutting hip and eyed him with contempt.

"What are you looking at?"

"When do you get that dressing changed?" he asked.

"I go back tomorrow."

"Did they say how serious it is?"

"They say there's not going to be a scar, if that's what you're worried about."

Shelter could feel himself blushing and was powerless to stop it. She'd intuited what he was thinking from a simple remark.

Nicki locked her bike to a pole, and they walked a block and a half down Broadway to a greasy spoon. Shelter chose a table in the window, well away from the other patrons. He was silently impressed by the size of the lunch Nicki ordered: soup, a clubhouse sandwich with fries and a strawberry milkshake. He asked for a burger with a salad and coffee.

The restaurant was half full of a working-day mix of office workers, a city maintenance crew and a couple of lone men sipping coffee at the counter. He pulled out his black notebook and a pen and put them on the table beside his plate. Nicki took a big bite of her sandwich.

"You okay to work?" he asked, observing her.

Nicki looked up at him. "I'm okay," she said with a smile that made Shelter wonder if he was being mocked. "I can take it."

"I need you to go through everything that happened yesterday," Shelter said. "Starting from when Rory first contacted you."

"He didn't contact me. I phoned him."

"You called Rory?"

"I've been texting and calling him every day, but he never texted back or answered my calls. This time he picked up."

Shelter shook his head, and his brow furrowed. Crystal had been doing freelance investigative work when she was killed. Now her sister was playing the same game. The bullet aimed at her the day before proved how dangerous that was. "Why were you calling him?" It came out as a low, annoyed hiss. "I told you to leave the investigating to us."

"He knew what happened to Crystal, and I needed him to tell me. I wasn't giving up on that."

"Why would he tell you anything?"

"Because we'd known each other from way back. And he's always told me a lot about the shit he was into. He was proud of it. I would have got it out of him."

"What if he killed Monica and Crystal?"

Nicki was sucking milkshake from a straw. It made her eyes open wide as she studied his face. She set the glass down slowly and wiped her lips with a napkin. "He would have lied about it. He was going to lie one way or the other. But in the lie would be something to..." Her voice trailed off.

"To go on," Shelter said. "Hey, I don't want you to get killed too. Promise me you'll leave finding the killer to us."

Nicki slouched on her chair and cast her eyes to the ceiling. "Are you armed?"

"Am I armed?"

"Yeah, like are you carrying a gun right now?"

"Yes."

"Good. Because there is someone running around town killing people. And he could be sitting over at that table right now for all you know."

She got to her feet and left the restaurant. Shelter threw thirty dollars on the table and went after her. She was standing on the sidewalk with her shades down.

"What did he say to you?"

"He was scared shitless."

"Did he give you a name? Who he'd been talking to?"

"No. But I told him he had to call you. At first, he said no way. Said that's the last place he was going. But I gave him your number again. You know the rest. I met him a couple of blocks from the square, and we came together. I set him up to get killed."

"No, you didn't, Nicki," Shelter said, softening his voice. "You were doing the right thing by getting him to come in. Anything else you can remember about that call you made to him? Anything at all?"

She chewed her lower lip, her eyes on the key to her bike lock in her hand. "Yeah. He was at the track."

# EIGHTEEN

On his computer screen, Shelter studied a newspaper photo of Charlie Osborne from a few years before. Osborne was one of three men seated behind a table at a press conference in a downtown hotel. He was on the right, unsmiling in a leather vest over a Western-style shirt. According to the photo caption, the man in the middle was Lyle Mackay, chief of the Lone Pine reserve. He was much younger than Osborne, probably in his late thirties. His hair was cut short, and he wore a dress shirt. He looked to be in a jovial mood, smiling and saying something to the other man in the photo, a federal official named Stephen Miller. Bald, middle-aged, and looking to be about thirty pounds overweight in his jacket and tie, Miller fit the stereotype of a grey, overfed bureaucrat. The caption said he was the assistant deputy minister in the federal Indigenous Affairs department.

Shelter scanned the short article under the photo. The press conference had been called to announce a land settlement between the Lone Pine First Nation and the federal government. Ottawa was handing over $21 million in recognition that the community — like other First Nations in Manitoba — had received only a fraction of the land it should have had under historic treaties. Besides the cash, the Lone Pine First Nation also received close to ten thousand acres of Crown territory added to its land base. McKay was quoted as saying the money would be used to improve the lives of his people, including the many who lived off the reserve. Shelter scrolled down the article and found a brief mention of Osborne, saying he favoured using part of the money to establish an urban reserve in Winnipeg.

A reserve inside Winnipeg? A vision of gravel roads, unpainted plywood houses, and people motoring around on ATVs came to Shelter's mind — the stereotypical image of reserves in the North.

He plugged the term "urban reserve" into Google and was surprised to learn several had been established in Manitoba and other western provinces and that they bore no relation to the reserves he was thinking of. Instead, they were commercial developments integrated into the cityscape. The idea was that a First Nation band negotiated with the federal government to have a piece of urban land designated as a reserve. After negotiating a deal to pay for municipal services, the First Nation attracted both Indigenous and non-Indigenous businesses. Shelter found an article that portrayed urban reserves as a success story. It said they provide business opportunities and jobs to people who had left remote reserves in large numbers to come to the city, as well as much-needed revenue for First Nations communities.

Shelter glanced at Traverse, who was seated at his desk a few metres to his left. "Hey, Gabe," Shelter said. "I'm just reading up on urban reserves here."

Traverse looked up and nodded. "A lot of people think they're the way forward, or one of them, anyway." He paused before adding, "There are a lot of misconceptions about them, and they take time to negotiate, but they seem to be working where they've been set up."

Shelter closed his web browser. "Let's go over what we know again. Charlie was using Rory for hookers and coke. He was in the hotel room that night with Monica Spence, Pam Daniel, Bill and another man."

Traverse nodded. "After she talked to Pam, Crystal knew Sinclair was pimping Monica and Charlie was with her."

"She goes to see Charlie to get answers about Monica," Shelter said, squeezing a paper clip, deep in thought. "Crystal ends up dead, and Rory finds himself on the line for both murders." He stood up and stretched. "Let's say he meets Charlie or someone else from the hotel room and decides he's being set up. He knows who the third man was that night, and he's coming in to give them all up to us."

Traverse put his hands on his hips. "Charlie's spent his whole life in Lone Pine. Chances are he's pretty good with a hunting rifle."

Shelter locked eyes with his partner. "Any luck tracking him down?"

Traverse shook his head. "He's giving us the run-around. The only home address I could find is in Lone Pine. I called the band office, and they say he's in the city. The receptionist at their office in town says they don't know where he is."

Shelter called to Jennifer Kane at her desk. "Jen, I need you and Ian to get over to the Lone Pine First Nation office and find out where Charlie Osborne stays in Winnipeg. Put pressure on. Talk to the chief, okay?"

Turning back to Traverse, he said, "Nicki says Rory was at the track yesterday afternoon when he called her," Shelter said. "There were no races yesterday."

"Didn't Jasmine tell us Charlie likes the ponies?" Traverse asked. "Let's go."

The racetrack was on the western outskirts of the city. Portage Avenue traced a straight line from downtown to open prairie twenty kilometres to the west. Winnipeg's planners had never embraced the sixties craze for freeways and travelling Portage Avenue was a stop-and-go grind past a succession of undistinguished low-rise businesses and strip malls. Traverse drove and Shelter dozed, still feeling the effects of hitting the ground with Nicki the day before. The sound of Traverse's voice woke him. "What?"

"I was just thinking about the days Crystal was missing," Traverse said, steering the car with one hand. "The mud in her car. If she was up at Lone Pine, maybe she was trying to find out what Charlie knew about Monica's murder."

"Maybe she had a source up there feeding her information."

"A source in the community," Traverse said, following Shelter's train of thought. "She goes up there to see that person. Or maybe she went up to see her grandmother. Don't forget, her mom had just committed suicide and she was upset."

Shelter sighed and tilted his head back against the headrest. "Did Sim get anything on those calls Crystal was making up there?"

"I don't know. I'll check when we get back."

The head of security at the track was an ex-cop in his early fifties named Rudy Stern. He was waiting for them in the air-conditioned entrance hall under the grandstand. He had a barrel chest and a beer gut — a weightlifter gone to seed. His arms strained the seams on his navy-blue sports jacket with a track logo on the pocket.

Stern had been thrown off the police force five years earlier. He and his partner had given a vicious beating to a teenager in the North End that had landed the kid in the hospital with a shattered nose and eye socket and two broken ribs. Stern and his partner had worked the kid over behind a convenience store in full view of a video camera. Stern managed to stay out of jail by testifying against his partner, who'd gone to Headingly jail for two years less a day.

"Rudy," Shelter said.

"Mike." Neither man extended a hand to shake. Stern nodded to Traverse. "Gabe."

"How'd you get this job?" Shelter asked, eying Stern's outfit.

Stern gave a chuckle. "They needed someone who knows what they're doing."

"And they settled for a gorilla with a drinking problem."

The security officer's face turned red, and he took a step toward Shelter.

"Relax. Where's your boss?"

A man who'd approached silently from behind said, "That would be me." He extended his hand to be shaken by Shelter. "I'm Paul Kennedy, the general manager." He shook Traverse's hand and took a step back to stand beside Stern. Paul Kennedy was in his early forties, tall and slim, with salt-and-pepper hair parted in the middle and hanging over the collar of his yellow golf shirt.

Shelter said, "You guys know Rory Sinclair?"

"The gentleman who was shot in the Old Market Square yesterday?" Kennedy asked.

"Well, he was no gentleman, but he did get shot. In the hours before, he was out here."

"I saw the story in the paper this morning, but I didn't know him," Kennedy said. "You, Rudy?" Stern shook his head.

"How about Charlie Osborne?"

"Yes, Mr. Osborne is a good customer."

"Is he here today?"

"I haven't seen him." He looked over to Stern, who gave another almost imperceptible shake of the head.

"Was he here yesterday?"

"It's possible, but I can't be sure because Rudy and I were downtown all afternoon on business. Did you try his office?"

"Who was working the restaurant yesterday?"

Kennedy stepped back and conferred with Stern in a whisper. Shelter knew they were discussing whether to consult a lawyer before allowing the detectives to interview the staff. Kennedy turned back and smiled without showing his teeth. "This way, please."

He led them to the restaurant, where a waitress was serving late breakfast to a couple of tables of older men. She had no trouble remembering Rory and Charlie coming in at around one thirty the afternoon before and ordering drinks. They'd been arguing about something, but she'd been too far away to overhear what it was about. After twenty minutes, they'd paid the bill and left.

After letting the waitress get back to her tables, Shelter turned to Kennedy. "You've got video of this place, I take it?"

Kennedy led them to a small room where video equipment was set up. Stern worked the machines, and it took only a few minutes to pick up Sinclair and Osborne in a heated discussion in the restaurant. When they left the dining room, another camera captured them in the concourse, but instead of heading to the parking lot, they made a right turn and walked together out of the frame.

"What's over there?" Shelter asked.

"The stables are in that direction," Kennedy said.

"Let's see the video."

Stern punched up an image of the men walking through a large sliding door. "That's all we've got," he said. "No cameras inside."

"Who would they be visiting in the stables on a Tuesday afternoon?" Shelter asked, looking from Stern to Kennedy.

Kennedy cocked his head to the left just before answering, and Shelter knew he was about to lie. "Can't help you there, Officer," he said with a shake of his head and a smile.

"You're not trying hard enough," Shelter said. "You don't just walk into stables at a racetrack without a pass. I think we need to get some officers over here to interview everyone in this place."

"There are races tonight," Kennedy whined.

Turning to Traverse, Shelter gave a jerk of the head toward the door. "Let's go."

"Wait a minute," Kennedy said. He seemed short of breath. He gathered himself and said, "Mr. Osborne has been coming in the morning to watch the horses work out with one of the owners. They have breakfast together sometimes."

Shelter waited.

"Mr. Craig. William Craig," Kennedy said. "Bill Craig."

On the way back into town, Shelter thought about Bill Craig and what his involvement with Charlie Osborne and Rory Sinclair could mean. He glanced over at Traverse, who was steering with a forearm draped over the wheel. He could see from the lines on his brow he was concerned as well.

"What's a guy like that doing rubbing shoulders with Osborne?" Shelter asked.

"It's got to be money," Traverse said.

When Kennedy had said the name "Bill Craig," Shelter knew immediately he was the man with his profile to the camera in Pam Daniel's photo. Tall, with silver receding hair and a prominent pot belly, Craig was a real-estate developer in the city whose company had built whole suburbs in the city's south end. He'd married into one of Winnipeg's oldest families — one that had made its fortune in development and construction. Craig had often been in the newspaper for the role he'd played in a committee of prominent businessmen that had lobbied the government to bring the Winnipeg Jets hockey team to the city. Shelter also recalled seeing him and his carefully coiffed wife in the society page of the newspaper at black-tie charity fundraisers.

"They've got to be doing a deal. Some kind of a real-estate deal," Shelter said. "That makes sense, but where?"

Traverse gave a slight shrug. "Well, it's going to be in town, 'cause Craig's a city guy. Never heard his company operating in the country. And if it's in the city, it's going to be downtown or in the North End, because that's where Charlie Osborne would operate, right?"

As soon as they got back downtown, Shelter collared MacIsaac and sat him down in his office. The demeanour of the two detectives warned the inspector they had some serious news, but he wasn't ready to hear the name of Bill Craig. He groaned and screwed up his face as if he'd sucked on a lemon. MacIsaac slouched in his chair and rested his head on a fist.

Shelter ran through what they'd seen on the video at the track and what Kennedy had told them about Charlie Osborne's morning visits with Bill Craig.

MacIsaac exhaled sharply. "But there's no video of Craig with them yesterday," MacIsaac said.

Shelter shook his head. He knew where MacIsaac was heading with that comment.

"What do we have on Craig?" MacIsaac asked. "A picture of the back of someone's head in a hotel room and a few meetings at the track with Charlie Osborne. It's nothing."

"It was him in that hotel room," Shelter said. "And a guy like Craig doesn't spend his time chatting about the ponies. Those two are up to something. We've got to bring them in."

It was MacIsaac's turn to shake his head. "We've got Osborne in relationships with Monica Spence, Crystal Rempel and Rory Sinclair. That's our prime suspect."

"Craig was in that hotel room with Monica," Shelter said, struggling to keep control. "She ends up dead a few days later, and Crystal starts digging into it. Craig is just as much a suspect as Osborne."

"No."

"What do you mean, no?"

"You can bring in Osborne. But no action on Craig until we discuss it at the senior management committee. And I mean no action, including discussing it with the team. If Craig's name gets out in connection with this case, we're all going to be in shit."

# NINETEEN

By the time Shelter got home, ordered a pizza, and scarfed it down with a bottle of beer, he was having trouble keeping his eyes open to watch an old movie on Netflix. He let himself drift off on the couch. He was wakened by the telephone ringing. He pushed himself off the couch and saw by the clock on the wall in the kitchen it was almost 5:00 a.m.

"Hello."

"It's Joan." Shelter could hear panic in his mother-in-law's voice and came fully awake. "It's Kelsey. She didn't come home."

"Didn't come home?" Shelter struggled to process the information. "Where is she?" he said before he could stop himself.

"If we knew that, I wouldn't be calling you," Joan Arnason said. It was a stupid question, but it was unusual for Joan to snap at him. Shelter's heart rate spiked. Fear constricted his breathing. "When was the last time you saw her?"

"At dinner time. She said she was going to the beach to see Samantha." Samantha Lockhart was her best friend in Gimli.

"We spoke to Samantha," Joan said. "She was at the beach — the kids are there every night — but she never saw Kelsey. And she's not answering her phone. We've been calling everyone we can think of, but no one knows where she is."

Shelter's mind raced through the possibilities of where she could be. Run away. Abducted. He recalled the veiled threat Rory Sinclair had made after tracking her down on Facebook. Could her disappearance have anything to do with the case? He couldn't see why the killer would take his daughter. What could he hope to gain by it? But maybe it wasn't a rational decision if he thought Shelter was closing in on him.

"Michael. Are you there?" Joan's voice had gone up in pitch.

"Just a minute, I need to think."

Shelter took a deep breath and made a conscious effort to calm himself. What was the most logical explanation? He knew only a tiny minority of teenage disappearances were abductions. It was far more likely Kelsey had gotten drunk and fallen asleep at a friend's house.

"She probably will show up soon or at least call," Shelter said with more confidence than he felt. "Did anything happen yesterday?"

"She came home with a nose ring and piercings in her ears. She told us she's getting a tattoo as well. Didn't ask us. Told us."

Shelter became aware that this sweet, sensitive woman was overwhelmed.

"Sig was pretty harsh. You know his temper. He told her she was grounded for the weekend. But Kelsey wouldn't hear it. She just left without eating dinner. You can't control a fifteen-year-old. We learned that with Christa."

Shelter let that sit. He couldn't blame his in-laws. They were seniors. They'd raised their children and shouldn't have to deal with a rebellious teenager.

"We thought she'd be home after she cooled down. But she never came back."

He was struck by a thought. "The last time I was at the house, you were teasing her about a boyfriend. Who's that?"

"That's a good question," Joan said. "We don't know. It's just little signs, like she's begun to wear makeup and wants to buy more clothes. But it's strange because Samantha says Kelsey doesn't have a boyfriend." She gathered her thoughts. "She's become more and more secretive. We don't always know where she is."

"I'm going to call the RCMP and get them to start looking for her," Shelter said. "I'll stay here for now. If we don't hear anything by noon, I'll head up there. What's Samantha's phone number?"

As Joan gave him the number, Shelter sensed she was close to tears. "I'm sorry you and Sig have to go through this. But I'm sure Kelsey will be okay. I'll call you soon."

Shelter slumped in a kitchen chair and gave his throbbing hip a rub as he again went over the possibilities. He picked up his cellphone and sent Kelsey a text. *Where are you? Please get in touch.*

He called the number, but it rang through to Kelsey's cheerful voice asking callers to leave a message. It was recorded a couple of years earlier — the voice of a little girl. Christa was still alive then, and there'd been much debate over whether Kelsey needed a phone and the expense. Christa had taken Kelsey's side and won, of course. She'd also paid for a replacement when Kelsey lost her first phone after two weeks. Shelter left the same message he'd texted.

He went to the computer in the upstairs office and looked up the number of the Gimli detachment of the RCMP. The duty officer sounded young but asked the right questions about Kelsey's living arrangements, her friends and signs of rebelliousness. In an off-hand way, he asked if Kelsey had a phone. Shelter silently kicked himself for not thinking of it sooner. You could track the phone, assuming it was turned on. He discussed with the Mountie how to find it using an app. The officer assured him they'd start looking for her around Gimli right away and keep him posted.

Christa had paid for Kelsey's phone and used to check her account from time to time to see how late she was staying up texting with her friends around the neighbourhood. On a few occasions, she'd seized the phone for a couple of days when she'd discovered Kelsey had stayed up hours past her bedtime. When Christa got sick, she'd transferred her bills to Shelter, and he'd paid them ever since by automatic withdrawal but had never checked Kelsey's account.

He opened the grey metal cabinet where Christa kept her meticulous files. He pulled out the one marked *Kelsey's phone* and found instructions in his wife's beautiful printing on how to access the account. Turning to the computer, he opened the account to look at her recent activity on the phone. He found a long series of texts and phone calls from the day and evening before, all to just two numbers. Messages to one of the numbers ended at 5:16 p.m., around the time Kelsey had left the house. His daughter's phone showed sporadic texts to the other number through the evening and night up until 2:30 a.m. Shelter looked at previous days. Her communications had been almost exclusively to the same two numbers. He went downstairs, made some instant coffee, and took it on to the back deck with his phone. He sat in an Adirondack chair and dialled the number for Samantha Lockhart's house in Gimli. The Lockharts were cottagers from Winnipeg, and Shelter knew them casually from chatting during play dates when the kids were younger. It was Jackie Lockhart, Samantha's mother, who answered.

"It's Mike Shelter."

"Have you found Kelsey?"

"Not yet."

"I can't believe this is happening."

"We'll find her," Shelter said. "I need Sam's cellphone number."

"Why? She's right here."

"I need it to check something. Do you have it?"

Shelter followed the digits on the piece of paper in front of him as Jackie recited them to him. It was the number Kelsey had been communicating with through the evening. He asked Jackie to put her daughter on the phone and get on the extension.

"Hello?" The girl's voice was quavering, barely audible.

"Samantha, it's Kelsey's dad. I need to ask you some questions so we can find her, okay?"

"Okay."

"When was the last time you saw Kelsey or heard from her?"

"She texted me last night to say she would meet up with us in town. We always meet up downtown and go to the beach. But she never showed up."

"You never texted her or spoke to her after six o'clock?" Shelter asked.

Samantha answered in a whisper. "No."

"I have Kelsey's cellphone records in front of me, and I know that's not true, Samantha. You have to tell me where she is."

He heard the girl's mother gasp. "Sam. What's going on?"

The girl began crying. Shelter waited, giving her time to realize it was useless to keep lying.

Finally, she spoke. "I told her not to do it. But she wouldn't listen. She said she'd never speak to me again if I told."

"Told what?" Shelter asked calmly.

It took another few seconds of sobbing before Samantha came out with it. "She's gone to Winnipeg with a boy."

"What boy?"

"His name is James. I don't know his last name. He's a townie. He has a motorcycle."

"Motorcycle?" Shelter said.

On the extension, Shelter heard Jackie Lockhart draw in her breath and whisper, "Oh my God."

"How old is this boy?"

"I don't know. I only met him once. But he's a lot older than us. Maybe twenty. They met a couple of weekends ago, and she's been riding around with him. She says she loves him."

Shelter shook his head. Samantha told him they'd left in the early evening, heading for Winnipeg with a plan to go to Calgary and find work. An angry Jackie Lockhart cut in. "How could you get involved in this?" she demanded.

"Let's just find her," Shelter said. "Where is she right now?"

"They're getting ready to go, I think. They want to leave this morning. But I don't know where he stays in Winnipeg."

"Okay. Leave it with me. It's going to be okay," Shelter said before hanging up.

He was confident Kelsey could be tracked down. The technology unit could monitor her phone and track it as soon as it was turned on. She couldn't live without using her phone. If that failed, they'd be picked up on the Trans-Canada Highway before they made it to Portage la Prairie. But before bringing the Winnipeg police into it, he decided to make one last try at reaching her.

He punched her number on his cellphone and waited until it rang through to her voice mail. He was careful to keep a calm, reassuring voice. He knew the teenage mind was prone to rash decisions, and he was hoping she might be having second thoughts now that the reality of what she'd gotten herself into was sinking in. "Kel, you've got to call me back. I know you're with a boy named James and you're planning to leave town. I'm not mad. I love you. But we have to talk right away. Everyone's worried." He followed up with a text, urging her to listen to his message.

He glanced at his watch. It was almost eight o'clock, and his shift would be starting soon. Traverse was already in his car and heading to the office when Shelter reached him. As Shelter described the situation, Traverse clucked and hummed with concern.

"What do you want me do?" Traverse asked.

"For now, I'd like to keep this low-profile. Can you get the technology unit to track down these two cellphones?" He read out Kelsey's cellphone number and the other one she'd been communicating with before she disappeared — the one he assumed belonged to James. After ending the call with Traverse, he took a deep breath and punched in James's number. As expected, he didn't answer the call — no one under thirty ever did. Shelter's call rang through to voice mail. He felt his anger building as he listened to the recorded voice of the young man who'd run off with his daughter.

"James, this is Kelsey's father," he said. "Get in touch with me before this goes any further. Kelsey is a young girl, and she needs to come home." He also sent the message as a text and then waited for them to talk it over and decide what to do.

He thought about how to handle the call when it came. While the age of consent in Canada is sixteen years old, Shelter knew there was an exception for fourteen- and fifteen-year-olds. They could consent to sex with a partner less than five years older. So if James were twenty, it would depend on their birthdays. But Shelter didn't want to escalate the situation by making threats. He knew it was important to be calm, reassuring and focused on Kelsey's safety. But it was going to take every bit of his self-control. After five minutes had passed, Shelter prepared to call the police command centre to get started on locating the couple when his phone buzzed.

"Kelsey."

"Hi."

He felt relief wash over him. She was alive, not spattered on a highway after a motorcycle accident. "Where are you? Everybody is really worried."

"You know where I am, Dad. I'm with James." Her tone was petulant, angry.

"Why did you leave without telling anyone? Your grandparents are terrified."

"They're trying to control everything I do. I'm not a kid anymore."

Shelter got off the couch and walked to the window. The street was bathed in golden early morning sunshine. He struggled to keep his tone even.

"I know you're not a kid anymore. Your grandparents just want what's best for you. We all do. We can work this out, but you have to come home."

"No. We're leaving today."

Shelter was tempted to tell her she wasn't going anywhere. Instead, he said, "Let's just get together and talk about it."

"Why do you care anyway? You stuck me up there and just forgot about me."

He felt as if he'd been stabbed. His mind raced. What to say? A long moment of silence passed as he thought about it. He pictured his daughter at the end of the line.

"I've let you down." He felt his throat tightening. "You're so precious to me. It's been hard for both of us since Mom died. But I know I haven't done enough to take care of you."

When Kelsey answered, her voice had softened. "I'm sorry I scared Grandma and Grandpa." She began crying. "I don't like it here. They had a party last night, and it was full of creepy people drinking and doing drugs."

Shelter searched his mind for a way to get her to come home that would allow her to save face. "Come and stay here for a while," he said. "It will be quiet, and we can figure out what you want to do. I'm sure your grandparents will understand." He paused before asking, "Can I come and get you, sweetheart?"

When she answered yes, it was barely audible. She gave him an address in the St. James district. When Shelter pulled up to the rundown bungalow, Kelsey looked like a lost little girl, waiting for him on the front steps with her school bag and a pillow.

"Hi there," he said. She stood up, and he took her into his arms, kissing her forehead. "I love you."

"I love you too," she whispered.

When she'd disengaged from his embrace, he asked, "Where's James?"

"He took off. He didn't want to meet a cop."

# TWENTY

Kelsey had been up all night, and after devouring a huge bowl of cereal, she retreated to her bedroom. Shelter made calls, starting with Joan Arnason. He told his mother-in-law he would be keeping Kelsey in Winnipeg for the time being. Joan agreed it was for the best and asked that Kelsey call her and Sig that evening. "We have a few regrets about how we handled things."

Shelter then called Gimli RCMP, Gabe Traverse and, finally, his mother to let her know what had happened. He'd have to count on Roberta Shelter to look in on Kelsey when he was at work. She was seventy-two years old but had grown more energetic since his father's death five years earlier. Between outings to the golf club, bridge games with her cronies and trips to the family cottage, she maintained a hectic social calendar. She didn't take kindly to interruptions to her carefully planned agenda, but she was crazy about Kelsey, and Shelter knew she'd rally in a crisis. When he got her on the line, she was getting ready to go the hair salon. He glossed over the scarier parts of what had happened the night before and emphasized that Kelsey was at home and safe. Still, his mother reacted with alarm.

"She's so young. How could this happen?"

Shelter sensed a suggestion that Joan and Sig Arnason were to blame. He decided to let it go. "She's fifteen, Mom. I was getting up to all sorts of hijinks at that age you and Dad didn't even know about."

"If you're talking about smoking marijuana and climbing out

the basement window at night, you'd be surprised what we knew about," she said, going over old territory they'd shared laughs about over the years.

"I'm going to keep Kelsey here with me," he said. "Can you come by afternoons and check in on her? Make sure she's eating and maybe take her out with you?"

"Yes, of course," she said. Then after a pause, "How long will this be for, do you think?"

"I'm not sure. It might be just until the end of the summer. She's talked about going to school in Gimli in the fall."

"Gimli? That's not a good idea." Roberta Shelter had never been one to hide her feelings. "She needs to go to a proper school."

Shelter cut her off. "We'll see. Anyway, she'll be sixteen in the fall, and she's getting more and more independent."

"Do you need me to come today?"

"I'm going to head down to the office. I expect her to sleep all day, so I think we'll be fine."

He didn't share a lot with his mother about his work. She read the newspaper from front to back every day and always called when he was mentioned. But she lived in a world far away from the violence and crime that was a part of his everyday reality.

"I'm working on a big case, but I'll try to be at home with Kelsey as much as I can."

"Alright, dear. We'll speak soon."


Coming off the elevator at the office, Shelter bumped into Himmat Sharma. He could tell from the breezy greeting he got that news of his daughter running away hadn't hit the department. He knew Traverse wouldn't spill the beans, but he'd been worried it could have gotten back from Gimli — it was a small world. Shelter was relieved he wouldn't have to deal with sympathy and questions from his colleagues, at least for now. He'd probably tell Jennifer Kane about it in a few days.

Traverse was just ending a phone call when Shelter stopped by his desk. "How's she doing?" Traverse asked.

"She's sleeping it off," Shelter said with a shake of the head and a rueful half smile. He filled Traverse in on what had happened.

"How about you?"

"You know. Who needs sleep, right?" Shelter said.

"Well, you look like shit but no worse than usual." Traverse tapped his notebook. "Looks like Charlie's back on the reserve. I just talked to a Mountie up there. He hasn't seen him but says he might be in the bush."

Shelter sighed. "Hide and seek, eh? As soon as we know for sure he's there, I'll head up." Shelter crossed his arms and thought about the logistics of getting to Lone Pine. "How about Bill Craig?"

"Nothing in CPIC," Traverse said. "Pulled up some old articles. It's all stuff about bringing the Jets back to town and a couple of ribbon-cutting events at buildings with cabinet ministers and the mayor. He's a big booster of the downtown redevelopment plan." As he talked, Traverse plugged Craig's name into Google and was running the cursor over the various search results. He clicked on one, and a photo with a brief caption popped up on the screen. Shelter leaned in for a closer look. The photo showed Craig at the wheel of a vintage wooden powerboat, cruising with a blond woman who waved from the passenger seat. Shelter knew the boat was worth a fortune. The caption under the photo said it was taken on Lake of the Woods, the summer playground for Winnipeg's old-money set.

"Any court files on him?"

"I haven't had a chance to look." Traverse swivelled in his seat and looked at Shelter. "If we start pulling files, it could get back to Craig. MacIsaac said no action."

"One way or another, this guy is involved," Shelter said. "Let me make a call."

Shelter went to a closed office, shut the door and phoned Steve

Roth. He'd been friends with Roth since they were in primary school. They knew each other's secrets from their sex, drugs and rock 'n roll days and would trust each other with their lives. Roth had pursued the career that Shelter's parents wanted for him. He was a top-notch litigator with a downtown law firm and worked incredibly long hours. He knew everyone and had a razor-sharp memory and a taste for gossip. But he'd never betray Shelter's confidence.

Lawyers didn't have secretaries to screen their calls anymore. They did it themselves using call display, and Roth picked up on the first ring. "Yo."

"How's it hanging?" Shelter asked.

"I'd rather be at the lake," Roth said. "How about you?"

"Ah, you know. Trouble with Kelsey. But it's okay."

Roth made a sympathetic sound. "Something for me to look forward to." He and his wife had gotten started later on having kids, and their two were still in elementary school.

"Hey, listen. What do you know about Bill Craig?"

Roth was uncharacteristically silent. "You know who he is, right?" he said finally. "What do you want to know?"

"His name came up in a case."

"Hold on." He heard Roth putting the phone down, his chair squeak and then the sound of his office door shutting. He picked up the phone and said, "That's a serious dude."

"What can you tell me about him?"

When Roth spoke again, all the usual humour was gone from his voice. "Filthy rich, obviously. Real estate, construction and I think he even owns a quarry east of town. Two kids — Sam's a year older than us and went to Ravenscourt. Stacey was a year behind us at Kelvin. They're both in the family business. The old man is very well connected with the mayor and pro-development city councillors. They're always at his box at Jets games. Apart from that what can I tell you — a big cottage at Kenora — on Treaty Island. Yacht club.

Golf at Niakwa when he's in town."

"Who's his lawyer?"

"Oh, that's something," Roth said. "He's got a bunch of them. We do a bit of work for his company. But his main man is Derrick Alistair. He runs his own firm under his last name. We get files he's involved in, and that's how he signs everything — just Alistair. He's got a kind of a dicey reputation."

"Dicey how?"

"I heard he's an offshore specialist."

"Like offshore accounts?"

"That's what I heard. A stockbroker was talking about him at the squash club. It's just a rumour, obviously. He keeps a low profile, but he's got a big house in the old part of Tuxedo. So he's doing alright."

Shelter made a note. "Anything else?

Roth thought about it. "Well, you know about the break-up with his wife, right?"

"No. What about it?

"Oh, a nasty one," Roth said with relish. "She catches him fooling around with someone at the office and goes absolutely bat-shit." He chuckled. "Massive fucking scandal. Last I heard, it's headed to court. She wants to take him for half of everything, and that's a very big number, my friend."

Shelter made another note. "What's her name?"

Roth paused and then tried out a couple of names before coming up with it. "Shawna. Shawna Craig. Very old money. In fact, it's her family's company Bill is running. Daddy was a senator, a bagman for the Liberals, and she grew up on the Crescent. The place at the lake is on her side, too. Bill was a salesman when he met her, for Christ's sake."

"Okay. I hadn't heard anything about that," Shelter said.

"Oh, yeah. Very messy. She's trying to get him out of the company."

Shelter made a note. "Thanks, man."

"You got it. You and Kelsey need to come over for dinner soon. I'll call you, okay?"

"Sounds good."

Shelter called Traverse into the office and filled him in on the conversation.

"It's interesting, but it doesn't get us any closer to why Craig is hanging around with Charlie Osborne or who the other guy in that hotel room was," Traverse said. "I don't believe these guys would kill somebody — let alone two women — to keep coke and hookers quiet. No way."

"There's got to be more," Shelter said. "Let's check out the court records on Bill and see what we can find."

He turned to his computer. The civil records showed a lengthy list of lawsuits and other proceedings stretching back twenty years. Shelter wasn't surprised to see the litigation. It wasn't unusual for construction companies and real estate developers to get into beefs with suppliers, subcontractors and disgruntled clients. He ran his eyes down the first page of the search results. It was Traverse who spotted it. "Hey, I've seen that number before."

"What number?" Shelter asked.

"This one." Traverse reached over Shelter's shoulder and touched the screen. It was a long string of letters and numbers that ended with 01-06933. Traverse pulled a set of keys from his pocket and unlocked a filing cabinet. He returned to the desk with a manila file folder. Inside was a copy of the paper they'd found in the laundry room at Crystal Rempel's apartment block. He pointed at the sheet. "Here. It's the same number," he said, his voice betraying his excitement.

Shelter grabbed the mouse and clicked on the entry. Details of the court record appeared on the computer screen. "It's the divorce proceedings," Traverse said.

Shelter nodded, leaning back in his chair. "Let's see what's in the file."

Court records in Manitoba were stored at the Law Courts building, a short drive through the downtown core. Shelter submitted a slip of paper with the file number to a clerk. She returned with a tan-coloured folder containing records from divorce proceedings between William and Shawna Craig.

Shelter carried it to a desk and scanned the documents, stopping at an affidavit filed by Shawna Craig.

"She's accusing him of hiding assets," he said after skimming the document. He flipped back to the beginning, and he and Traverse read it together paragraph by paragraph. Her lawyer's dry rendering of his client's allegations had the odd effect of making them all the juicier. It was clear the document was calculated to inflict maximum embarrassment and legal damage to Bill Craig.

"Oh, wow," Traverse said, tapping a paragraph with his finger.

*In 2002, Mr. Craig purchased a safe and had it delivered to his office at the company's headquarters. It is Mr. Craig's practice to keep large sums of cash in this safe. The amounts exceeded $25,000 at times. To Mrs. Craig's knowledge, these sums were never accounted for in the company's financial statements, or in any tax return.*

Shelter ran his finger down to another paragraph.

*It was Mr. Craig's practice to use workers employed by the company to effect renovations on the couple's residence on Wellington Crescent and their cottage at Lake of the Woods. These renovations included, but were not limited to, an addition to the residence, the construction of a swimming pool and the installation of a new kitchen and the renovation of two bathrooms. At the Lake of the Woods cottage, a large boathouse was constructed. None of this work was reported in the company's records, and the workers were paid in cash. No taxes of any kind were paid, nor were the usual payroll deductions made.*

On the next page, Shelter's eyes were drawn to a subject heading: *Agassiz Holdings.* "That name was in Crystal's notes," he said. He pulled out the sheet of paper from the file folder and pointed to it.

They read the passage in the court proceeding.

*During the course of her duties, Mrs. Craig had occasion to view references to an entity by the name of Agassiz Holdings registered in the Bahamas. Mrs. Craig believes that her husband and certain of his business associates are the beneficial owners of Agassiz Holdings and have used this corporation to illegally hide the proceeds from their dealings from Mrs. Craig and Canadian tax authorities — an amount of at least CDN$1.5 million.*

Shelter whistled. "I wonder what else she knows about?"

"There's no sign from the database that a tax investigation is going on."

"It's a pretty recent document," Shelter said. "I guess no one knows about it."

"Crystal knew," Traverse said.

Shelter nodded. "What I don't get is how Crystal knew it's Bill Craig in the photo?" Traverse asked. "Rory and Charlie wouldn't have told her, and Pam only knew him as Bill."

"Maybe someone else was feeding her information," Traverse said. "Someone who knows what they were doing in that hotel room."

# TWENTY-ONE

Shelter tapped on Inspector Neil MacIsaac's door. "What?" MacIsaac barked.

Shelter looked at Traverse and raised his eyebrows. He peeked his head into the office and found MacIsaac glaring.

"We've got something in the Crystal Rempel case."

MacIsaac frowned and waved at the two chairs on the other side of his desk. When the two detectives were seated, their boss couldn't contain his anger. "I spent the last hour and a half being interviewed by the goddamn search committee for the new chief," he said. "There's not a police officer among them. Did you know that? They don't have a bloody clue."

Shelter nodded but remained silent. Of course, he knew the search to replace Chief Gordy Taylor was being conducted by a civilian oversight body appointed by city council and the province. The composition of the search committee was irrelevant to MacIsaac's chances of landing the job. He was all wrong for chief of a modern police department. He was too old-school, too unpolished, too grumpy. Shelter was taking a guilty pleasure in watching his boss's career dreams go up in smoke before his eyes.

MacIsaac looked down at his desk, gave a shake of his head and brusquely gathered some papers into a pile. "Taylor's lucky to be getting out. Now what do you two want?"

"It's Bill Craig. We've found evidence of some pretty serious tax evasion," Shelter said. "We've also established that Crystal Rempel knew about it." He ran through Shawna Craig's allegations against her husband. "The tax evasion gives us leverage to get search warrants and bring Craig in."

MacIsaac had been shaking his head as Shelter spoke, and his shoulders were rounded, as if he were carrying a great load. "We talked about Craig this morning, and Chief Taylor was adamant that we are not to take any premature action," MacIsaac said. "We still haven't established a firm link between Craig and the homicides."

"We have him in a hotel room with Monica Spence," Shelter said. "And Crystal Rempel was investigating him and his business dealings."

"You say he was in the hotel room, but we don't have any hard evidence of that fact."

"Come on, Neil."

"Come on yourself. I'm not saying we're never going to talk to Craig. Let me take this new evidence up the chain. But for the moment, it's hands-off."

"Jerk," Shelter said to Traverse under his breath as they walked back to his desk. "This is all politics. He's so scared of the chief. But Taylor is going to be gone in a couple of weeks."

"I guess old habits die hard," Traverse said.

Shelter considered their options. One was to simply bring in Craig against orders and let the chips fall where they may. He was running the investigation, and it was highly unusual for this kind of roadblock to be put in his way. But it would be a big move, one that could land him back in a uniform or end his career altogether. Shelter stared at Traverse as his mind turned.

"What?" Traverse said finally.

"Let's go see the wife."

"MacIsaac said to leave Craig alone."

"He didn't say anything about his wife," Shelter said. "She seems to be in the mood to talk about her husband."

Traverse smiled. "I like it."

"I know where she lives, assuming she's keeping the house in the divorce. And I think that's a pretty safe bet, given the tone of those proceedings."

It was mid-afternoon by the time they had set up an appointment to see Shawna Craig at her house on Wellington Crescent. Traverse parked in the circular driveway in front of the three-storey mansion, and the two detectives climbed the broad limestone staircase. Shelter rang the bell and then turned to survey the lawn shaded by enormous oak trees. In the distance, a jogger passed on the boulevard that separated the two traffic directions on the Crescent. He heard the door swing open and turned to find a deeply tanned woman in a mauve T-shirt, knee-length khaki shorts and white canvas sneakers. Shawna Craig's shoulder-length blond hair had been simply but expensively cut and dyed with highlights. Deep wrinkles around her eyes and mouth were evidence of a lot of time in the sun, but with an upturned nose and broad lips, she was still a handsome woman in late middle age.

"You were lucky to catch me," she said after Shelter had made the introductions and she'd ushered them into the house. They stood under a chandelier in the entrance hall, facing a wide staircase leading to a landing, where an antique grandfather clock ticked. To the right through an archway was a dining room with a long mahogany table and a hutch where expensive china was displayed. To the left was a large living room made gloomy by drawn curtains. "I'm just on my way to the lake for a few days. But I'm pleased the police are taking an interest in this. Thank you for coming. We can sit in here."

She led them into the living room. Shelter felt his shoes sinking into the deep pile. Two couches upholstered in shiny gold and cream stripes faced each other across an oval coffee table. The furniture looked as if it had never been used, and when Shelter sat down, the stuffing was stiff against his backside. He and Traverse turned down an offer of iced tea.

"My lawyer was alarmed when I told him I was meeting you this afternoon. But I don't give a damn. My husband's the one who should be worried."

"Mrs. Craig, we have some questions to ask about an affidavit you filed in your divorce proceedings against your husband," Shelter said. "You've made allegations about tax evasion and assets held in a shell company."

"Oh, they aren't allegations," she said. "They're facts. My husband is quite allergic to paying taxes. He always has been." She looked from Shelter to Traverse. "It's so short-sighted of Bill to cut corners. I tried to get him to stop, but he just laughed at me. Now he will have to pay the price."

"How did you learn of these matters?" Shelter asked. "Do you work in the business?"

"Our construction company was founded by my father. When I was younger, I worked in the office. I don't have any brothers or sisters, and my father thought it was a good idea for me to understand how the business works. I trained as an accountant."

She rummaged in a handbag, bringing out a package of menthol cigarettes, and lit one. "Sorry. A disgusting habit," she said, exhaling smoke away from the detectives. "I started again after I kicked Bill out. So that's another thing I can thank him and his little cunt for." As she drew on the cigarette, her eyes narrowed through the smoke and the corners of her lips turned up, evidently pleased by her profanity. "I made a habit over the years of going through his papers and asking about various deals. You can't be too careful. I inherited half the company from my father; he has the other half. So you see, I have an interest in knowing what he's up to."

She leaned forward and tapped her cigarette on a heavy crystal ashtray. "Of course, I knew the work on the house and cottage was all done under the table," she said. "But he's also adept at making arrangements to win contracts."

"What kind of arrangements?" Traverse asked.

"Rigging bids with other contractors. And bribing public officials."

Shelter glanced at Traverse. "Oh, yes," she said. "It goes much further than what's in the affidavit. We had to be careful, though. I didn't want to be sued over something I couldn't prove."

"What can you tell us about Agassiz Holdings?" Shelter asked.

Craig ground out her cigarette and leaned back, crossing her legs. "He was stupid enough to leave his email account open. That's how I found out about his affair with that woman in the first place. I also found a message from Alistair."

"The lawyer," Shelter said.

"Yes. Revolting human being. He'd written it in a cagey way. No details, but it referred to Agassiz Holdings and a $1.5 million wire transfer to the Bahamas. It's all done with front names, but our supposition is he's been hiding money down there."

"In the affidavit, you mentioned other individuals might be involved with that company," Shelter said.

Craig shrugged. "We don't know who's involved. But now that you're on the case, perhaps you can find out. Do you have enough here to charge him?"

Shelter and Traverse had been vague about their interest in Bill Craig. Now, Shelter considered whether to tell her they were homicide detectives and run the danger it would become a topic of gossip.

"We'll definitely have to look into that," he replied. "Are you familiar with a man named Charlie Osborne?"

"No, I don't believe so. Who is he?"

"He is a band councillor for the Lone Pine First Nation," Shelter said.

"An Indian?" She raised an eyebrow. "No, I'm sorry. I don't know anything about him."

Shelter nodded and made a note. "When was the last time you saw Mr. Craig?"

"The night I put him out of this house. That's been six months."

"We're interested in who he does business with and who he socializes with. Are there any names that come to mind?"

"We're in the construction business, but he doesn't like to mix with that gang," she said. "He's got a few cronies he plays golf and drinks with in the city and at the lake. And, of course, there's his horses. He's always at the track. But I don't know anything about that side of his life."

"If you could make a list of his friends and associates, we would appreciate it."

Shelter examined her face as she took out another cigarette and lit it. The smoking was deepening the lines, aging her. She turned slightly to face Shelter. "Do you think my husband killed Crystal Rempel and Monica Spence?"

Shelter blinked, looked at Traverse, and then back at the woman, who hadn't taken her eyes off him. When she spoke, the tone was harsh. "When the police call out of the blue, of course I'm going to have my lawyer find out who they are and what they're up to."

"We're just following up various leads, Mrs. Craig."

The same cynical chuckle. "You wouldn't be asking me all these questions if you didn't think Bill was involved."

"We can't discuss our investigation," Shelter said. After a moment, he asked, "Did you speak to Crystal Rempel?"

She ran a hand up and down her arm as she considered the question. "Yes. She contacted my lawyer, and we spoke by telephone a few weeks ago. She said she'd seen the papers we filed in the divorce."

"How did she find them?"

"I'm sure I don't know. She said she had information about my husband that might help my case. And that I might be able to help her with something she was working on. She wanted to meet."

"Did you agree to meet her?

"Yes. She was to call me back with a time and place. But she never did."

"Did you ever speak about her to your husband?

"I don't speak to him except through my lawyer. And the answer is no."

Shelter closed his notebook. "It's important our conversation remains confidential."

She considered this. "It's important I get control of my father's company back from that man. I'll do whatever is necessary to do so, including going to the press."

"Please don't do that, Mrs. Craig," Shelter said. "It won't help you, and it could jeopardize a murder investigation."

"We shall see, Detective. Now, you'll have to excuse me. I have to pack for the lake."

In the passenger seat, Shelter was lost in his thoughts, trying to pull the pieces of the case together. He glanced at Traverse and said almost in a murmur, "Okay. We've got to get Bill Craig in for an interview. MacIsaac can't stall any longer."

Traverse nodded and turned the car onto the Maryland Bridge. The sun was still high, but the trees along the river cast long shadows, and the breeze was slightly cooler than earlier in the afternoon.

"I've had it, Gabe," Shelter said. "Can you drop me off at home? I'll call MacIsaac and brief him on what she had to say. I'll write up the interview in the morning."

When Shelter came through the front door, the curtains were drawn and the house was in semi-darkness. He threw his briefcase on the couch, kicked off his shoes and wiggled his toes with relief.

"Hello!" he called. Silence. His brow wrinkled. He called out again as he climbed the stairs two at a time. The door to Kelsey's room was open, but her bed was empty. He stood on the landing and called out, "Kelsey!" Nothing.

Then from below, a faint "What?"

He found his daughter still in her pyjamas in the cool, musty basement rec room. A sitcom rerun glowed on the TV in a corner of the room, but Kelsey was intent on her phone.

"Why didn't you answer me when I called you?" Shelter asked, trying to keep his voice even.

"I did," she shot back. He again noticed the nose ring and two piercings in her ear. He felt a sharp desire to go up to his bed and close his eyes.

"How are you?" he asked.

Kelsey, her face illuminated by the glow of her iPhone, ignored him and continued to punch in a text. Only after she'd finished did she look up and offer, "I'm fine." Her phone pinged with an incoming text, and Kelsey's eyes were back on her phone.

"Put that thing down," Shelter said.

"No," she said in a tone that suggested his command was absurd.

"I said put it down," Shelter said, his voice rising.

"Jesus. Relax."

"Don't tell me to relax. What you did last night had us all scared to death."

"I was fine. I said I'm sorry."

"I want to be able to trust you." He became aware of how angry he was and tried to bring himself under control. "You ran away without..."

"I didn't run away, Dad. I was going to call you."

Shelter was astonished. He realized she didn't understand how much trouble and pain she'd caused. How serious it was. Even as upset as he was, he knew taking away her iPhone was the nuclear option. He could ground her, but would she obey him?

"Who are you texting? Is it James?"

"That's none of your business. And no, it's not James. He's gone."

"Stop speaking to me in that tone," he said, making up his mind. "I don't want you to go out for a few days. Grandma Roberta is going to come by and get you lunch."

She kept her eyes on the TV, refusing to look at him. "You can't keep me a prisoner."

"I'm painfully aware of that. Now call your grandparents in Gimli and apologize for what you put them through."

She looked up at him with alarm. "I'll do it later."

"You'll do it now," he said. "They've been worried sick, and I promised you'd call."

Kelsey rolled her eyes but didn't protest further. Shelter dialled the number to the house in Gimli, and after a few words with Joan Arnason, he handed the phone to Kelsey. When she said hello, it was in a shy little girl voice, as if she'd been caught stealing candy.

Shelter wondered how Christa would have handled the situation if she were alive. She would have known what to do to express disappointment without pushing her away. After the call, Kelsey went to her bedroom while Shelter poured a double vodka and tonic and made a perfunctory search of the kitchen for something to make for dinner. No delicious food had magically appeared in the cupboards or fridge overnight. He found a menu for a pizza place in one of the drawers.

The order placed, he dialled MacIsaac's cellphone and filled him in on the interview with Shawna Craig. MacIsaac conceded the bid-rigging and bribery allegations were serious and instructed Shelter to contact the RCMP commercial crime division to let them know and see what they had on Bill Craig. "I'll make some calls," MacIsaac said. "But plan on bringing him in as soon as we can tomorrow."

"I'll start preparing for the interview."

# TWENTY-TWO

The next morning was overcast and cooler. Shelter was dressed for work and spooning coffee into a filter when he felt his phone vibrating in his pants pocket.

"Hello, Mike," Gordy Taylor said in his familiar baritone. "I just got off the phone with Neil. He was telling me about your conversation with Shawna Craig. You're bringing Bill in today?"

Shelter wondered where this was heading. It occurred to him that Taylor was calling to make him put off the Craig interview. "He's involved in business dealings with this guy Charlie Osborne from the Lone Pine reserve. They were both in a hotel room with Monica Spence and Rory Sinclair. And Crystal Rempel was looking into it. So we've got connections among all of them."

"I personally think Bill Craig is a bastard," Taylor said. "We're on a couple of boards together. Your father knew him too."

Shelter expected more about Craig, but Taylor paused for a long second before asking, "What about this Osborne character? How close are we to bringing him in?"

"We've been trying to track him down, but he's not making it easy. We think he's up on the reserve, and we want to get up there and interview him."

"Alright, then. How's that daughter of yours?"

Shelter was surprised again. How could Taylor have known about Kelsey running away? Had MacIsaac heard about it and tipped him off? He weighed confiding his worries about Kelsey to Taylor. Shelter respected his opinion, and the police chief knew Kelsey as well as if she were his own granddaughter. He'd watched her grow up during many dinner parties over the years both at his home and Shelter's parents' house.

"You heard what happened?" Shelter asked.

"No. What?" The alarm in Taylor's voice was instantaneous.

"She took off from Gimli with a boyfriend I didn't even know about."

"Is she okay?"

"Yeah. I tracked her down, and the boyfriend took off. She's at home now, and I'm going to keep her with me."

After a pause to digest the news, Taylor said, "I know it can't be easy for you, raising her alone. I fought with both of mine at that age." The son and daughter he'd raised with his first wife were now adults who'd started their careers. "When they were teenagers, I put them to work to keep them busy. Made sure they had summer jobs. I got Richard going on a lawn cutting business, and Julie was a lifeguard. It helped keep them out of trouble."

"Kelsey's going to be at loose ends," Shelter said. "I don't know what I'm going to do with her."

"Maybe I can help. We need someone to walk Heidi."

Heidi was Taylor's Golden Lab, a dog Kelsey had known and loved since she was a little girl. "She's getting old and can't make it through the day anymore without going out for a pee," Taylor said. "Janet has to come from the office on her lunch hour to let her out. If Kelsey could come by in the morning and later in the afternoon, that would help us out and give her a bit of spending money. She could even stay for dinner if she wants. We'd love to have her."

Shelter felt relief spreading through his body. His shoulders dropped as he let go of tension he wasn't even aware he was holding. Taylor's house wasn't too far, and he was sure Kelsey would love to spend time with the dog.

"That would be great. Let me talk to her about it tonight, and I'll get back to you. Thanks, Gord."

"Don't mention it. It'll be a pleasure to have her around." After a pause, he added, "It sounds like you're on the right track with this case. Keep it up."

Shelter wolfed down a bagel and drank his coffee standing at the counter. He called his mother and arranged for her to come over at noon and make lunch for Kelsey. Before leaving, he peeked into his daughter's room and could make her out through the gloom under a sheet. He'd intended it to be only a quick glance but found himself looking at her for a long time before gently closing the door.

After the morning status meeting, Shelter called Craig's office and was told he was in a meeting. Shelter thought it would probably take him about an hour to talk to his lawyer and get back to him. He was right, almost to the minute. His telephone rang, the caller ID showing the name of Craig's company. Shelter took a deep breath and reached for the phone. It was the beginning of a chess match.

"Michael Shelter."

"Bill Craig. I hear you're looking for me." The tone was chipper, friendly.

"I'm with the police homicide unit. And we'd appreciate it if you would come downtown to answer a few questions in connection with an investigation we have underway," Shelter said, maintaining a neutral, polite tone.

"What investigation is that?"

"The murder of Monica Spence last month. I guess you've probably seen it in the news?"

"Yes. But what could it possibly have to do with me?"

"Let's cross that bridge when we come to it. Will you come down this afternoon?"

Craig hesitated. He could either refuse to cooperate and signal he had something to hide. Or he could agree to come in and risk saying more than he wanted to. How arrogant was he? Did he think he could outsmart the police?

"No problem," Craig said. "What time do you want me there?"

The meeting was set for 2:00 p.m. Shelter and Traverse spent the morning and right through the lunch hour preparing. They went over newspaper clippings and press releases on Craig and his company. They reviewed the evidence they'd collected so far and drew up a list of questions. They were simple, open-ended. Twice a year, Shelter ran a two-day training course on interviewing. It was hugely popular, a plum reserved for rising stars in the department. He'd earned a reputation as the best interrogator in the service by doggedly pursuing and wringing confessions out of dozens of suspects, applying low-key psychological pressure. The last thing Shelter wanted was a Hollywood-style grilling — accusations, charged words and leading questions. All those tactics would do was drive Craig into a defensive shell. The blander the questions, the more likely he would get him talking and giving up critical information.

Craig arrived twenty minutes late dressed in a navy-blue suit, expertly tailored to hide his belly. He was just over six feet and still powerfully built in his early sixties. With a quick glance, he inspected Shelter from head to toe as he approached the detective. Shaking hands, Shelter's overwhelming impression was of whiteness. An ivory shirt open at the neck, gleaming teeth and a fringe of snowy hair around a bald, tanned head. He was accompanied by Derrick Alistair, who looked to be about the same age. His charcoal suit was expensive too. It was accented by a discreet blue striped tie and matching puff in his breast pocket. He was even taller than Craig and had a priestly presence, pale and thin with an eagle's beak, ruddy cheeks and an annoyed squint behind gold-framed glasses. He was a tax specialist, and Shelter wondered if either of the men had been in a police station before. Craig would have been better off hiring a criminal defence lawyer for the occasion.

Shelter led Craig and Alistair into an interview room and closed the door. MacIsaac and Traverse would be watching the live video feed in a room down the hall. Shelter gestured to two seats on the near side of a steel table screwed into the floor. Alistair took the seat nearest the wall and set his briefcase on the table. When Craig was settled in the seat beside him, Shelter pulled a chair on wheels from the other side of the table and positioned it at the end. He was now facing Craig, with only a small space separating their knees. Shelter gestured to three paper coffee cups sitting on the table beside plastic water bottles.

"I got us some coffee," he said. "Would you like a cup?"

"Sure. Why not?" Craig said with a smile.

"Nothing for me, thank you," Alistair said, a note of annoyance in his high-pitched voice.

"Thanks for coming in today," Shelter said as he passed a coffee to Craig and pointed to cream and sugar on the table. "Before we get started, I'd just like to let you know our conversation is being recorded on video." He pointed to two cameras positioned in upper corners of the room. "Now, Bill, I'm going..."

Alistair interrupted him. "Mr. Craig."

Shelter kept his eyes on Craig and said, "Bill, I'm going to go through your rights in this situation under the Charter of Rights and Freedoms." Alistair let out a sigh of irritation. "Obviously, you're not under arrest here today. You're free to leave at any time, and you don't have to answer any of my questions. We can stop at any time, and you can talk to Mr. Alistair or another lawyer in private. Do you understand that?"

"Yes. Of course." Craig appeared calm, self-assured. His hand was steady as he pulled off the lid of his coffee and added milk and sugar. "You're Tom Shelter's boy, aren't you? Insurance."

"I'm his son, yes."

"Great guy. We did quite a bit of business together over the years."

It was a prepared gambit to put Shelter off his game. With a curt nod, he put it out of his mind.

"I'm a homicide detective, and we are investigating three cases. They are the deaths of Monica Spence, Crystal Rempel and Rory Sinclair. These cases have been in the news, so I guess you've heard about them?"

Craig didn't respond. Alistair made a note on a yellow legal pad he'd brought out from his briefcase.

"Let's start with Monica Spence. Monica was found dead in a culvert just inside the city limits, on June 17th. She had been strangled." Shelter was careful to keep the description of a brutal murder as factual and neutral as possible.

"Crystal Lynn Rempel's body was found on the banks of Omand's Creek near Portage Avenue on July ninth."

"Officer." It was Alistair. The lawyer opened his briefcase and brought out a single sheet of paper. "Before you go on, my client would like to read from a prepared statement at this time," he said. "But before he does, I would like to emphasize the importance of discretion in this matter. Mr. Craig has done a great deal for this city, and he wants to continue to contribute in ways big and small. His good reputation is obviously very important to him, and his ability to do his work. We are counting on you and your colleagues in the police service to be discreet."

"We'll be as discreet as we can be."

Alistair nodded to Craig and handed him the paper. He pulled a pair of reading glasses from his shirt pocket and began reading in a halting voice.

"On June 9th of this year, I met with a man named Charles Osborne in a room at the Bond Hotel to discuss a business arrangement. When we had successfully concluded our discussions, we had a drink to celebrate." He stopped to take a sip of coffee and continued. "I was unaware of it at the time, but Mr. Osborne had taken it upon himself to invite two young women to the hotel room. They arrived in the company of a man. I became aware the women were prostitutes, and the man also produced a quantity of cocaine. I was very uncomfortable and considered leaving immediately. To my ever-lasting regret, I did not do so. While I did not ingest cocaine, I did accompany one of the women to an adjoining room and had sex with her. That woman was Monica Spence. The man was Rory Sinclair. I am aware both of these individuals are now dead, but I never saw either of them after that evening and have no knowledge of how they were killed or who killed them."

Craig turned over the sheet and glanced at the blank reverse side. "And that's it," he said with a mournful half smile. "I'm sorry for what I did, but I really can't help you with the deaths of these two women or Mr. Sinclair."

"Thank you for that," Shelter said. "I have a few questions."

Before he could go on, Alistair cut in once again. "We're here to cooperate with your investigation, but as Mr. Craig just mentioned, he doesn't know anything about the deaths of these individuals."

Shelter was about to argue the point when Craig raised his hand. His expression was mild as he looked from Shelter to his lawyer. "I guess I could field a few questions."

Shelter opened a beige folder and glanced at his list of questions. His mind was racing, going over what Craig had just disclosed. He would have assumed he'd been caught on CCTV entering the Bond Hotel, along with Charlie, Rory, Monica and Pamela Daniel. But his statement had gone further than that. He'd admitted to cocaine being in the room. So he must know about the photo Pam Daniel had taken. How? Had he learned about it from Monica Spence? Had she contacted him, and that was what ended up getting her killed? And Crystal too when she followed the trail?

One by one, Shelter asked Craig about where he'd been and what he'd been doing on the dates Spence, Rempel and Sinclair had been murdered. The businessman was well-prepared. He'd been at his cottage, his golf club or at work, where he'd been seen by friends or employees. Each alibi would be carefully verified, but the specificity of Craig's explanations told Shelter they would all check out. He took a drink of coffee and flipped the page on his notebook.

"What was this business arrangement you were discussing at the hotel?"

Craig again looked to Alistair. The lawyer nodded for him to answer.

"I've agreed to partner with the Lone Pine First Nation on the development of an urban reserve downtown. We see it as an important part of the mayor's plan to bring the city's core back to life and at the same time improve the lives of the Indigenous community."

"What does it entail?"

"The details are private, but I can tell you we're talking about an important project — several tens of millions of dollars with retail, residential and a multipurpose entertainment facility."

"A casino."

Craig smiled. "We're very excited about the project, and so is the mayor."

"Why would you meet in a hotel room rather than in your office or his office?"

"These were very confidential negotiations. We preferred a neutral location."

"What is Agassiz Holdings?"

Craig blinked, and the corners of his mouth turned down for an instant. It was an almost imperceptible reaction before he arranged his face into a quizzical expression. He shook his head. "I have no idea."

"Agassiz Holdings is a Bahamian-registered corporation. The

identity of the shareholders is secret, but we believe it's controlled by you, Bill. What's its purpose?"

"No. You're mistaken. I don't know anything about it."

Shelter looked at Alistair. "I understand setting up offshore entities is one of your specialties, Mr. Alistair."

Alistair's features pinched into a frown. "As Mr. Craig just told you, we don't know what you're talking about, Detective."

Shelter looked from Alistair to Craig. "Are you aware that a photo was taken in the hotel room?"

Craig crossed his arms and looked at Shelter steadily. "A photo taken in the hotel room? I don't remember anyone taking pictures. May I see it?"

Shelter sensed he was lying. "I'm afraid that won't be possible. Did Monica Spence ask you for money in return for the photo?"

Alistair broke in. "Mr. Craig has just told you he has no knowledge of a photo and had no further contact with Ms. Spence after June 9th."

Shelter nodded. "We believe there was another man in the hotel room with you. Who was that person?"

Craig gave another regretful shake of his head. "Again, I don't know who you've been talking to, but there was no one else." Shelter noticed his arms across his chest tightened ever so slightly.

"Two people who were in that room are already dead. You should think about that."

"I can assure you we are being as cooperative as we can be," Alistair said.

Shelter gave a quick nod before asking, "What was your relationship with Crystal Rempel?"

"There wasn't any relationship. I didn't know her."

"She never contacted you?"

"I never spoke to her." Shelter noted Craig hadn't answered the question, but Alistair had begun to fidget and glance at his watch.

Craig volunteered, "Of course, she knew Charlie, and I know she'd talked to him a number of times about Monica Spence's death. She was accusing him of having a hand in it."

Shelter struggled to hide his surprise at this admission. He glanced at Alistair, who was looking at Craig. Shelter sensed he too was surprised.

"How do you know about these conversations?"

"Charlie told me. He was upset and was wondering what to do about her. Obviously, I couldn't give him any advice. I told him to go to the police."

Alistair snapped the catches on his briefcase and put a hand on his client's shoulder. "Mr. Craig has another appointment."

Shelter said, "What else can you tell me about these interactions between Crystal and Charlie Osborne?"

Craig looked down as if debating with himself, trying to make up his mind. Then he said, "To be perfectly honest with you, I'm concerned about the role Charlie has played in all this."

"What do you mean?"

"On the day Crystal's body was found, Charlie was supposed to be up on his reserve. That's what he'd told me. But he wasn't. I was surprised to see him downtown, crossing Hargrave Street."

"You spoke to him?"

"No. I was in my car. I didn't think too much about it at the time, and I'm sure it doesn't mean anything, but I thought you should know."

# TWENTY-THREE

Shelter took his usual booth in the Peking Garden and ordered a large bowl of hot and sour soup from Arthur Yee. He'd missed lunch and needed some time alone after the interview. What was Bill Craig up to? His alibis for the three murders looked tight, so why would he turn on his partner in a multi-million-dollar construction deal? Shelter's instincts told him Craig was doing it to protect someone else — the other man in the hotel room that night.

Shelter judged it unlikely Monica Spence or Crystal Rempel would have shown Pam Daniel's picture to any of the men in the room that evening, so they wouldn't have known who could be identified in it. A record of them together in a secret meeting would be enough to cause a scandal and sink their deal. Monica Spence may have thought she was blackmailing them over hookers and coke, but it could have been business that got her killed. And Crystal too, when she started asking questions.

As he ate his soup, he went through his email on his phone. A reply had come in from an RCMP constable on the Lone Pine reserve. Charlie Osborne had been spotted at the band office, and his truck was in front of his house. Shelter sent a return email, telling the officer he would be leaving for the reserve the next morning.

His phone signalled an incoming text. It was from Nicki. *Hey, not working tonite. Something to tell u.*

An image of Nicki came to his mind. He couldn't deny he wanted to see her, and he'd be dropping off Kelsey at his mother's place for the time he'd be at Lone Pine. He composed a text. *Can meet you at nine.*

Even as he sent the message, doubt crept into his mind. What the hell was he doing? He should be meeting her with Traverse if she had information. Agreeing to see her alone was contrary to procedure and doing it at night was exposing her to more danger from the killer. He visualized the scene in Market Square and thought of the bullet narrowly missing her head. He dropped the phone on the table and ate a couple of spoonfuls of soup. The phone signalled another text. *Ok. Meet me at vimy ridge park at 9:30.* He knew he should call off the meet but made no move to pick up his phone and send her another text.

Back at the office, Shelter had just tapped in his password to sign into his computer when Traverse approached his desk.

"Just had the Land Titles Office on the line. I had them run through large land purchases downtown in the last two years or so, and one stands out."

Shelter stopped typing. His partner had his full attention.

"Someone has put together a full city block north of Ellice. It's a frickin' huge piece of land." Traverse turned back to his desk and pointed to a Google map of downtown Winnipeg on his computer screen. "Right here." Shelter stood up to take a closer look.

"These are all parking lots," Traverse said, running his finger lightly across the screen, "except for a couple of rundown buildings here. The buyer got it for a song. It might have nothing to do with the urban reserve project, or someone might be getting ready to make a killing if they flip it."

"Who bought it?"

"It's a numbered company owned by someone named Thomas Walsh. He paid cash. Jennifer is checking him out right now. We'll know more soon."

"Okay. Keep on it," Shelter said. "I'm heading up to Lone Pine tomorrow morning to talk to Charlie."

He returned to his desk to make preparations for the three-hour drive north to the reserve. He called his mother and arranged for Kelsey to stay at her house while he was gone, telling her he hoped to be back late the next evening but might have to stay overnight. When he got off the phone, he found Jennifer Kane waiting a discreet distance away, tapping her foot with excitement.

"This Thomas Walsh is a real-estate broker with an office on Pembina Highway." She flipped a page in her notebook and added with a smile, "Guess what? He took a fifteen-month disciplinary suspension of his licence back in 2011."

Shelter stopped packing papers into his carry bag. "Go on."

"A friend of his lent a lady ten thousand for the down payment on a house Walsh was selling. The lady was supposed to pay it back when the mortgage closed with the cash back she got from the bank. That's totally illegal."

Shelter nodded and returned Kane's smile. "Not bad. Nice work. Small potatoes, but once a crook..."

"Always a crook. You think he's fronting for someone?"

Shelter shrugged. "Could be. Let's bring him in and find out why the sudden interest in downtown real estate and where the money came from."

From the mugs in the sink and food containers left on the counter, Shelter saw that Kelsey hadn't done anything all day except eat TV dinners and drink tea. He found her in the darkened basement, still in her pyjamas, with the cat on her lap, watching YouTube videos. He would have liked some downtime himself, but he forced himself to throw together broccoli and chicken pasta. At the dinner table, he broke the news to her that she'd be staying at her grandmother's house for a day or so while he went out of town. She rolled her eyes and sighed but didn't put up a fight. She enjoyed spending time with her grandmother. Roberta Shelter had the means to spoil her with lunches and shopping trips to the mall.

"Does she know what happened?" Kelsey asked.

"I told her but spared her the details," Shelter said.

She took that in without replying, her eyes on her plate. Shelter resisted the urge to go over just how serious Kelsey's actions had been. He was reluctant to drive the wedge between them any deeper. He couldn't read what she was thinking. Could she just be waiting to take off again?

"I talked to Gordy Taylor this morning, and they're looking for someone to walk Heidi. You interested?"

She raised her head and studied his face, obviously curious. "Like for money?"

"That's the idea."

"How much?"

"I have no idea. But he's a generous guy, and it's not as if you're raking it in now. It would be a walk before lunch and then again in the late afternoon. Heidi's getting old, and she needs to get out more often. I'm sure she'd enjoy your company too."

"I'll think about it."

From the way she said it, Shelter knew she liked the idea.

After dinner, Shelter made a quick call to his mother while Kelsey was getting dressed and packing an overnight bag. After cleaning up the dinner dishes, he climbed to the second floor to see what progress Kelsey had made in getting ready. He found her kneeling by her bed with her head resting on her hands. A photo album was open on her bed. She must have come across it as she packed. Shelter took a step toward her. Her head came up at the sound of him in the room. She was crying, and Shelter could see over her shoulder she was looking at a picture of Christa holding her when she was a toddler. He felt a wave of tenderness. He took another step.

"Kel." It was all he got out.

"Get out!"

"Kel. Let's talk about it."

"No. Leave me alone." Her voice was choked, and she dragged the back of her hand across her eyes.

Shelter couldn't go forward but didn't want to retreat.

"I said get out."

Shelter turned and left the room. He stood hurt and angry in the hallway. He held himself back from marching back into the room and telling her, "You're not the only one who lost her." Instead, he went downstairs and kicked open the screen door to the patio. Over the course of ten minutes, his brain slowed and he could breathe normally again. *Nothing to do tonight except not make it worse*, he thought.

Standing at the bottom of the stairs, he called up to Kelsey, telling her it was time to go. She didn't reply but showed up on the landing a few seconds later. Shelter didn't take his eyes off her as she descended but said nothing. Kelsey kept her eyes lowered until she'd reached the second to last stair. She glanced at him with a frown that he took to be a sign of regret. It was enough for now.

Shelter sat beside Nicki on top of a picnic table, their feet resting on the bench. They were surrounded by tall oak and elm trees in the gathering darkness enveloping Vimy Ridge Park. Sitting close to her, with moonlight shining through the branches, his doubts about meeting her alone evaporated. He felt no awkwardness from her and didn't feel any himself.

She was telling him a story about a patron at the bar, laughing so hard she could barely get the words out. He was laughing too, but mostly he was studying her face. White teeth, full lips and golden skin. The story was about a guy who'd had his penis tattooed.

"He was telling the whole table about it. Very proud."

"Ouch. A tattoo of what?"

"A dragon. Or so he said. I didn't have a look," she said, breaking up again.

"Fire-breathing, I take it," Shelter said, shaking his head. He added, "Just so many questions."

"Like what?"

"Did he have to be erect to get it done?"

"Someone asked him that, as a matter of fact. Know what he said?"

"What?"

"How long could you stay hard with needles stabbing into your penis? Apparently, the artist just pulls the skin tight."

"Oh my God. Okay. That's enough," Shelter said, wiping tears from his eyes.

"What did you have for me?"

Nicki turned to look at Shelter. "Somebody contacted me from the Lone Pine reserve about my sister."

"Who?"

"A lady who lives up there. She says Crystal stayed on the rez a couple of days, just before she was killed."

"Okay. We thought it was a good possibility she was there. But how come this lady hasn't contacted us before? It's been in the news for a week."

"I don't know. Maybe she didn't know it was important. Maybe she was scared. Anyway, she called Moses for more info, and he gave her my number."

"She knows Moses?" Shelter asked.

"Well, mostly Crystal, I think. She's active in women and child welfare issues on the rez. Crystal was helping her with that — mostly finding ways of keeping kids in the community instead of being sent into care in Winnipeg."

Shelter wasn't surprised the woman had gone to Moses Kent to find out what was happening. Crystal Rempel's ex-boyfriend would have been a natural choice to find out more about her killing. But he was disappointed Moses hadn't come to him with the information. "What's this person's name?"

"Doris Bear."

"Okay. We've been trying to get through to a number up there belonging to someone with that name." Judging by the cellphone records, Doris Bear had spoken several times with Crystal Rempel in the weeks before her death. It seemed possible she was Crystal's source on the urban reserve deal and the involvement of Charlie Osborne and Bill Craig. It could have been the information that got Crystal killed.

"Did she say why Crystal was on the reserve?"

Nicki reached behind her for a small backpack on the table and pulled out a cigarette pack. She lit one and, exhaling, held it up to Shelter. "Down to two a day. I'm getting there." After another drag, she continued. "Crystal just showed up out of the blue. Doris says she was very upset about Mom's death and wanted to see our grandmother."

Shelter nodded. "Right, your mother's mother is there."

"I've never met her, but Crystal had been getting to know her. She'd always wanted to connect with her."

"How come you never met your grandmother?"

"My mom didn't want to go back to the rez, and then my grandma moved to Saskatchewan to be with a brother of hers. She's only been back a few years. I've just never had the chance."

Shelter wondered about Nicki's mother. How could she have become so estranged from her home and family on the reserve? What had happened to Anne Alexander at Lone Pine that she'd never returned, even just so Nicki could meet her grandmother and see where she grew up? Anne had been lost in a world of drug and alcohol addiction for much of her life. Maybe being closer to her community could have helped her and made Nicki's life easier.

"What happened when Crystal went up there this last time?"

"Doris said she spent a lot of time at our grandmother's house. She slept there two nights." Nicki took another pull from her cigarette, and after looking at the glowing tip, she flicked it into the grass. "She also went to see Charlie Osborne." She pushed herself off the bench, walked over to where the butt had landed and ground it out. "On the third morning, she took off for the city." Turning and taking a couple of steps toward Shelter, she said, "Doris doesn't know what was bothering her or what she talked about with Charlie."

"Hopefully that's what I'll find out. I'm going up there tomorrow."

After considering this, she said, "I'm going with you."

Shelter shook his head. "No way."

Her eyes narrowed and her chin tilted up. She was standing close to him, just a foot or two away, a hand on one jutting hip. "Doris won't talk to the cops without me there. She told me that. And besides, you can't stop me. If you don't take me, I'm going on my own."

Shelter sighed. "You have to let us do our work, Nicki. I can't do it if I have to watch out for you at the same time."

"I been taking care of myself since I was eight years old."

"Okay. But this is different. This is a murder investigation, and it's—"

She interrupted him. "It's not different. It's my sister, and that reserve is where my people are from. I'm going."

Shelter stared into her dark eyes. He could smell tobacco on her and found it strangely enticing. Something in her fierce expression sent a wave of excitement through him. He dropped his eyes, worried she would sense the attraction he was feeling. From where he sat, he could reach out a hand, take hold of her wrist and pull her to him. His pulse was racing. He hadn't felt this way about a woman since Christa. Finally, he looked up and shook his head in surrender. Smiling, he said, "I guess you're going to do what you're going to do."

Nicki's face softened, and then she smiled too. "You're finally starting to get it."

In that moment, Shelter thought he sensed desire in the way she was looking into his eyes. Or was he just projecting his emotions onto her? He felt his cellphone vibrate in his pocket. "Sorry."

The number on the display was from an unidentified caller. It was a woman, verging on hysteria. He recognized Pam Daniel's voice. "He did it again."

"Did what?"

She gasped for breath. The words came out as a scream. "Killed my girlfriend."

# TWENTY-FOUR

By the time Shelter got to the emergency room, Donna Davis was out of danger. She'd been through a sexual assault examination and was now asleep in a private room. Her face and neck were badly cut and bruised, and her windpipe had been nearly crushed by the force of hands around her throat.

She was alive because she'd been spotted by a security guard making rounds of an industrial park near the airport. He'd seen the tail lights of a car exiting a parking lot of an empty warehouse and found her lying unconscious beside a dumpster in the rear. She was naked below the waist, her black miniskirt pulled up and a torn pair of panties beside her. A health-care card in a tiny purse found under her body gave her name. Donna Davis was sixteen.

This information came from Detective Sue Marek, a veteran of the Sex Crimes Unit who'd been surprised and displeased to see a homicide detective show up at the Health Sciences Centre. In her early forties, Marek had an athletic build and light brown hair to her shoulders. She had a prominent nose and an angry scar that ran from the right corner of her mouth to just below her ear. It had faded only a little in the ten years Shelter had known her. How she got it was a secret; he'd made a few discreet inquires over the years and come up empty. She had a fearsome reputation for taking no bullshit and, as he did each time he spoke to her, Shelter struggled to keep his eyes off the scar and on her brown eyes.

"How did you hear about this?" she demanded after a curt handshake.

"I have a source in the Monica Spence case who heard about it," Shelter said. "She was worried and gave me a call."

"Who's this source, and how did she hear about it so fast?"

Traverse arrived, and he and Marek shook hands.

"Her name is Pam Daniel, a friend of Spence's — they were in the business together," Shelter said. "From what I can piece together, your team found Pam's phone number in Donna's bag and called her. She phoned me in a panic."

Marek nodded. "The girl on Furby Street. She wouldn't talk to us." Marek considered the situation, looking down at a black leather boot she was tapping lightly on the cement floor. "Davis was picked up for streetwalking a couple of months ago. We're heading over to Furby to interview Pam Daniel."

"I'm not sure she'll talk to you, if she's even there when you arrive," Traverse said.

Marek scowled, looking from Traverse and back to Shelter. Traverse continued, "She's scared. We have a relationship with her. Let us talk to her, and we'll keep you posted if she has anything."

Marek's face was drawn into a frown, but she couldn't argue with Traverse's logic. She briefly ran down the extent of Donna's injuries without emotion, including indications she'd been raped.

Shelter thanked her and promised to brief her on whatever they found from Pam Daniel.

"Yeah, just don't forget who's running this investigation."

On the drive over to Pam's apartment, Shelter considered the similarities between the attacks on Donna Davis, Monica Spence and Crystal Rempel.

"All three were strangled," he said to Traverse, who was driving. "Donna and Monica were Indigenous and sex workers and it's possible they both knew Crystal. It's got to be all tied together. One killer."

"But what's the motive?" Traverse asked. "Donna and Monica were sexual assaults but not Crystal." They pulled up to a brick walk-up apartment block in the city's West End. "And what's the connection to the land deal? If Monica, Crystal and Rory were killed to keep it quiet, how does Donna fit in?"

It was just after 1 a.m. when Shelter knocked on the door of Pam's third-floor apartment. "It's open," a voice called from inside. They found Pam Daniel seated at the kitchen table with a little dollar-store notebook in front of her. The room was painted a dingy yellow, with grease stains on the walls above the stove. The sink was filled with unwashed dishes, and a plastic garbage receptacle was overflowing. There was a faint odour of cat urine but no sign of the animal. Pam alternated between taking drags from a cigarette and toying with her lighter.

She knew the girl as Donna Star. They'd met at Portage Place Mall, and Pam had been crashing with her in this dump for the last few days. Pam wore a pink tube dress. Her eyeliner was smeared and her hair dishevelled. Her eyelids were droopy, and she raked her fingers through her long hair in a languid gesture.

"It was the same system you used with Monica Spence, right?" Shelter said.

Pam nodded. "We worked diagonal corners."

"Where?"

"Out here on Sargent," she said, jabbing with her thumb over her shoulder.

Each time a man picked up one of them, the other made a note of the licence plate number. It was just after 7:00 p.m. when Donna hopped into the vehicle.

"What kind of car?" Traverse asked.

"An SUV. Don't ask me what make," Pam said, flicking the wheel on her lighter to make sparks. "Brown, but a light shade." She fired up another cigarette, inhaling sharply and then exhaling a long stream of smoke. "He pulled up down the block from where she was, so it was a fair distance away. But I'm pretty sure this is it." She tapped a page on the notebook, where a licence plate number was noted in a childish scrawl. She pushed it across the table to Shelter.

"I'm giving you this but keep me out of it. I didn't see the guy."

Shelter nodded. "Can you give me anything? Hair colour? Glasses? How big he was?"

"Uh-uh. It was too far."

Shelter picked up the notebook and handed it to Traverse with a nod. His partner took it into the living room, where Shelter could hear him calling to verify the owner of the vehicle.

"Did Donna know Monica or Crystal?" he asked.

Pam bowed her head and examined the cigarette smouldering between her fingers. "Not that I know of. I met her after Monica was gone." She rubbed her temples before giving her head a shake.

"You going to be okay?" Shelter asked.

She gave a short, sharp laugh. "No, but what fucking difference does it make, right?" She took another drag. "I'm just trying to stay alive out here."

"There's help, Pam. Let me put you in touch with someone."

Her eyes dropped again. "I'll let you know, okay?"

When Traverse returned, he stood in the door frame without speaking. He locked eyes with Shelter and gave a slight nod. Shelter felt a surge of adrenaline. Pam must have sensed it, because she swivelled to look at Traverse and then back at Shelter. "What's going on?"

"Nothing. But we have to head out now. Where are you going to go? You don't look like you're in any shape to be alone."

"Don't fucking give me that," she said, jabbing two fingers at Shelter, the cigarette between them. She turned to Traverse, who'd moved into the room. "What did they say on the phone about that licence number? You know who the fucker is, don't you?"

"We need to do some more checks," Traverse said.

She ground out her cigarette in an ashtray and glared at Traverse. "Who is it?"

"Pam, it's too early. And what difference would it make anyway?"

She scowled and crossed her arms across her chest. "You'd have jack shit without me."

Shelter became aware how young and alone she was. Her anger was all she had. When he spoke, he kept his tone low and gentle. "We know that, Pam and we're grateful. Where are you going to stay tonight?"

"I'll sleep here and go back to the motel in the morning."

"You sure you don't want to ride over there right now?"

She shook her head. She held her head in her hands, her long hair forming a curtain hiding her face.

"Alright, stay off the street. We'll be in touch."


"A 2005 Toyota RAV4. Tan-coloured," Traverse reported as they crossed the street to the car. "Registered to Daniel James Stokes, age forty-four. He was picked up last year in Operation Clean Sweep and had his car seized. The same SUV."

"Sent to John School?"

"Yup. That's how he got the car back."

Clean Sweep was one of the periodic round-ups of men soliciting prostitutes. First-time offenders were usually sent to the one-day program run by the Salvation Army designed to teach them the consequences of prostitution, known as John School. If they attended the program, the solicitation charge was dropped and they got their car back — after paying a hefty fine.

"He was also given a suspended sentence on a domestic assault in 2007. He beat up and choked his wife," said Traverse, who steered the car down the wide expanse of Portage Avenue. "He lives off St. Mary's Road, on the other side of Fermor."

"Give it to Marek. That should brighten her mood a bit."

As Traverse punched in the phone number, Shelter reminded himself the assault could have nothing to do with the Spence and Rempel homicides. Assaults on sex workers were common and often involved choking. It would take work to establish it was Stokes driving the car and that he was the one who beat and raped the girl.

Traverse ended the call. "She's going to set up surveillance on the house and will try to get him ID'ed by the girl in the morning."

"Chances are he's a random john," Shelter said, trying to tamp down his hopes. "Even if he picked up Monica Spence, what would the connection be to Crystal?"

"Maybe he got girls through Rory Sinclair," Traverse said. "That would tie them all together."

Shelter nodded. But could the murders really be the act of a random bad trick with nothing to do with Charlie Osborne, Bill Craig and the urban reserve deal?

"Weren't you supposed to be going up to the reserve?" Traverse asked.

"Yeah. That's off. I'll have to let the Mounties know. And Nicki."

"Nicki?"

"I'm giving her a ride up there. She wouldn't take no for an answer."

Traverse was silent for a few seconds. "She's the sister of a homicide victim and might be a witness. What are you doing, man?"

"I can't stop her from going up there," Shelter shot back.

"When was this decided?"

"Hey, what business is it of yours?" Somewhere in the back of his mind, Shelter already knew it was his exhaustion talking, but he couldn't stop himself.

Traverse gave a violent shrug. Shelter had rarely seen him this angry. "You're so full of shit. I saw the way you were looking at her at the hospital. You seeing her on the side?"

Shelter shook his head. "I'm going to bed, and you should too."

"I'm telling you, for your own good, don't get involved."

"I'm not getting involved. So don't worry about me."

A tense silence fell between them as Traverse turned onto Shelter's street and pulled up in front of his house. Something in the intensity of Traverse's reaction made Shelter wonder if it was more than Nicki's involvement in the investigation that was bothering him.

"What?" Shelter said.

"Are you taking advantage of a situation?"

Now, Shelter was well and truly pissed off. "I'm not doing anything, okay?" He got out of the car. "I'll be at the office by seven."

Traverse remained silent, looking straight ahead.

On the drive into the office the next morning, Shelter went over the fight he'd had with Traverse the night before. He had to admit his partner had hit a nerve. It was the first time he'd felt attraction to a woman since Christa's death, but he couldn't deny that acting on it would be a mistake. Not only were the power dynamics between him as a police officer and Nicki as a witness all wrong, but he wasn't even sure the attraction was mutual. But the desire was strong, and a part of his brain refused to let go of the idea of taking it further with her. Stopped at a red light, he stretched and shook his head to clear his mind.

Traverse arrived at the office just after eight and went straight to his desk without a word. Shelter decided to keep his distance. He focused on the information he'd pulled up on Daniel Stokes, going over the details of the solicitation and domestic assault charges and noting he made his living as a long-distance truck driver.

The sound of chatting and squeaking chair wheels signalled the team was gathering in a semi-circle for the morning meeting. Shelter briefed them on the events of the previous night, emphasizing that for them nothing had changed. They were stretched badly by the unsolved homicides, with dozens of leads and tips to follow. And they worked under the knowledge that soon other killings would inevitably be added to the workload. Still, news of the sexual assault had them looking at one another with raised eyebrows.

"Strangulation is the same M.O. as in the Spence and Rempel cases," Ian Sim said, stating the obvious.

"And we know Monica worked that strip," Jennifer Kane added.

"We know she worked in the area, but we don't know where she was picked up," Shelter said. "Let's just keep working our cases and see what sex crimes comes up with."

Back at his desk, Shelter was working on an email to the RCMP detachment on the Lone Pine Reserve to say he couldn't make it as planned when he heard a faint tapping behind him. He turned around to find Sue Marek at his office divider. She took a step forward, and the corners of her mouth turned up in an uncharacteristic show of good humour.

"Hey, just wanted to let you know the girl picked Daniel Stokes out of a photo pack this morning. No doubt in her mind," Marek said. "Thanks for the tip."

"No problem. You have eyes on him?"

"He's in his house. Mom and the two boys have been in and out. But he hasn't budged."

Detectives from the Sex Crimes Unit would be bringing Stokes in as soon as Marek could get a judge to sign warrants to enter the house and search his vehicle. He would be brought down to the PSB and booked with sexual assault. The SUV would be towed to a garage the Ident unit maintained for forensic examinations.

Shelter would have loved to be in the room when Stokes was interviewed, but this was Marek's investigation and he had to respect that line. A few hours later, he got confirmation the arrest had gone down without a hitch in an email from MacIsaac that went on to tell him to be in a conference room on the second floor in fifteen minutes. When he got there, MacIsaac was already set up at the head of the table with a notebook and a cellphone laid out in front of him. Sue Marek sat on the side of the table closest to the windows. Her body language was foreboding. She had her arms crossed tightly across her chest and a tense look on her face.

Shelter gave her a nod of greeting, took a seat across from her, and angled himself to face MacIsaac. "What's up?"

"The Stokes case," MacIsaac said. "Ident just found a roll of blue duct tape and a sheet of clear, plastic tarp concealed in the spare tire well."

Shelter was stunned. He glanced at Marek and back to MacIsaac, who was nodding. In his mind, Shelter saw Monica Spence and Crystal Rempel lying encased like mummies.

"Holy fuck."

"Yup."

"He's got two little kids, so the passenger compartment is a gross mess," Marek said. "But Ident is pulling fingerprints, hair and fibres as we speak." The tone was harsh, and when she finished, her lips were tightly pursed. Shelter could sense the disappointment coming off her. She was a competitive detective, and she was losing a huge investigation. But Shelter could barely contain his excitement.

"You and Traverse will conduct the interview," MacIsaac said.

# TWENTY-FIVE

Interview room two's only furnishings were a grey steel table and a chair bolted to the floor. Shelter and Traverse rolled office chairs into the room. Traverse closed the door while Shelter arranged a red file folder and yellow legal pad on the table. The top page was blank. His interview plan and questions were scrawled on the pages that followed, but he rarely needed to look at them.

Shelter examined Stokes as he introduced himself and Traverse. This was Shelter's first glimpse of the man except for a mugshot. He was no more than five foot eight inches, and he looked to have put on weight in the three years since he'd been photographed after being charged for soliciting a prostitute. His face was jowly, like a Boxer dog, and he had only a few strands of greasy brown hair running across his scalp. He had a thick brush of a moustache and bulky shoulders. The stubby fingers folded on top of his basketball of a belly had black hair growing from the knuckles.

Shelter passed him a bottle of water.

"Daniel, you've been charged with sexual assault, and you've spoken to your lawyer," Shelter said for the benefit of the video camera. "We can stop the interview at any time, and you can talk to your lawyer for as long as you like. Do you understand all that?"

Stokes's cinder block of a head had been bowed as Shelter spoke. Now he raised it and fixed pig eyes on Shelter. "Does this one have to be here?" he said, pointing a finger at Traverse but not looking at him.

"You have a problem with Detective Traverse being in the room?"

"Shouldn't he be in a bar drinking with his buddies?"

Shelter and Traverse stared at him in silence.

"What?" Stokes said, still addressing Shelter. "When his people aren't lying drunk on Main Street, they're cruising around town in taxis to the liquor commission or the bar, and it's all paid for with our fucking tax dollars." Stokes turned toward Traverse for the first time, his eyes in a defiant squint, his chin extended. "But you're a good little Indian, eh?"

Traverse's face was impassive, his gaze unflinching. "If you're finished, Daniel," Shelter said in a calm voice, "we've got some questions to ask you."

Stokes shrugged and lowered his head again, making a show of examining a hand balled into a tight fist on his thigh. Shelter noticed the thumbnail had been chewed to the nail bed.

Stokes had declined a lawyer. Shelter assumed it was a combination of overconfidence and not wanting to spend the money. Whatever the reason, having him alone improved the chances of getting him to talk, and his racist outburst was another good sign. He was already talking. Far from being upset, Traverse would be pleased.

"You're a truck driver, yeah?" Shelter said.

"No comment."

"Listen. I know your lawyer told you not to speak to us, and that's fine. That's your right. But we need to confirm some basic information. Now, you're a truck driver for what company?"

"I don't work as a driver no more."

"Why?"

Stokes was silent. He opened his hands and closed them so tight, they turned red. "Because of my son. He's autistic. Too much for my wife to handle alone."

"So where do you work now?"

"In a cold storage warehouse, freezing my ass with a bunch of pakis and chinks. And even some of yours, when they can drag themselves out of bed," he said, glancing at Traverse.

"Where were you on Saturday night?"

"Home with the wife."

Shelter looked down at the legal pad before locking eyes with Stokes.

"We have a witness who saw you pick up a girl about 8:00 p.m.," he said. "The girl you picked up has identified you as the man who beat and choked her behind a building on Stevenson Road, near the airport."

"No comment."

Shelter sighed and tapped his pencil on the table. "Our guys are tearing apart your car right now, and they're going to find this girl's fingerprints and DNA all over the vehicle. And there are video cameras throughout that industrial park."

A knock on the door interrupted the interview. Shelter nodded to Traverse, who exited the room, only to stick his head in a minute later to ask Shelter to step out. In the hallway, Jennifer Kane was waiting with Traverse. She was holding a notebook in her hand, and Shelter noticed her hand was trembling.

"Ident made a positive match to the rear left wheel of his vehicle and the tire track lifted near Monica Spence's body. They've also got a match from the passenger compartment for almost a full set of Donna Davis's right-hand fingerprints." The three detectives were standing in a huddle, looking at each other. They had their man. Shelter felt relief wash over him. "Get them to send up pictures of the tire and the tracks."

He followed Traverse back into the interview room. Stokes ignored them, keeping his head bowed and raising his thumb to his mouth to inflict more damage on his ravaged nail.

"Sorry about that," Shelter said. "Can I get you some coffee? Need to go to the bathroom?"

Stokes shook his head. "When can I talk to my wife? She's alone with my son. He screams all day long and throws himself around."

"We'll see about that in a little while," Shelter said. "Daniel, I want you to look at a couple of pictures for me." Shelter pulled the red file folder out from under the legal pad and opened it. He laid two eight-by-ten photos on the table side by side. They were the same photos that had been in newspapers. Both women smiling brightly, Monica in her grade twelve high school picture, Crystal in her graduation photo from law school. Shelter tipped the red file folder toward himself and examined a sheaf of documents inside.

"Do you know who these women are?"

He studied the images only for a moment before dropping his eyes to his lap. "No comment."

"This one is Monica Spence, and this one is Crystal Rempel. Monica was found dead in a culvert just inside the Perimeter Highway. Crystal was found at Omand's Creek near Portage Avenue."

"I've got nothing to say to you two."

"What were you doing on June 16th, a Friday night, a little over a month ago?"

"How the fuck would I know? Probably sitting at home watching TV."

"You know Plessis Road in St. Boniface, right? When was the last time you were out there?"

Stokes lifted his head slowly, his eyes narrowing with suspicion. "It's been years."

Shelter referred to his notes again. "Did you get your snow tires taken off that SUV of yours this year?"

Stokes shook his head and grunted.

"Do you remember the brand of tires on your truck?"

"They're Michelin. What's this about?" He said it in a growl of annoyance, but Shelter detected uncertainty, even fear in his voice. Still, curiosity was getting the better of him. Again, there was tapping at the door, and Jennifer Kane stuck her head in and called Shelter out of the room. She handed him a grey folder and briefed him as he examined the photos inside.

Shelter returned to the interview room and slid the two pictures of the women back into the red folder. He replaced them with two photocopied images from the grey one. One was a close-up of a rear tire on a vehicle and the other a tire track in heavy mud just off a paved road.

"Take a look at these pictures. This one was taken from your SUV this morning, and this one was taken on Plessis Road on the morning of June 17th. That was the day that Monica Spence was found dead in a ditch a few metres from where this picture was taken."

"They're both winter tires. Now look at this." Shelter used his pen to point to several wear marks and a shallow but distinct cut across one of the treads. "Our forensic guys tell us these two tires match perfectly. But you said you haven't been to Plessis Road in years. How do you explain that?"

Stokes stared at the images but said nothing.

"We also found a roll of blue duct tape and a plastic tarp in your trunk this morning. The bodies of both Monica and Crystal were wrapped in plastic, which was then secured by blue tape in exactly the same way." He paused and then continued in the same calm, quiet voice. "How do you explain that?"

Stokes sat for long minutes, his eyes on his lap, tightening and loosening his fists. Finally, Shelter said, "Daniel! Look at me."

Stokes raised his head with a jerk.

"Where are we going with this? It won't take us long to match the tape to what was used to wrap those women. And their DNA is going to be all over your car. You know it is."

Stokes had crossed his arms and hunched his shoulders, as if trying to shield his body. Another minute of silence passed before Stokes raised his head and nodded toward Traverse. "I'm not saying a fucking word with him in the room."

Shelter glanced at Traverse. He knew his partner was used to dealing with racism, even though it was rarely expressed this brazenly. It was sickening to hear, but the important thing was to get a confession.

Traverse stood up, his face impassive, picked up his notebook and left the room without a word.

Shelter let Stokes sit in silence for another full minute before saying, "Daniel. Tell me what your concerns are?"

Shelter waited and watched the war within the man — sighs, frowns and even a rueful laugh as he searched the room with his eyes. Finally, he said, "It's my wife. She's had enough pain. I don't want you guys tearing up our house."

"I understand what you're saying, Daniel. We have no intention of causing any unnecessary pain to your wife or family. Look at me. Let's start with Monica. Where did you pick her up?"

It was like he was on the edge of a cliff, trying to screw up the courage to jump. When the two words came, it was in a whisper. "On Ellice."

Shelter maintained a poker face, but he knew officers monitoring the interview by video feed would be hooting and hollering in victory. Once the dam had broken, Stokes described in a flat, unemotional voice every detail of how he'd murdered Monica Spence. How he'd driven her to a vacant lot in the Point Douglas area by the Red River to have sex. How he'd refused to pay her, and when she tried to get out of the car, he'd pulled her back and choked her to death. How he'd driven the body to his garage and wrapped it in plastic and secured it with duct tape. How he'd taken her to a stretch of Plessis Road and forced her body into a culvert.

Shelter only needed to interject occasionally with clarifying questions. When Stokes was done, Shelter glanced at his watch. It was mid-afternoon. Much more work would have to be done on the

Spence murder, but he was anxious to keep Stokes going, to move on to the Crystal Rempel and Rory Sinclair killings. "How are you feeling? Do you want to take a break here or go on to talk about Crystal Rempel?" he asked.

"What about Crystal Rempel?"

"How did you meet her? What happened?"

"I never met no Crystal," Stokes said, his eyes boring into Shelter's.

"Come on, Daniel. Let's not go through this again." Shelter flipped open a file and glanced at a timeline of the Rempel murder.

He looked up. "Let's start with where you were on the evening of July 8th, a week ago last Thursday."

Stokes narrowed his eyes, a sly expression Shelter hadn't seen before. "That's easy. I was in a hotel room in Edmonton."

Shelter felt blood rushing to his face. "Edmonton?"

Stokes watched him, drawing out the moment. "We were looking at houses and schools," he said. "Alberta's services for autistic kids are way better and cheaper. We're moving next month."

Shelter stared at Stokes for long seconds in a state of shock. He stood up abruptly and gathered his papers.

"You're not going anywhere."

# TWENTY-SIX

Shelter was in the bathroom splashing cold water on his face when Traverse came through the door. Shelter dried his face and then set both hands on the counter. He was angry at himself for his overconfidence, for letting his hopes cloud his judgment. The possibility Crystal Rempel's murder had been made to look like Monica Spence's had always been there. Not only were there the differences in the profiles of the victims, but also the discrepancies in how the killings had been carried out. "A god-damned copycat," he said to Traverse's reflection in the mirror.

Traverse nodded. "Jennifer is checking out Stokes's Edmonton story, but it looks that way."

Traverse had been all business with Shelter since their confrontation over Nicki, and the tension was weighing on Shelter. He was still stinging from the rebuke he'd received in the car the night before. Now Shelter had to admit to himself that Traverse had always been more skeptical about the theory that one killer had committed the Spence, Rempel and Sinclair murders. His instincts had turned out to be right and Shelter's wrong, and it burned.

"Assuming Stokes was in Edmonton, we've got to get up to the reserve and interview Osborne right away," Shelter said. "You coming?"

"You still planning on taking Nicki with you?"

"I told you. I have no choice."

Traverse wheeled to face his partner. "Mike, if you don't get your head screwed on right about this woman, you're going to find yourself out on the street."

"What are you talking about?" Shelter asked. Then, after a pause, "What's this really about, Gabe? Is it because she's Indigenous?"

Traverse let out a harsh bark of laughter and shook his head. "You gotta be kidding me. You know as well as I do you can't be involved with her. End it now."

"There's nothing to end. And as far as finding myself out on the street, you're the one who's talking about quitting."

"Don't throw that in my face," Traverse said, his features contorted into an angry glare. He looked down at his cowboy boots, and when he spoke, it was in a low, resigned tone. "You're a big boy. You do what you want. As for the reserve, I'm staying here." He turned, threw the door open with a bang, and was gone.

Shelter looked at himself in the mirror. His heart was thumping, and his shoulder muscles were knotted with tension. Traverse had put his finger on Shelter's attraction to Nicki and was right about the potentially dire consequences. But it was more than that. Shelter knew his anger was a reaction to his failure to take the possibility of a copycat seriously enough in the Rempel murder. He had to admit his desire to wrap up the case had overwhelmed the basic skepticism that's so fundamental to police work. The Spence attack had been unplanned, brutal, messy — a frenzied crime. She'd fought back, and her body and face were bruised from a beating before she was strangled with bare hands. Crystal Rempel's murder had been clinical. Her skull had been fractured from behind by a sharp blow, apparently knocking her unconscious, because there were no signs of a struggle with her assailant. She'd been strangled with a two-inch-thick strap or belt. Both bodies had been wrapped and taped with blue duct tape in exactly the same way, but Crystal's had been carefully washed before. As for Rory Sinclair, Stokes had been a doubtful fit for the shooting in Market Square.

His anger at himself had come out in the confrontation with

Traverse. He regretted the shots he'd taken about Nicki being Indigenous and Traverse's desire to leave the police force. Still, it wasn't going to stop him from going to Lone Pine with Nicki. She was the key to Doris Bear, and that could open the door to finding Crystal Rempel's killer.

He walked into the homicide unit to find a sombre mood had descended on the other detectives as late afternoon sun beat down on the desks. They were slumped in their chairs, silently pretending to work on their computers or do paperwork. Shelter felt it too, but despite his disappointment, he knew he had to inject some energy into the detectives' room, or the investigation could founder.

"Let's bring it in."

The six detectives pulled their chairs into a semi-circle. "We've got Daniel Stokes on the sexual assault of Donna Davis and the murder of Monica Spence," Shelter said, looking at each detective in turn. "That's a huge win for us. Let's not forget that. But obviously, the Crystal Rempel and Rory Sinclair cases are still open." The detectives looked distracted, apathetic.

"We've got to get right back at it," he said, rising from his chair and going to a whiteboard screwed to a wall. He wrote down *Monica Spence* and *Daniel Stokes*, drew boxes around them and connected them with a line. Then he wrote *Crystal Rempel* and *Rory Sinclair* and drew boxes around those names. He pointed to Monica Spence's name and turned to face the detectives. "Stokes confessed to killing Monica Spence, but he was out of town when Crystal was murdered. The Rempel murder is a copycat, but we never released the details about the duct tape or the plastic tarp to the media." Shelter knew this would have been on their minds almost from the minute they heard Daniel Stokes wasn't in Winnipeg the night Rempel was killed. They would have already chewed it over at length amongst themselves. A leak in the police department was the elephant in the room.

"We've already had information leaked from this investigation,"

Himmat Sharma said.

"But not these kinds of details," Jennifer Kane said. "Those were known to only a few people."

Shelter had already considered this. "Actually, the number is well over a dozen if you include the medical examiner's office, the Ident team, the homicide unit and senior management."

The meeting fell silent as the detectives considered the possibilities. Shelter had always assumed the leaks were coming from someone trying to embarrass the department over a grudge. But revealing the use of duct tape and a tarp to wrap Rempel's body had taken the leaks into a whole new realm of troubling possibilities. Someone with knowledge of the investigation was in direct contact with the killer. They had to find the source. It was their best shot at solving the case.

"The professional standards unit is already working on the leaks," Shelter said. They'd be going over phone, email and banking records of anyone involved in the investigation, including him. He slowly exhaled. He looked around the circle of detectives. "We know Crystal Rempel was conducting her own private investigation into the Monica Spence killing. It looks like she spooked someone, and he came up with the idea of making her murder look like it was done by the same man."

Shelter turned around, wrote the names *Charlie Osborne* and *Bill Craig*, and made boxes around them. "We're right back here," he said, tapping the whiteboard beside the two names with the marker.

Shelter had just sat down at his desk when the phone rang. He was surprised to see on the call display that it was his mother calling.

"Hello, dear. I have a casserole ready for Kelsey. What time are you picking me up?"

Shelter was at a complete loss. Then it came to him. He brought the heel of his hand to his forehead and mouthed a silent curse. It was Gordy Taylor's retirement party that evening. He'd received his invitation a month before and agreed to take his mother, who had also been invited. Then he promptly forgot about it. He reviewed his options for getting out of it and concluded there were none.

"Michael, are you there?" Roberta Shelter said. "You didn't forget about the party, did you?"

"No. I was just thinking about what the best time would be. Let's say seven."

"Alright. I don't know why I'm even invited to this thing. He was your father's friend." After a moment she added, "You didn't want to go a little earlier? Cocktails begin at seven."

Shelter couldn't help but smile to himself. His mother detested Taylor but loved a party and had obviously been anticipating this one.

"Okay, Mom. Let's make it six thirty. How's Kelsey doing?"

"Well, we can talk about it tonight. Do you want to talk to her? She's right here."

While he waited for his daughter to come on the line, Shelter went over the mad rush he faced in the next two hours. He'd have to get home, shower, change into a suit and get over to his mother's house. It would be no small feat. Was his blue suit even clean?

"Hey."

"How's it going?"

"Okay. But I want to come home."

"Why?"

His daughter dropped her voice to a whisper. "It's so boring over here. There's no internet, and Grandma won't leave me alone. She always wants me to go shopping with her."

"Sounds like a pretty nice life to me."

"I'll be fine at home, and I start the dog-walking at Mr. Taylor's this afternoon."

Shelter considered this. She had a point. The school year was coming, and if she stayed in the city he'd be forced to give her more and more freedom with just the two of them at home. After the day he'd had, his resistance was low. "I'll talk to Grandma this evening, but I'm not making any promises." They both knew this amounted to total capitulation.

Gordy Taylor's retirement reception was to be held at the Bison Club. It had been built before the First World War as a private men's club, a place for the city's elite to drink, play snooker and talk business discreetly. On the way downtown, Shelter discussed Kelsey with his mother. She made it clear she favoured moving her back to his house to preserve the sanity of both grandmother and granddaughter.

"She's a lump around the house," Roberta Shelter complained. "I don't know how a girl can spend so much time staring at a phone and watching TV. She needs stimulation — more than I can give her."

"The dog-walking job will help." Earlier, Kelsey had headed over from her grandmother's house to walk Heidi. "It gives her something to do."

Roberta nodded. "Where are her friends?"

"They're mostly at the lake or working, the ones who have turned sixteen. Fifteen is a tough age. I'll tell her to come home from Gordy's and pick up her stuff when I drop you off tonight."

Shelter pulled into the circular driveway in front of the Bison Club to drop his mother off. Couples in evening wear were climbing the wide staircase and entering the three-storey brick building. He was lucky to find street parking just a few minutes away, and as he walked back to the club, he steeled himself to get through the next few hours. He knew the crowd would be a mix of senior police officers, city officials, including the mayor, and pillars of the business community, all a generation or more older than him. He was there because of the close relationship between Taylor and his father and the role the chief had played in bringing him along as a young officer.

On the front stairs, Shelter called Kelsey before entering the club. She was still at Taylor's house, keeping the dog company. "I talked to your grandmother, and we decided it's best if you come home. I'll pick up your things when I drop Grandma off." Shelter ended the call and entered the club's brightly lit entrance hall, where a noisy crowd was having drinks and chatting. He scanned the faces, looking for his mother, and was delighted to spot her chatting with his friend, Steve Roth.

"Hey, look who I found wandering around alone," Roth said, shaking hands with Shelter.

"Don't worry. Mom can take care of herself," Shelter said. "What are you doing here?"

"I'm standing in for one of the senior partners. We do a lot of work for the city, and this is what you call mixing business with pleasure." Roth smiled at Shelter's mother. She'd known him since he was a boy, playing hour after hour of street hockey in their driveway with other friends from school.

An elderly woman approached their group. "Bobby," the woman said to Roberta Shelter. "Oh, thank goodness. Who are you sitting with?"

Shelter checked to see Roth had a full drink and headed for the bar. When he'd delivered his mother her rye and water and took a sip of his beer, he said to Roth, "A well-heeled group."

"You bet." Roth put a hand on Shelter's arm, gently drawing him aside. He lowered his voice. "Did our conversation about Bill Craig come to anything?"

"Yes and no," Shelter replied. "You were right about the divorce. The wife has filed some incredible allegations about him in the proceedings. But we still don't know if or how he fits into our investigation."

Roth scanned the crowd. "I wonder if he's coming tonight. Have you heard about this urban reserve project north of Portage Avenue?"

Shelter turned his body to shield the conversation. "How do you know about that?"

"There's a lot of buzz about it around town. Apparently, the feds are on board, and Craig's the developer."

"With the Lone Pine First Nation."

"Exactly. I'm hearing they're getting ready to make an announcement in the next few weeks."

Shelter's attention was drawn to a commotion near the door. He turned to see Gordy and Janet Taylor entering the club to loud greetings and congratulations from nearby guests. Taylor looked distinguished in a tuxedo and Janet elegant in a long, emerald sequined gown. They looked as if they were on the red carpet at the Oscars. They advanced through the crowd, shaking hands, dispensing kisses to cheeks and waving.

"I guess I better make the rounds," Roth said. "We're going to be called for dinner soon." Shelter watched his friend approach a group of three couples and easily join the conversation. Shelter went to his mother, who introduced him to a woman she played bridge with and her husband, a senior engineer with the city.

The grand ballroom ran the length of the south end of the building on the second storey. The tables were set for a four-course meal with heavy white linen, silverware, crystal glasses and centrepieces with pink and white roses. Floor-to-ceiling windows offered a distant view of the river in the soft light of the setting sun. The appetizer was a delicious crab and avocado creation followed by a main course of filet mignon. The wine was excellent and plentiful. Shelter and his mother were seated near the back of the room with a surprisingly lively group that included a vice president of the Jets who cheerfully indulged Shelter's suggestions on how to make the hockey team better. He periodically scanned the room, but there was no sign of Bill Craig. A series of speeches paying tribute to Taylor's long, colourful career, including one by the mayor, were mercifully short and good-humoured. Shelter was surprised to find he was actually enjoying the evening.

During a speech by the deputy police chief, Shelter slipped his cellphone from a pocket of his suit jacket and texted Nicki. *Heading to the rez tomorrow. You still in?*

The answer came back almost immediately. Yup.

*Be ready at nine. Pick you up outside your building.*

He was finishing up his dessert — light, cream-filled puff pastry balls drizzled with chocolate — when he felt a hand on his shoulder. He looked up to find the imposing figure of Gordy Taylor looming over him. Because of the direction he was seated, Shelter hadn't noticed the police chief making the rounds of the tables to greet and thank the guests.

"Bobby, nice to see you," he said to Shelter's mother. "You're looking terrific. Thank you for coming."

"Congratulations, Gordy. Such a beautiful evening."

Taylor made similar comments to the other guests around the table. When he came to Shelter, he said, "Mike, I wonder if I might have a word."

The police chief led Shelter out of the ballroom and down a long corridor that overlooked the entrance hall. "You've been here before?" he asked as they strolled.

"I was here once with my grandfather when I was a boy," Shelter said. "He let me roll the pool balls around."

"In this room," Taylor said, opening a door on the opposite end of the building from the ballroom and ushering Shelter into the billiard room. The room wasn't in use and was illuminated by only a few dim lights. Shelter could almost smell the cigar smoke and whiskey. The dark wood panelling, brass fixtures and six massive snooker tables with their ornately carved legs and tasselled overhead lights gave Shelter the impression he was stepping into the 1920s.

"I want to show you something," Taylor said, switching on the lights. He led Shelter between the tables, stopping beside a cue rack on the far wall. He pointed upward to where framed portraits lined the wall above the panelling. "These are all the past presidents of the club. And that's your grandfather."

Shelter studied the photo. It was taken in the 1960s, when his grandfather was still in his prime. He was slim and handsome in a suit with his hair combed straight back in the style of the day.

"I knew him quite well, you know," Taylor said. "Very much the British gentleman and a heck of a storyteller."

"That's the image he liked to project," Shelter said, smiling. "His father owned a factory in London, so he wasn't exactly of the aristocracy."

"Well, he did well for himself." Taylor walked over to the closest snooker table and leaned his big frame against it. "I need to get back, but I wanted to talk to you about this case with the Indian girls. I heard we have a copycat situation. It's hitting the media tomorrow, and I may need to make a statement. Where are we at with it?"

"As you know, we have an offender charged in the Monica Spence homicide. But that individual was not involved in Crystal Rempel or Rory Sinclair. We're continuing to investigate a land deal to establish an urban reserve downtown involving Charlie Osborne and Bill Craig. Rempel was aware of possible financial irregularities with the deal, and we believe there could have been a motive there."

Taylor nodded. "I read the transcript of your interview with Craig but haven't seen anything on Charlie Osborne."

"I'm heading up to the Lone Pine Reserve tomorrow to interview him."

"Good. I want you to call me when you've talked to that guy," Taylor said.

He pushed himself off the snooker table and turned for the door. His face had become stern. "We're getting killed in the media on this," he said as they walked back to the party. Once again, Shelter became aware how much the chief had riding on the investigation — a victory to cap his career or a humiliating failure staining his legacy.

# TWENTY-SEVEN

Shelter had packed the night before and was up by six to get ready for the trip. He wrote out a list of meals for Kelsey and made sure everything was labelled and easily accessible in the cupboards, fridge and freezer. He'd heard her still moving around her bedroom at one in the morning, so he decided against waking her to say goodbye. Instead, he left a note telling her he hoped to be back that night but could possibly be away until the next day. He added the phone numbers of his mother and two close neighbours, told her he loved her and to be safe. Then one last line: *P.S. Don't open the door to ANYONE.*

He gassed up his Toyota Camry and picked up road supplies for both him and Nicki — coffee, water, potato chips and trail mix. Shelter thought about the three-hour drive ahead and felt surprisingly buoyant. He liked to drive and anticipated a rare respite from daily life. The forecast was for a hot, sunny day and Nicki was waiting on the boulevard outside her apartment building in a pair of jeans, cut-off just above the knees, a sleeveless T-shirt, her Yankees cap and aviator sunglasses.

"What's the situation for tunes?" she asked before Shelter had a chance to say hello.

"We've got the radio," he said, handing her a coffee.

"Come on. We need some road tunes," she said, sliding the coffee into a cup holder. "Is there somewhere to plug in my phone?" She leaned over to peer at the dashboard.

Before he could answer, she'd found the plug, tapping it with her finger. She threw off her seatbelt, twisted in her seat, and grabbed her pack from the backseat. She pulled out a cord and plugged her phone in. In a couple of seconds the car filled with the sounds of an electric guitar backed up by a moderately driving beat. A man's voice kicked in. After a couple of seconds, Shelter decided he liked it.

"Who's this?"

"Ryan Adams."

"It doesn't sound like Bryan Adams."

"RYAN Adams, you idiot," she said, laughing. "Okay, let's roll."

Shelter was laughing too as he pulled out, turned up a side street, and headed north. Within half an hour, they were leaving the city on a two-lane highway that would bring them to the Lone Pine Reserve. Vast fields of wheat and bright yellow canola stretched to the horizon on either side of the road, interspersed with scrubby forests of poplar and jack pine. The farmhouses were modest; this had always been a tough, inhospitable environment to scratch out a living ever since Eastern European settlers broke their backs clearing the bush at the turn of the last century. The traffic was so light that Shelter had the feeling they were alone on this grey ribbon under an immense blue sky. The windows were down, and Nicki's hair was blowing in the wind. She had her bare feet up on the dashboard.

For the first hour, they hardly spoke. Shelter tried asking her about work, but that brought a perfunctory response. He let it go and let his mind wander to the day ahead.

Eventually, Shelter said, "You told Doris we were on our way up today?"

"Yup. She's waiting for us."

"You've never been to the reserve?"

"We had no connection to that world when I was growing up," Nicki said, dropping her feet to the floor and angling herself toward him. "It was Crystal who got back in touch with our grandmother.

She was going to take my mom and me to see her, but she never got the chance."

Shelter thought about Crystal's neat apartment on Edmonton Street with her law degree framed on a wall and the work she'd been doing at Anishinaabe Awakening. His mind went from there to the body he'd seen laid out on the medical examiner's steel table. What a waste. His desire to solve the case had intensified as he got to know Nicki and learned the details of Crystal's life. It had become an overwhelming, all-consuming imperative from the instant Daniel Stokes had let him know the killer was still out there.

"How are you doing with what happened to Crystal?"

"It comes and goes, you know? I was just numb all the way through the protest march and funeral — busy organizing shit and working."

"And chasing Rory."

"And chasing Rory. Then I walked into her apartment last week and saw all her stuff. It hit me hard."

"It takes time. I don't think I'm over my wife dying, and it's been more than a year."

"That's not a long time. Not over it how?"

"I'm just not interested in anything. Things I used to do after work — curling, running, drinking with my buddies. I dropped all of that when Christa got sick, and I just don't feel like it anymore. And then there's my daughter." He looked over and raised an eyebrow.

"What?" she asked.

"Um, let's just say it's been hard on both of us. She's a teenager and a handful right now, I guess."

"I like her already," Nicki said with a smile. "How old is she?"

"Fifteen but acts like twenty-one."

"If she's anything like I was, you got to give her space to make her own mistakes."

"I know. But it's not easy, especially when you're doing it all alone."

"No matter how hard you think it is, she's needs you to be strong. So be strong."

Shelter took that in silence. His first reaction was to resent her lack of sympathy, but as he thought about it, he knew she was right. This wasn't the time for self-pity. He had to be there for Kelsey and get her through these years.

Nicki pulled down the bill of her baseball cap. The next time he looked over, she was asleep. After an hour, they were entering the small farming town of Tracy, the last stop before the reserve began. Shelter parked the car diagonally in front of a cafe on the main drag. He touched Nicki's shoulder, and she came awake with a jerk.

"We're getting close. You want something to eat or keep going?"

"Pee break," she said. "But let's keep going."

"Okay. How do you want to handle it when we get there?"

"I'm going to Doris's house as soon as I get there. She's waiting for me and going to introduce me to my grandma. You can drop me off there and meet up later."

"Okay. But don't tell her I'm here to interview Charlie."

"You don't think she'll find out? It's a small place."

"I want to keep it quiet."

She nodded and gave him a smile. "If you say so."

The Lone Pine reserve covered a swath of land west of Lake Winnipeg, a mixture of sparse forest, grassland, marshes and ponds designated for the band in the late 1800s. Nine hundred community members lived on the reserve and a thousand more in Winnipeg and elsewhere. The main public buildings were scattered along a half-kilometre stretch of highway: a modern-looking school complex, a fire department, hockey arena, band office and RCMP detachment. Shelter pulled into the parking lot of a large general store with gas pumps, where Nicki got directions to Doris Bear's house. The prefab bungalow was only ten minutes away at the end of a gravel road. Shelter waited until a middle-aged woman admitted Nicki to the house and waved to him that all was well.

RCMP Constable David Petrovich was in his mid-twenties, tall and well-built, with wavy brown hair. Dense multicoloured tattoos ran from both wrists up under the short sleeves of his uniform shirt. In one smooth movement, Shelter ran his eyes over the tattoos, up the black flak jacket to meet the Mountie's gaze. He was wondering how a young officer could afford that much intricate ink work as they shook hands.

"Detective Shelter," Petrovich said.

"Make it Mike."

"Dave. I'm ready to go."

Shelter had briefed him on the phone with as much information as he could about the investigation but had been vague about his interest in Osborne. He referred only to some financial dealings that may or may not have a bearing on the Crystal Rempel murder.

Keeping the peace on reserves could be tough, dangerous work for young Mounties who moved from community to community across Western Canada, gaining experience before moving up in the service.

"I'm pretty sure he's at his house," Petrovich said over the roof of his cruiser car. "I went around this morning, and his truck was there."

"You get a lot of action out here?" Shelter asked, settling into the passenger seat.

"It's not bad compared to the fly-in reserves up north. Some drug busts and kids pulling B&Es or getting rowdy. And, of course, the domestic and child welfare stuff." He shot Shelter a glance.

Shelter nodded as the car picked up speed on the highway. He'd been mentally preparing all morning for the meeting with Osborne but still felt jumpy. The evidence against him in the Rempel and Sinclair murders was fragmentary, far from enough for an arrest. Shelter remembered seeing Osborne with Rory Sinclair in the pool hall — how nervous he'd been and how uncooperative. He'd used Sinclair to get Monica Spence and Pam Daniel to the Bond Hotel, and Crystal Rempel knew that. She also knew Charlie was tied up in a land deal with Bill Craig. Did she have other evidence that Shelter was unaware of? Had she confronted him with her suspicions when she travelled to the reserve in the days before she was murdered? Osborne knew her well enough to have lured her away from the bar that night. And living on the reserve all his life, he likely had the skills for the long-range rifle shot to kill Rory Sinclair. But there was the blue duct tape and plastic tarp. Could he really have a source in the police department?

"What's your impression of Charlie?"

"I'm from a small town in Saskatchewan, and that's essentially what you've got here," Petrovich said, gesturing with a sweep of his hand. "With all the gossip, jealousy and politics that go with it. We try to keep our noses out of the politics and stick to policing. But there are opposing clans and an election for band council early next year. Whoever controls council controls the budget, so the stakes are high. Just between you and me, Lyle McKay is the chief, but they say Charlie is the real power, and he likes it that way — a low profile. He probably already knows you're on the reserve, by the way."

"How about Doris Bear?"

"A great person," he said without hesitation. "She tries to keep kids in the community. She's also been pretty critical of the band council — the salaries they pay themselves while some of the people are living in terrible housing conditions. The rumour is she's going to run for chief." He hit the turn indicator. "She's tough. But I like her."

Petrovich pulled off the highway onto a gravel road, and after a few minutes they came to a large two-storey house sheltered on three sides by poplar and pine trees. It was a more impressive structure than Doris Bear's home, with a two-car garage and spacious deck visible at the rear. A recent-model Dodge Ram pickup was parked on the driveway. Getting out of the car, Shelter kept his eyes open for dogs, but all was quiet.

Petrovich knocked on the aluminum screen door, and after a moment a boy of perhaps ten appeared.

"Your dad around?"

Without answering, the boy skipped into the house, calling, "Dad."

A few moments later, Charlie Osborne came to the door. He was dressed in clean but well-worn jeans and a cowboy shirt stretched over his huge gut. He looked from Petrovich to Shelter without greeting them or giving any other reaction.

"Hello, Charlie," Petrovich said. "This is Detective Michael Shelter from the Winnipeg Police Service. He wants to ask you a few questions."

Osborne had his hand on the inside door and looked ready to close it. "Questions about what?" he asked. His lips barely moved as he spoke. Shelter took a half step forward. "We met at the Double Deuce a while back. I'm still looking into the Crystal Rempel murder."

"Don't know anything about that. You're talking to the wrong guy." He started to close the door, but before he could, Shelter said, "I'm surprised you don't want to cooperate. Someone you knew well, someone with roots in your own community with such a bright future."

Osborne let out a sigh and rolled his shoulders. "You want to talk about Crystal, talk to the chief. He's the official spokesman for Lone Pine."

"One of your buddies seems to be trying to pin it on you," Shelter said. He'd prepared the line to get Osborne's attention. He knew it was a gamble, but he had to do something to keep the door from being slammed in his face. Osborne's reaction was almost imperceptible — a slight muscle spasm near his eye.

"Which buddy?"

"Why don't you just come down to the detachment and we'll go through it?"

"I'm not going to no police station."

This was progress. Osborne was now entertaining the idea of talking. Shelter sensed he was nervous, anxious to know what the investigation had turned up. "Okay. We can do it in your kitchen if you like."

Osborne considered this. "We can talk out here," he said, pointing to his driveway.

He abruptly closed the door. Shelter led Petrovich down the stairs and across the driveway to where the cruiser was parked. After a couple of minutes, the door swung open and Osborne emerged in a pair of worn work boots. He circled the two police officers to lean an elbow on the hood of his pickup. "Who's this buddy?"

"Bill Craig, a business partner of yours, I hear," Shelter said. "He told us you were supposed to be on the reserve July 8th. That's the day Crystal was killed. But he saw you in downtown Winnipeg. The question is, where were you the evening of July 8th?"

"I was on the road, coming back here. I had a business meeting and then headed back after dinner."

"Can anyone confirm that?"

"My wife can confirm I came home."

"At what time?"

"Around ten, maybe."

"You admit you know Bill Craig."

Osborne's chubby face cracked into a thin smile. "He's our partner in developing an urban reserve downtown."

"Why is he telling us you were in Winnipeg when you weren't

supposed to be?"

"That's your interpretation. I don't tell Bill every time I change my plans."

Shelter nodded and decided to change tacks. "There's a picture of you with Bill in a hotel room at the Bond Hotel with two prostitutes. One of them was Monica Spence. Your friend Rory Sinclair was there too."

Osborne shrugged and remained silent. He looked off toward the stand of trees on the other side of the road.

"Crystal believed you killed Monica because she was blackmailing you with that picture. That's why she came up here — to confront you."

Turning to look at Shelter, Osborne let out a brief, bitter chuckle. When he spoke, it was louder, more forceful. "Is that really all you guys got? Blackmailing us about what?" The corner of his lip lifted in a sneer. "That little girl couldn't have blackmailed a bag of chips off her best friend." He crossed his arms and kicked some gravel with the toe of his boot. "I know you've been sniffing around our business with Bill's company. Go on and sniff, man." After a beat, he jabbed a finger at Shelter. "Nobody's going to stop that project."

He put the glasses back on and started walking toward the house. When he was at his front steps, he turned around and called to them. "She came out here, just like you, making accusations. Don't make 'em true. Not then. Not now."

# TWENTY-EIGHT

By the time Shelter and Petrovich got back to the RCMP detachment, the sun was high. Shelter let the Mountie go ahead into the building, and standing in the parking lot, he pulled out his cellphone and punched in Nicki's number. As he waited for her to answer, his eyes picked up a battered Chevy racing down the highway. A man, maybe eighteen or nineteen years old, was in the passenger seat. He locked eyes with Shelter as the car approached and made a gun out of his hand, thumb in the air, index and middle finger pointed through the open window. He fired a shot at Shelter.

"Hey," Nicki said. The car was gone around a bend.

Shelter closed his eyes behind his sunglasses, hot wind on his face. It took a moment to collect his thoughts. "How's it going with Doris?"

"Good, she's been telling me about Crystal's time up here. How about Charlie?"

He was wary of Nicki getting any more involved in the investigation than she already was. But Osborne had been open enough about his relationship with Bill Craig and the land deal in Winnipeg. He knew it was a matter of public record and would be making news soon enough.

"He wasn't helpful. But it was good to talk face-to-face."

"Hold on," Nicki said. She listened to someone in the room with her. She came back on the line. "Doris says you should come over, and we'll go to my grandma's house together. It's close by."

Shelter thanked Petrovich and told him he would be in touch.

Five minutes later, he was knocking at Doris Bear's door. She was in her late fifties, with plump cheeks and a warm smile. Her brown hair was cut around her ears and parted down the middle. She was short, barely reaching Shelter's shoulder, and dressed in a white blouse and jeans. She ushered Shelter into a living room that was simple but kept with care. A worn couch and armchair set were grouped around a coffee table. On the walls were framed photos of children at various ages: a boy in hockey gear, a girl in a T-shirt and shorts standing on a beach with a baby in her arms. On an end table was a family shot: the two children, Doris and a heavy-set man Shelter assumed was her husband. Nicki joined them from the adjoining room, where she'd been sitting, looking through a photo album.

Shelter glanced over at Nicki and gave her a quick smile. When he looked back to Doris, he caught her giving a clandestine nod to Nicki. It occurred to Shelter that she and Nicki had become more intimate confidantes than he'd realized, brought together by the death of Crystal Rempel. They would have discussed everything that had gone on in Winnipeg, including his suspicions about Charlie Osborne.

"Doris was showing me pictures of her family and some community events," Nicki said. "Treaty days begin on the weekend."

"Big celebration?" Shelter asked.

"Dancing, a feast, a baseball tournament," Doris said. "It goes on for a week."

"Band members have been getting paid by the government every year since the treaty was signed in the 1870s," said Nicki, clearly intrigued by this piece of her history.

"It's symbolic," Doris said, smiling. "Five bucks a head. Enough to buy an ice cream sundae. It's our connection to the Crown and a reminder to everyone we signed a treaty nation to nation. We were never conquered. But you knew that already, right, Mr. Shelter?"

It was a jab, but a good-humoured one. She pushed her hands

into the pockets of her jeans. "Have you eaten?"

Doris had made a plate of egg salad and ham-and-cheese sandwiches. They sat around the dining room table, munching and sipping coffee. Doris explained her husband had died two years earlier from a heart attack brought on by diabetes. Her children had left for the city, her daughter to study nursing in Winnipeg, her son to start a construction business in Calgary. She found herself alone and threw herself into community activism with a small group of friends.

"There's a lot of pressure on the young people. We start early, finding good foster homes for kids who've been taken from their parents either here in the community or in Winnipeg. We also try to help young people who've gotten into trouble. We get them out of the gangs, out of prostitution, off the drugs."

"Is that how you met Crystal?" Shelter asked.

Doris passed the plate of sandwiches. "We met in Winnipeg at the Friendship Centre. She ran a legal aid clinic every Tuesday with her boyfriend, Moses. We started talking, and she told me her mother was from Lone Pine." She glanced at Nicki and smiled. "I'm close to the grandmother of these girls. She's an elder and a spiritual leader here."

"What do you know about Charlie Osborne and the urban reserve project?" Shelter asked.

"Charlie and I have a lot of history, none of it good," she said, pursing her lips. "He's gotten involved in a lot of shit, and I don't trust him. But the band council is talking up the urban reserve, and it's been good for other communities. We've been asking for more visibility on the finances."

"When you say he's involved in a lot of shit, like what kind of shit?"

She looked at him and shook her head with a grim smile. "That's our business."

"But you're worried about the urban reserve project financing?"

"I'm always worried when it comes to money."

"Crystal made several calls to the reserve to a number belonging to Joseph Bear. That's your line?"

Bear nodded.

"You knew Bill Craig had been selected as the developer of the urban reserve. You told that to Crystal."

Doris looked down at the coffee mug she was cupping in her hands. She raised her eyes to meet Shelter's and nodded. "Crystal started looking into the court records and found some divorce papers," she said. "We were preparing a file to go to the band council and the police."

"Crystal also told you about a party at the Bond Hotel?" Shelter asked. "About Monica Spence being there?"

Again, Doris nodded. "It was all in the file."

"That's why she was so upset when she left that day?"

"No, she was upset when she got here. You have to remember that Crystal came up after her mother committed suicide. She was with her grandmother for two days before she went back to Winnipeg. The next thing we heard was the news she'd been killed."

"What did they talk about during those days?"

"Her grandmother won't tell me, but she hasn't been eating, and she spends her time praying."

"Did you talk to Crystal before she left?"

Doris shook her head. "She just got in her car and was gone."

"What's her grandmother's name?" Shelter asked.

"Mary Alexander."

"She's not well," Nicki said.

Shelter looked to Doris Bear and saw that her face had become clouded with concern. "She's been weak ever since we told her about Anne committing suicide."

They walked to Mary Alexander's house. The road went from gravel to rutted dirt track shaded by trees. They followed a bend, and when it straightened, Shelter could see where it came to an abrupt end at a rough shack. When he saw the dilapidated condition of the cabin, he was concerned for the old woman's well-being, especially during the brutal winters. He couldn't see any insulation to keep out the cold.

"The band has tried to get her into a new home, but she won't move," Doris whispered as they approached the house.

Only bits of white paint remained on the walls, and the roof had patches of emerald-coloured moss. A stove pipe jutted from its peak. Shelter spotted an outhouse in the rear and noted abandoned objects strewn around the grounds: a rusted lawn mower, an ancient drum washing machine, and in the high grass, the hulk of a seventies vintage Dodge Dart, its engine removed.

Doris tapped on the screen door and called out to Mary Alexander in Ojibwe. She entered without waiting for a reply. Shelter and Nicki held back, waiting on the stairs. The wind rustled the poplar leaves, and a cicada gave a high-pitched whine that grew in intensity and then was gone. Shelter could hear Doris speaking to the old woman in low tones but couldn't make out the words. The contrast between the sunshine and the gloom of the room beyond the screen door made it impossible to see inside.

After a couple of minutes, Doris appeared, nodded and pushed the door open. Shelter followed Nicki into the cabin. The room was cool and almost dark, the windows covered with heavy curtains. Shelter smelled something sour, and his attention was drawn to a thin, congested cough to his right. As his eyes adjusted to the light, he saw the two women sitting close to one another. Doris, perched on the end of a couch, held the hand of an old woman who was made even smaller by the massive armchair where she sat.

Nicki advanced toward her grandmother, and Doris whispered something in Ojibwe. Mary released Doris's hand and raised a thin arm to Nicki, who knelt before her. The old woman took Nicki's face in her hands, looked into her eyes and said something Shelter couldn't understand. "*Noozhishenh*," Doris repeated. "My grandchild." The old woman pulled Nicki close, kissed her cheek and wrapped her thin arms around her neck, hugging her for a long minute. The skin on her hands was translucent, the knuckles knobby.

When the woman released her, Nicki was sobbing. Doris moved down the couch, making space for Nicki, and then looked up and nodded to Shelter to come forward. Again, she spoke quietly in Ojibwe. He bent, shook her hand and, smiling, introduced himself. He noticed for the first time that her pupils were cloudy.

"Bring this chair," Mary said in English, pointing to a straight-back chair positioned against the wall on the other side of the room.

The main living space was open, with a dining room table beside a pot-bellied, wood-burning stove in the middle and the kitchen in the back. Three closed doors along one side of the house would be bedrooms and a bathroom.

Mary held Nicki's hand and spoke to her quietly, pronouncing the words slowly. "Now, you will come and stay with me." Her face was deeply lined, and her grey, braided hair ran down her back. A spasm of coughing wracked her body under the shawl she wore despite the heat. Nicki used the back of her hand to wipe away her tears and nodded.

Mary reached out and caressed Nicki's cheek. "When Crystal came, she brought me a picture of you and your mother. I see her in you."

"I'm sorry our mother couldn't be with us."

"Her spirit has been with me since she was taken from us."

Shelter thought about Crystal and Nicki's mother. Her efforts to get Crystal back after she'd been adopted. The descent into addiction and finally suicide. Why had she left Mary and this reserve in the first place? And why had she never returned? He cleared his throat, and the three women turned their heads.

"I'm sorry, ma'am, but I must ask you some questions about

Crystal to help us find whoever hurt her." The old woman nodded. She kept Nicki's hand gripped in both hers. "I understand Crystal came to visit you on a few occasions. I want to ask you about the last time, about ten days ago. What do you remember about the visit?"

She released Nicki's hand and began playing with a corner of the shawl. She took a long time before answering. When she did, the words came slowly.

"Crystal was upset," she said, glancing at Nicki, who nodded for her to go on. "We sat together here, and then when the moon was high, we went outside, and I burned sweetgrass and we prayed together to the creator. She could not sleep, and we talked through the night."

"Talked about what?"

"Many things. My parents. The old ways. The residential school where we were sent." She looked at Doris and then Nicki. "And about Anne, her mother. Stories of how she was when she was young and of how she was taken from me."

"May I ask what happened with your daughter? Why was she taken away?" Shelter asked.

She bowed her head. She had an embroidered handkerchief hidden in the sleeve of her blouse, and she brought it out, touching it to her lips.

Shelter waited. "Perhaps we could..."

The old woman interrupted him. "Anne was very young. Still a child." She stopped, and Doris spoke to her in Ojibwe in an encouraging way. She began again in a quiet but clear voice. "It was a very cold night, winter. It was late because she'd been to the hockey game at the arena." She was wringing the handkerchief, her eyes on her hands.

"Anne told me later that a car came up beside her, and a man offered to drive her home, a white man. She didn't want to, but it was so cold." Mary raised her eyes to meet Shelter's, and he felt his stomach tighten with a sensation that was something like fear. "He didn't take her home."

Shelter nodded for her to go on. "He was drunk, and Anne told me he only laughed when she begged him to take her home. He said her parents would never find her if she didn't do as he said or if she told anyone after. And he showed her a gun."

Now she stopped for a long time. Shelter could hear the whine of the cicada again. He glanced at Nicki. Her eyes were locked on her grandmother.

"He made her go to the backseat and take off her clothes. Anne was a virgin."

The cicada stopped, and the room was silent except for the distant sound of the wind stirring poplar leaves.

"When she was late, we knew she was pregnant. They found Anne a place in a school in Winnipeg, and she went there until it was time for the baby to come. They took the baby, and Anne stayed in Winnipeg. She never came back here."

Nicki was crying, and Shelter was at a loss. After a while he managed, "This is what you told Crystal?"

"Yes. She was very angry. She wanted to know who the man was."

"You know who he is?" Shelter asked.

"Not the name. But he is in the picture. We looked at it together. I pointed to him."

The picture? Shelter was confused. Did she mean the picture from the Bond Hotel? Could Crystal have shown it to her on that last visit? The only white man in that photo was Bill Craig. Could he have been on the reserve in the 1980s? Maybe working on a construction project? His age made it possible, but it seemed implausible.

"A picture taken in a hotel room?" he asked the old woman.

"Hotel room? No. The picture here, on the wall in the hockey arena."

# TWENTY-NINE

Mary Alexander hobbled to the car with one hand on a cane and the other on Doris Bear's arm. Shelter, who had made the ten-minute walk back to Doris's house to get the car, held the passenger door while Mary awkwardly climbed in and got settled.

The arena was a modest structure that dated from the seventies. Shelter had been in dozens of similar buildings as a teenager when he was playing hockey. The entrance hall was built of cinder blocks. Benches ran along the walls, where you could pull on your skates. At the height of summer, all was quiet. A janitor was probably dozing in an office somewhere. But it wouldn't be long before they began making ice for late-summer hockey camps and practices in preparation for the season.

At the end of the room, a set of steel doors led to the rink. To the left, stairs descended to what Shelter knew would be the dressing rooms and showers. Doris steered Mary to a staircase leading to a second floor. The old woman made slow progress upward, taking the stairs with the same foot each time and stopping to rest halfway. At the top, Doris flipped a light switch, revealing a bar and restaurant area with picture windows overlooking the rink. During the hockey season, parents could have a beer or coffee and a bite to eat while they watched a game or practice. Now, chairs were upturned on tables and dishes, glasses and equipment stowed.

A trophy case stood in the far corner beside the bar. On the walls were dozens of framed photos of hockey teams from years past. Mary led the way toward the trophy case, stopping in front of the second to last column of pictures on the wall. She moved closer, her eyes only a few millimetres from the middle picture in a column of three. Giving a slight shake of her head, she stepped to her right to examine the next one in the row. She tilted her head, looking at the photo above.

"Here," she said, pointing to the image.

Shelter, Nicki and Doris gathered around the old woman to peer at the picture. Yellowed and dated from many decades before, it captured a team of smiling teenage boys in their hockey equipment. They were grouped haphazardly on the ice after the final whistle of a championship game. One group of boys kneeled or sat on the ice in a semi-circle around a trophy, while another row of players stood behind. Some of the boys were waving or giving a thumbs-up. Doris pointed to a boy standing in the middle with a C on his jersey. "Is that Charlie Osborne? It is. I'm sure of it."

But Shelter's attention was elsewhere. His eyes had been drawn to a young man standing in a long coat to the left of the celebrating players. He was taller than the tallest of the boys, even in their skates, and was obviously the team coach. The thick neck and barrel chest, visible despite the coat, had remained through the years, even as the other features had been remoulded by time.

The word came out of Shelter's throat in a long, low, guttural exhalation. "Jesus."

Nicki turned to look at him. "What?"

Shelter was too shocked to answer.

"What is it?" Doris asked.

He raised a hand and with a finger touched the glass under the face of the man in the picture. "This is Gordy Taylor."

Nicki looked at the picture and then turned her head with a jerk to look at Shelter again.

Shelter's stomach was clenched, and his heart was pounding. He had to open his mouth to catch his breath. He looked down at Mary, whose head was bowed. It was Doris who spoke to her, asking a question in Ojibwe. The answer came out in a few grunted syllables.

Doris's finger moved across the glass like on a Ouija board until it came to rest under Taylor's face. She asked Mary a question.

The old woman glanced up and gave a one-word affirmation.

"This is the man who hurt Anne," Doris said.

Shelter nodded as he studied someone else in the photo, another man standing on the other side of the semi-circle of boys. Shelter recognized him as well. It was a young Ted Wright, the priest who'd been with Gordy Taylor at Crystal Rempel's memorial service. He turned and spoke directly to Mary. "You showed this picture to Crystal, and she recognized this man, yes?" he said, pointing to Taylor.

She nodded and spoke in Ojibwe. The only word Shelter could understand was "Crystal."

"Crystal knew the policeman," Doris translated.

"What did Crystal do when she realized this was the man who had hurt her mother?" Shelter asked.

Mary answered in English. "She left for Winnipeg."

All three men, Gordy Taylor, Charlie Osborne and the priest, Ted Wright, together in the same place, at the same time. Shelter stepped away from the wall and turned to face the three women. He could tell from the expression on Nicki's face that she was in a rage. Shelter urged Nicki and Doris to remain calm. It was essential for them not to discuss what they'd discovered with anyone.

He went down the stairs and found the caretaker. He showed his ID and asked him to accompany him up to the restaurant. The caretaker took down the photo and gave it to Shelter. The detective turned to the women.

"Let's get you home," he said, looking from Doris to Mary.

The car was quiet on the way back to Mary's house. Shelter was lost in his thoughts, considering the chain of events and weighing his options. Gordy Taylor would have been a young RCMP officer stationed at Lone Pine at the time the picture was taken. But how would you prove he'd raped Anne Alexander thirty years ago? There would be no physical evidence, just the word of an elderly woman against that of Winnipeg's chief of police, one of the most respected men in the province.

Shelter knew Crystal had been full of anger over her mother's suicide. She'd probably confronted Taylor as a rapist and threatened to go public. The media coverage alone would have been enough to ruin his reputation just as he was preparing to retire. Was it enough to make Taylor a murderer? Shelter didn't want to believe it. But Taylor knew the M.O. used in the Monica Spence killing, and he was a crack shot with a rifle. He thought back to Taylor's intense interest in the case, the leaks to the media. What role had the priest and Charlie Osborne played in the killing of Crystal Rempel, if any? Was it even connected to Crystal's mother — the rape and adoption all those years ago? Or was it still the land deal in central Winnipeg that held the key?

After helping Mary inside and into her easy chair, Shelter spoke to Doris outside with Nicki looking on.

"I'll be in touch as soon as I know something." They shook hands. "Thank you for everything, and please keep this to yourself until you hear from me."

When Nicki was in the car, Shelter stuck his head through the driver side door and said he had to call his boss in Winnipeg. She stared straight ahead, not acknowledging him. Her arms were crossed tightly across her chest, and her face was fixed in a tight, fierce expression. Shelter walked to the tree line, dialling. MacIsaac picked up on the third ring with his usual abrupt "Yup."

Shelter filled him in about Gordy Taylor and the photo in the arena. "Neil, we're going to have to bring him in."

The line was silent as MacIsaac digested the news. "You want to bring Taylor in as a homicide suspect on the basis of a thirty-year-old picture and the word of some old lady? Are you fucking crazy?"

Shelter struggled to keep calm. "Crystal Rempel knew about the rape allegation, and she was heading back to Winnipeg to confront him…"

MacIsaac cut him off. "You know what kind of a shit storm you're talking about? We can't bring him in. You don't have nearly enough. And it's not that easy. We'd have to get the professional standards unit involved, and the justice minister. Jesus!"

"Neil, we can't wait. If he hears about…"

"I said no. We need more evidence."

Shelter felt his face get hot and the muscles in his neck tighten. "You know what I think, Neil? I think you're worried about not getting the chief's job." He stopped himself from going further. "We've got to get him off the street."

When MacIsaac spoke again, his tone was low-pitched and menacing. "Be in my office at eight tomorrow morning. Until then, no action. You got it?"

Shelter's jaw was clenched, and his back was drenched in sweat. He knew he'd taken it too far in accusing MacIsaac of ulterior motives.

"I said, you got it?"

"Yes." Shelter had barely got the word out before the line went dead.

He took a minute to calm himself before punching Traverse's number into his phone. He filled Traverse in on the photo in the arena and his confrontation with MacIsaac.

"Gordy fucking Taylor?" Traverse said. "You've got to be shitting me."

"We need to find out about Taylor's time in the RCMP — where he was stationed and for how long. Then we're going to have to cross-reference with sexual assaults. And can you find out where this priest lives? Ted Wright." Shelter spelled the last name out for his partner and said he'd be back in the city by early that evening. Once off the phone, he considered going back to Charlie Osborne's house to confront him with the information and rejected the idea. He had to get back to the city, and he couldn't risk Wright and Taylor being tipped off.

Once on the highway, Shelter pushed the car to well over the speed limit. He wanted to be back in the city in under two hours.

"Dirty bastard. Should have known it was a cop," Nicki said, apparently oblivious to the insult to Shelter.

"We need evidence," Shelter said. "You're going to have to be patient until we figure this thing out."

"Fuck that, man. It's all there in front of your nose. He raped my mom, and that priest brought her to Winnipeg to have the baby and keep it quiet."

"We don't know for sure what happened, Nicki. Leave it to us to investigate. We'll find the truth."

"Look, you've been straight with me. I know you've been trying. But above you, they're going to do everything they can to bury this. I know they are. They're going to protect him." She pulled her phone out and screwed headphones into her ears. For the rest of the trip, she kept a sullen silence, staring out the window at the passing fields. As he drove, Shelter vowed to himself that the scenario she had described was not going to happen. He dropped her off at her apartment building with another warning to do nothing until he got in touch with her. It was early evening when Shelter dialled Traverse's cell.

"You find out where that priest lives?"

"He's in Riverview."

"I want to see him. Now."

# THIRTY

Shelter rapped on the front door of the bungalow and took a step back to stand shoulder to shoulder with Gabriel Traverse. The house was in an old, self-contained neighbourhood in a bend in the Red River. Shelter studied a small brass cross that the priest had nailed to the door. What was its purpose? To tell the mailman a man of God lived here? Shelter had lost whatever faith he had in his early twenties, and indifference to the innocuous theology of his family's Protestant denomination had hardened to militant, if quiet, atheism with the grotesque revelations of child sex abuse and cover-ups in the Catholic church. When Christa was hospitalized, he'd felt only annoyance at the minister from his family's church, who seemed to think it was his duty to call once a week and on a couple of occasions stop by her hospital room unannounced because he was "in the neighbourhood."

The curtain over the window moved, and a pair of pale blue eyes behind rimless glasses examined Shelter and then darted to the left to take in Traverse. The deadbolt lock turned, hinges squeaked. Shelter felt an air-conditioned breeze hit him in the face. Ted Wright wore a beige cardigan over a checked flannel shirt. He was short and round, with a hooked nose. Shelter was struck again by the resemblance to an owl.

Wright opened the screen door and peered out. "Yes. May I help you?

Shelter made the introductions. "We met at Crystal Rempel's memorial service," he said. "May we come in?"

"What's this about?" Wright's voice was nervous, eyes moving from Shelter to Traverse.

"We just have a few questions to ask you."

The small living room was crowded with a large chocolate-brown couch and two matching easy chairs. Wright pointed the policemen to the couch. Shelter surveyed the room as the priest settled in one of the chairs. On a hutch stood framed snapshots of Wright in his vestments, surrounded by parishioners. On a side table on the other side of the room was a large, formal portrait of Wright standing stiffly beside Pope John Paul II.

"I see you met the pope."

Wright followed Shelter's line of vision to the table and the photo. "Yes. It was during a year I spent at the Vatican in 1993. The highlight of my life." The priest coughed and shifted on one hip in his seat to remove a white cloth handkerchief from the pocket of his corduroy pants. He touched it to his lips and laid it on a knee.

"You're still a priest, I take it?" Shelter said.

"I'm retired. Now, how may I help you gentlemen? I haven't had my dinner."

Shelter ignored this. "I was interested to see you with Chief Taylor the other day. Where did you meet?"

Wright's brow furrowed, and his eyes narrowed at the question. "We've known each other for many years."

"But how did you meet? Mr. Taylor isn't Catholic, so I'm curious."

"We met on the Lone Pine Indian Reserve. I was the priest there."

"What year was that?

"Oh my goodness, it was the eighties. I served on a number of reserves when I was a young man. I'd like to know why you are asking these questions."

"You coached the hockey team at Lone Pine?"

The priest's lips tightened in annoyance. He was used to deference, not having his questions ignored.

"Not really. I just helped out." The tone was cool, clipped. "Driving the boys to games and getting them hot chocolate when they were finished playing."

Shelter leaned forward and opened a notebook he'd placed on the coffee table. He was unsure of how to proceed. His first impulse was to go hard at Wright. To frighten him. But looking up from the notebook, he found those blue eyes studying him. There was something cunning in the look. He decided to go cautiously.

"We are tying up a few loose ends on an investigation, Mr. Wright."

"What does Gordy Taylor or a boy's hockey team thirty years ago have to do with your investigation?"

Shelter was careful to keep a blank expression. He felt a chill on his back and sensed cooled air being pumped from somewhere behind him. "There was a teenage girl on the reserve at that time named Anne Alexander. Do you remember her?"

A slight upward movement of the eyes. "There were so many children. I can't say I remember the name in particular, no."

Shelter leaned forward and raised his voice slightly. "Mr. Wright, we know you arranged for the adoption of Anne Alexander's child. We also know that child was Crystal Rempel. These facts aren't hard to verify."

Wright removed his glasses and examined the lenses before blowing on them loudly to remove nonexistent dust. He picked up the handkerchief from his knee and polished the lenses as if cleaning a chalice during Mass. When he looked up, Shelter noticed his round face had turned red, and his stomach was rising and falling.

"Why don't you tell us what happened on the reserve from the beginning?" Shelter said.

Wright examined his hands, apparently considering his options. How much to say? How much to hide? "Yes. You're correct. I did make arrangements for the girl. She was in trouble and needed help."

"She'd been raped, and you helped cover it up."

Wright's jaw tightened with anger. "That's an outrageous accusation. I did no such thing. The girl got herself pregnant, like so many others." He pushed himself out of his chair. "You have no right to come into my home and speak to me in that way. I think you better go now."

"Sit down," Shelter commanded in a low voice. The priest sagged, as if the air were escaping from a tire. When Shelter spoke, it was as if he was musing to himself. "We can take you downtown right now and continue our discussion there."

Shelter waited while Wright arranged himself in his chair again. "The question is, why would you cover up a rape?"

Wright began to speak but stopped himself. He seemed confused, and again his cheeks coloured. He kept his eyes on Shelter. Something in that look gave the answer.

"Because you were abusing children too."

Wright shook his head and looked from Shelter to Traverse. "No."

"It was either help him cover up the rape or be exposed yourself. That's how it was, wasn't it?" Shelter turned to Traverse. "Gabe, I think we need to look into Father Wright's career, starting with the reserves he worked on. They do still call you 'Father,' yes? Or have you been defrocked?"

"I *am* a priest," he said, trying to preserve some dignity, but it came out as a whine. The fight had gone out of him.

"We can start with a call to the diocese and squeeze what they know out of them," Traverse said.

Shelter nodded. "It shouldn't be that hard to make a case. They've been handing out harsh prison terms for child abuse. And the publicity — just incredible."

Wright brought his hands together, raised them to the tip of his nose, and closed his eyes.

Shelter knew the priest was wrestling with his options, trying to find a way out. Now was the time to wait.

The priest's hands dropped to his lap. He picked up the handkerchief, removed his glasses and mopped his face. "I need immunity from prosecution."

"Right now, we're interested in the murder of a young woman. Why don't you tell us what you know? And we'll worry about the rest later."

"No. I need assurance that I won't be prosecuted." It was the same petulant tone as before.

"We'll consider it," Shelter said. "But one thing's for sure. If you don't help us get a killer off the street right now, we can't help you."

Again, he silently weighed his choices. A minute passed. Two minutes. Then finally, he said, "It's not hard to imagine, Detective. He was a young man with a lot of power. When she became pregnant, it was something he needed taken care of."

"By 'he' you mean?"

"Gordy Taylor, of course." Wright stopped speaking for another long pause and then continued. "An evil man. A dangerous man." He paused. "There had been a complaint against me."

"It wasn't the first time. You had a lot to hide." Shelter said it as a fact, not a question.

"But you're still a priest," Traverse said, his voice tense with anger. "The church didn't do anything?"

"Yes, I'm still a priest. But the church has taken measures to help me with my..." he stopped to search for a word, "...personal problems."

Shelter said, "You took the girl to Winnipeg, and when the time came, you arranged the adoption to the Rempel family."

"Through the proper authorities," Wright said. "The mother and child were well taken care of."

"Earlier this month, we believe Crystal Rempel found out about her mother's rape and the circumstances of her adoption. Did she contact you in the days before her murder?"

Wright shrugged and smoothed the handkerchief on his knee. "She was irrational."

"What did she want?"

"She'd started looking into Gordy Taylor's activities on other reserves and certain business dealings that I know nothing about. She was preparing a file to take to the police."

"And you told Taylor about it?"

Wright hesitated.

"I'm sure it won't be hard to establish your contacts with Taylor through your phone records," Shelter said. "By the way, where were you the evening of July 8th?"

"I was right here, Officer, the same as every evening. I lead a quiet life."

"Did Gordy Taylor kill Crystal Rempel?"

The pale blue eyes were watery behind the lenses. The priest looked to Traverse and Shelter again. "I can't do your work for you, Detective."

Shelter considered whether to arrest Wright on the spot as an accessory to Crystal Rempel's murder. He'd tipped off Gordy Taylor to the danger Crystal Rempel posed to him, and he could do it again. On the other hand, taking him downtown would likely have the same effect — Taylor would find out within the hour.

"We'll be in touch, Mr. Wright. I'd advise you not to talk to anyone about this, especially Chief Taylor."

# THIRTY-ONE

It was almost 8:00 p.m. when Shelter climbed into the passenger seat of the Crown Victoria. He was dead tired and in need of a shower.

"Fucking little pervert," Traverse said, his features drawn into a tense frown. "He's not walking away from this. No way."

"I'm hearing you," Shelter said. "We'll deal with him once we've got Taylor off the street." After a moment, he said, "There's nothing to be done tonight. We're going to have to set up an off-site meeting tomorrow with the professional standards unit. Who's the inspector again?"

"Gary what's-his-name," Traverse said, pulling the car away from the curb. "Gary Gallagher."

"Right. Gallagher. He reports directly to Taylor, so we're going to have to be careful in laying it out for him. He'll have to bring in the Justice Department."

"Unbelievable," Traverse said.

The sun was setting as Shelter said goodnight to Traverse and slammed the car door. The smell of freshly cut grass was still in the air from his next-door neighbour's lawn. Shelter dug a handful of junk mail and a couple of bills out of the mailbox and picked the newspaper off the stairs. A teenager's ability to step over a mess and avoid even the simplest of tasks was a constant source of amazement. But he was relieved to find the door locked.

"Kelsey," he called out as he dumped his keys and phone and stripped off his blazer. He noticed none of the lights on the main floor were on. "Kelsey?"

Only Norman the cat responded to his call, rubbing against his legs for food as Shelter turned on the hall light. With all the activity, he hadn't texted his daughter all day. Upstairs, her bedroom door was open. She never left it open if she was using the room, but he checked it anyway. From the top of the stairs, he called her name again, this time louder to cover the whole house.

Descending to the kitchen, he found the sliding door to the backyard locked. There was no sign of Kelsey on the deck or in the yard. He wheeled around and headed for the door to the basement. Not bothering to throw the light switch, he descended the roughly cut staircase. In the gloom, he scanned the rec room with its old La-Z-Boy armchair and couch. He glanced at a jumble of sheets and blankets on a mattress where he or Kelsey sometimes slept to escape the summer heat and humidity. No sign of his daughter.

He climbed the stairs to the main floor in twos, pulling out his phone to text her. *Hi. I'm home now. Where r u?* As he stared at the screen, waiting for an answer, he realized the day's events had put him on edge. She was probably just at a friend's house or picking up something from the corner store. On the other hand, she could have run away again. He brought a hand to his face and rubbed stubble on his jaw and cheek as he tried to gather his thoughts. With a jolt, he remembered the dog-walking job at Gordy Taylor's house.

Now, his heart was pounding and his face grew hot. Adrenaline coursed through his body, making it hard to think clearly. She would have gone to Taylor's house in the late afternoon. Had he heard about their visit to the hockey arena on the reserve? Had the priest tipped him off? Could he be holding Kelsey? He felt panic clawing at his chest and made a conscious effort to calm himself. He punched Gordy Taylor's number into his phone. He answered on the second ring.

"I've been waiting for your call, Mike."

"I'm looking for Kelsey. Is she there?"

"Yes. She is." Taylor's words were slightly slurred and Shelter could tell he'd been drinking. "Janet's out for the evening, and I've had a busy day. So I asked Kelsey to stay for dinner and give Heidi her evening walk."

"I'm coming to get her," Shelter said, struggling to bring his breathing under control and keep an even tone.

"That's probably a good idea, Mike. We have some things to discuss. And for everyone's sake, I think it's best not to make any other calls tonight." The line went dead.

The threat was unmistakeable. It suddenly hit him Taylor might have offered Kelsey the dog-walking job as a way to keep her close to him in case he needed leverage over Shelter. He considered calling MacIsaac and getting backup at Taylor's house. But a heavy-handed response could trigger a hostage-taking situation. Shelter couldn't take that chance with Kelsey. Instead, he called Traverse and filled him in on the situation. "I'm going over there now."

"No, Mike," Traverse said. "Seriously, it's too dangerous. At least wait until I get there, and we can go together."

Traverse's farm south of the city was at least a forty-minute drive, assuming light traffic. "There's no time. I need to get her out of there now." Shelter realized how loudly he was speaking. He took a deep breath and steadied himself. In a calmer voice, he said, "Come now, Gabe. But wait outside the house where Taylor can't see you."

There was a pause. "Your daughter, your call. But I don't think you should go in there alone."

"No choice. I'll see you later, buddy."

During the familiar ten-minute drive to the Taylor's house on the other side of the river, Shelter considered how to handle him. He had to pacify Taylor, make him believe he had options, until he could get Kelsey away. He parked a short way down the deserted street and from the car examined the familiar three-storey stucco house in the dying light. The curtains were drawn and the front door closed. Shelter removed his holster from his belt, pulled out his Glock, and slid it into the waist band of his trousers, concealing it against the small of his back.

The heat and humidity were still high, and as Shelter approached the house, he felt beads of sweat running down his back. When the door swung open, Shelter found Taylor dressed in a flowered Hawaiian shirt untucked over jeans — an uncharacteristically casual outfit that made the situation all the more incongruous.

"That was fast," said a smiling Taylor, standing aside to let Shelter into the house.

Shelter smelled tobacco and alcohol as he passed the police chief. He swept his eyes over the living room. The hallway to the kitchen was in front of him. He turned to face Taylor. "Okay, where is she?"

"Oh, around here somewhere," Taylor said, raising his hands in a disarming gesture. He pushed roughly past Shelter and marched into the kitchen. Following, Shelter saw Taylor stumble as he circled the large kitchen island. On the other side, Taylor put both hands on the granite countertop to steady himself. His eyes were glazed, his face shiny with perspiration.

"We need to talk about the Crystal Rempel case," Taylor said. "You seem to be getting off on the wrong track there, Mike."

"We're not talking about anything until I get my daughter home. Where is she?"

"Stop worrying. She's watching TV."

Turning toward the front of the house, he took a step toward the kitchen door.

"Stay where you are," Taylor commanded. "I don't think you want Kelsey caught in the middle of this conversation."

Shelter wheeled to face him. His years of experience in volatile situations kicked in. He was focused, zeroed in on Taylor. Calmly and steadily, he said, "What's going on here, Gord?"

"What do you think's going on?" Taylor said, his head tilted and eyes squinting with disdain. He glanced down at his hands and released his grip on the counter. He swivelled his head so his chin was almost touching his shoulder, stretching his neck muscles. His shoulders dropped, and he bent to lean on the counter with his forearms. Shelter felt warm breeze blowing through the screen door that led to the deck attached to the back of the house. It was now almost completely dark outside. When Taylor spoke, the smile and lighter tone had returned.

"I hear you and that Indian girl took off from Lone Pine in a hurry this afternoon. Then I get a panicky call from Father Wright. He's worried about some of the accusations you're making. Accusations about him..." Taylor's smile fell away from his face. "And about me."

"I can't discuss an investigation here like this. You know that."

"I'm the chief of police, for fuck's sake. You can and will discuss the investigation with me."

The way Taylor was leaning, Shelter noticed for the first time a bulge at his hip under his shirt.

"Now, what do you think you've found?"

"Tell me where Kelsey is before this goes any further." Shelter kept his voice even. If Kelsey was in the house, why hadn't she heard him arguing with Taylor? Maybe she had headphones in or was somewhere upstairs in the large house, far away from the kitchen. Or maybe Taylor had her gagged and restrained.

"How about a drink?" Taylor said.

"It's not the time."

"Come on. It's always the time. Don't worry about your girl. She's fine."

The kitchen gave onto the dining room, and Taylor strode to a liquor cabinet in the far corner. He pulled out a bottle of Johnny Walker Black and a couple of tumblers and poured two hefty shots. He downed his in a gulp. He offered the other glass to Shelter.

"No."

"Have a drink. That's an order," Taylor said with a mirthless laugh as he refilled his glass.

He took another slug, turned his head and wiped his lips on the shoulder of his shirt, a coarse gesture. Shelter had never seen him act this way.

"Gordy…"

"Shut up! Now tell me your theory about the case."

Shelter shook his head. "I really don't think you…"

"I said shut up." Taylor took another gulp of whiskey. "Now, tell me your theory. Wait, I'll go first. That disgusting pig of a priest told you I made him bring an Indian girl down here to get rid of her kid."

Shelter remained silent, watching the police chief's movements closely. Taylor was losing control, and there was no way to know how far he would take it.

"Then what happened?" Taylor asked. "Still don't want to tell me? Okay. Next, your theory is that Crystal Rempel found out about it and came after me. And I killed her to keep her quiet."

Taylor looked to the ceiling as he fumbled in his pants pocket before bringing out a pack of cigarettes and lighting one. "How could you fall for this shit, Mike? Think about it. It was the priest who brought the girl down to Winnipeg. Why? Because he was the one who knocked her up." He took a deep drag from his cigarette, eyeing Shelter for his reaction. "You thought he was into little boys?" He let out a harsh bark of laughter. "That's your prejudice coming out. It's teenage girls he likes. When Crystal Rempel started snooping around, making wild accusations about what happened thirty years ago, Wright must have panicked and killed her."

"If you suspected him of killing her, why didn't you report it?"

"I'm telling you now. I only put it all together myself when he phoned tonight. He wanted me to stop you, and that's when I knew it was him."

"He called a police officer to save him from another police officer?"

"He's in a panic. He thought I'd help him."

Shelter considered Taylor. What he was saying made no sense. It was a wild attempt to save himself. Shelter had seen other offenders come up with similar outlandish stories when they were tied up in knots by their own lies. It was a Hail Mary pass. But Shelter had no choice but to play it out with him until he could get Kelsey from the house safely.

"Whoever killed Crystal Rempel knew the details of the Monica Spence murder — how her body was wrapped. Those details were never released to the public."

"He could have found out from someone on the force," Taylor said, circling Shelter to toss his cigarette into the kitchen sink. "Hell, maybe I mentioned it to him. I've been drinking more than usual these days."

Taylor's story was coming apart even as they spoke. Shelter knew if the forensics unit started working on his car, house and phone records, it wouldn't take long to put the pieces together.

"It's time for us to leave," Shelter said, taking a step toward the chief. "Just take me to Kelsey, and we will pick this up tomorrow."

Taylor put up a hand to stop him. "I need to hear you're going after the right guy on this."

"We're going to look at it from every angle."

Taylor glared at Shelter, his chest rising and falling with laboured breaths. He finished his drink. His cheeks were flushed, and he looked like he was making a decision. He dropped his hand to his hip.

"No!" Shelter hissed.

But it was too late. Taylor pulled his gun and pointed it at Shelter. "You fucking bastard. After all I've done for you."

"Put it down." Shelter couldn't reach for his own gun, and the door to the hallway was a good three steps from where he was standing. His only option was to keep him talking.

Taylor waved the gun. "Move to that corner. Now!"

Shelter glanced to where Taylor was motioning and saw a door that he knew led to the basement stairs. When he had moved, Shelter watched as Taylor lowered a blind to cover the window over the sink. Could he rush him while he was distracted?

At that moment, Shelter sensed movement on the deck outside the screen door. He shifted his eyes to the door without turning his head but could see only blackness. Could it be Traverse? Not enough time had passed from him to have reached the house. His mind must be playing tricks on him.

Taylor turned back from the window and took aim again at Shelter's chest.

"This has gone far enough," Shelter said.

"I need twelve hours to get out of the country." Taylor's eyes were red-rimmed, and his breathing was coming in puffs. "You armed?" Without waiting for an answer, he issued orders in a firm but steady voice — the old cop giving instructions to an offender. "Using two fingers, slowly take it out and put it on the counter."

Shelter reached to his back. He flipped the safety off the pistol so it was ready to fire before using his thumb and index fingers to place it on the granite counter.

"Push it over here."

Shelter gave the gun a hard shove, and it slid across the counter, coming to rest near the edge where Taylor stood. Now, he had to hope Traverse would ignore his instructions to stay away from the house and sneak around the back to investigate what was happening inside. That meant he needed to keep Taylor talking. "Tell me how it happened. Help me understand."

"In the basement," Taylor said, waving the gun toward the door in the corner.

"Ted Wright told you Crystal was preparing to turn you in, and you contacted her. She accused you of raping Anne Alexander on the reserve."

"Rape! The girl wanted it." Taylor gave his head a violent shake. "That Rempel bitch was crazy, out of her mind. She said she was going to the media. All that rape bullshit and threatening to expose my business dealings."

His business dealings? It only took a moment before Shelter had it. "The land deal downtown."

Taylor shrugged. "A little introduction, a little persuasion, and I'm set for a golden retirement."

"You introduced Bill Craig to Charlie Osborne, and they cut you in on a kickback," Shelter said. "You were the other man at the Bond Hotel."

"Bringing hookers and that little pimp into a room with the chief of police." Taylor shook his head at the memory.

"What about Rory Sinclair? You tried to frame him for Crystal's murder, but he figured it out. He was going to tell us you were in that hotel room."

"He got what he deserved," Taylor sneered.

"Did Charlie Osborne know about you and Anne Alexander, about the baby? Does he know what you did to Crystal?"

Taylor gave a loud, exasperated sigh. "Don't be stupid. Of course not."

Shelter saw how it had happened. Taylor had called Crystal and gave her the same story he'd just given him — accused the priest of raping Anne. It went against what her grandmother had told her, but he could have sown enough doubt in her mind to get her to meet him. From there it was a matter of picking her up outside the hotel that night and driving her to this house. Shelter felt his pulse racing and struggled to remain calm and focused.

"I don't know how you could have done it," Shelter said.

Taylor gave a dismissive shrug.

"You killed your own damn daughter."

A look of confusion came over Taylor's face. "What are you

talking about?" He looked shocked, bewildered. The gun drifted lower, and he raised his free hand to his jaw.

"Oh my God," Shelter said in a low voice. "You didn't know Crystal was Anne's daughter? *Your* daughter? Crystal didn't tell you?" Shelter paused a second for it to fully sink in and then ordered, "Gordy, put the gun down. It's over."

Taylor jerked, as if he'd been slapped. He raised the gun. "Nothing is over. Get down the stairs," he said, waving the gun toward the door.

"You know DNA is going to tell the story. There's no escaping it. You killed your own daughter."

"I said get down those fucking stairs. Now!"

Shelter turned and took a step toward the door to the basement stairs when he heard a sound from below. He felt his heart jump to his throat. There was someone on the stairs.

# THIRTY-TWO

Shelter pulled the door open and found himself looking into Kelsey's terrified eyes. She raised a trembling hand to shade her eyes from the overhead light. Shelter saw her look toward Taylor and the gun pointing at them.

"Dad!"

"Kelsey. Get back!" Shelter shouted. The girl jerked in shock.

But Taylor crossed the room with surprising agility. He shouldered Shelter out of the way and grabbed the teenager by the neck. He stepped back to the other side of the island, drawing Kelsey to his chest. He gripped her tight with his left arm across her shoulders.

Shelter took a step toward them before Taylor raised the gun and shouted, "Stop!" Kelsey must have been in the basement rec room, came up to investigate the noise, and been eavesdropping on the staircase. Now she was frantic with fear. "What's going on?" she said, her voice high-pitched and cracking.

"Shut up!" Taylor gave her a hard tug that made her head snap, sending blond hair flying into her eyes.

"Let her go!" Shelter shouted. "She's got nothing to do with this." Kelsey's panicked eyes searched her father's face for some clue about what was going to happen. A tear rolled down her cheek, and she let out a high-pitched squeal from deep in her throat.

Taylor waved the pistol at Shelter. "Downstairs. Move it. Now!"

Now Shelter was certain Taylor wanted them in the basement to muffle the gunshots and conceal the bloody mess. He had to rush him and hope Kelsey could get to the hall and out the front door.

He took two steps toward the basement door and then stopped and looked across the kitchen. "Please, let her go."

In a quick movement, Taylor put the pistol to Kelsey's temple. "I'll blow her fucking head off if you don't get down those stairs."

Shelter glimpsed a flash of movement behind Taylor. Snapping his head toward it, he saw a figure crash through the screen door. It was Nicki. She grabbed Shelter's gun from the counter where he'd pushed it. Taylor turned in shock and pointed his gun at her, but before he could fire, Shelter slammed into him and Kelsey.

Taylor lurched backward into a wall, releasing Kelsey. She dropped to the floor just as Shelter leaped again at Taylor. Shelter got one arm around his left shoulder and the other on his right wrist above the gun. Nicki was holding the Glock with both hands and circling the men. Taylor struggled to get his arm free, and his gun moved toward Nicki. She jumped back as it went off with a deafening explosion. The window shattered, and the air filled with the stench of gunpowder.

Taylor roared and wrenched his shoulder hard, loosening Shelter's grip on him. He swung his hand and caught Shelter under the chin with the butt of the gun, throwing him back against the fridge. Shelter slid to the floor, blood dripping from a deep cut in his chin. He glimpsed Taylor's gun swinging toward him. With a scream, Nicki tackled Taylor just as he pulled the trigger, sending a bullet into the fridge, inches from Shelter's head.

Taylor threw Nicki to the floor. She slid hard across the smooth surface, hitting the cupboard under the sink with a loud bang. Shelter's gun flew out of her hand and skittered across the floor. She frantically kicked herself behind the island. Taylor circled to get her in his sights. His gun exploded again, but Nicki had rolled. Chips of tile flew into the air beside her. Taylor rocked to his side, trying to get another shot.

Shelter scrambled on his knees to grab his gun from the floor.

With one movement, he stood and levelled the gun. Taylor turned and swung his gun toward him. Shelter fired twice, and both rounds hit the police chief in the chest, throwing him back against the sink. He slid to the floor.

"Oh, God!" screamed Nicki. Blood spurted from Taylor's wounds. Where he lay, a growing pool of crimson blood made a grotesque contrast with his snow-white hair. His eyes were open and his mouth gaped. He was trying to draw breath like a fish pulled from water. Shelter, trying to catch his breath, picked up Taylor's gun as he took his last breath.

Nicki was sobbing, huddled on the floor. Shelter went to her and helped her to her feet. It was the sound of sirens that brought him back to the moment. "Kelsey!" His daughter had disappeared.

He charged into the hallway to find Traverse barging through the front door, his gun drawn. The two partners pulled up at the sight of each other, both of them breathing hard. "Where's Kelsey?" Shelter shouted.

"She's okay. Outside."

"Taylor's dead. Help Nicki."

Shelter raced outside and down the front steps. Sirens were growing louder in the darkness. Groups of neighbours peered from their porches. He jumped to the sidewalk and ran into the street, searching the faces. He spotted Kelsey on a staircase across the street, surrounded by a neighbour's family. He met her on the sidewalk under an enormous elm tree. He took her in his arms and squeezed her as she wept for a long minute. When he opened his eyes, he saw Nicki watching them. He released Kelsey and hugged Nicki in the flashing light thrown by the police cruisers.

When they broke apart, Shelter nodded to Traverse, who was watching from a few metres away. He turned back to Nicki. "What were you doing there?"

"I followed him from downtown when he left work. I wanted to know what he was up to. And I didn't want him getting away."

"Followed him? How?"

"In Crystal's car. I got it back from you guys the other day."

"And he led you here."

"I saw you go in, and when you didn't come out, I knew something was up. I went around the back and saw you fighting with him."

Shelter thought about that for a second, looking into her eyes. Her black hair glowed under the streetlight, and she had her arms wrapped around herself. A grin spread across his face.

"What?"

"You're unbelievable."

# THIRTY-THREE

Shelter and Traverse sat in MacIsaac's office, waiting for their boss to return from a senior management meeting upstairs. It had been three days since Taylor's body had been taken out of his house, and Father Ted Wright had been arrested. "I'm taking a couple of weeks off," Shelter said. "Heading up to the lake with Kelsey." Traverse nodded without looking over.

Shelter was exhausted. Between the media storm, hours of questioning by investigators and making sure Kelsey was okay, he'd barely had time to think about what it would all mean for his and Traverse's careers. Would they be rewarded for exposing Taylor? Or would their careers be blighted for the embarrassment the department had suffered?

Sitting side-by-side with Traverse in the late afternoon gloom, his thoughts turned to his partner's future. Shelter knew the city would see no respite from the violence, the killing in the months and years ahead, and he needed Traverse for both his skills and his calm head. Was he still determined to quit? Shelter wasn't sure where they stood after the fight over Nicki but decided to go straight at the subject; Traverse was too smart not to detect a subtler approach.

"So, what are your plans? You still thinking of leaving?"

"I talked it over with Janice, and she says I'm going to be miserable if I quit. Can't say I disagree. I'm going to let it ride and see how it goes."

"That's good, I'm happy."

"I'm happy you're happy."

Shelter glanced at him again and couldn't help but smile.

"You've seen Nicki since the other night?" Traverse asked.

"I'm going to the bar when we're done here."

Traverse finally looked him in the eyes, but Shelter couldn't read what he was thinking.

At that moment, MacIsaac entered the office and snapped on the lights. When he was seated, he looked from Shelter to Traverse. "The Mounties are setting up a special unit to go through Taylor and Wright's years up north to see if we can match them to any other sexual assaults or homicides." He turned over a piece of paper on his desk and examined it before continuing. "The commercial crimes division is looking at Bill Craig, Charlie Osborne and the urban reserve project. So we'll see where that goes."

"Any word on a new chief?" Shelter asked.

"They've put the search on ice for six months until all this blows over." He looked at Traverse. "Mike's taking a couple of weeks off. You should take the rest of the week off too."

"What happens when we get back?" Traverse asked.

"What do you mean what happens? You get back to work." He paused and looked from Traverse to Shelter. "I've put you both in for commendations. That was a hell of a job you did. Now get out of here."

Nicki slid into the booth across from Shelter in the coffee shop at the City Hotel.

"How you doing?" she asked.

"Well, I got this," he said, pointing to a row of stitches on the underside of his chin. "How about you?"

"I'm still sore but okay."

He shifted on his chair and smiled. "You're quite a TV star. I saw your interview on *The National*."

Nicki rolled her eyes and gave Shelter a shy smile. "I'm getting a lot of action about it in there," she said with a nod toward the bar.

Shelter smiled, and then turning serious, he said, "I wanted to thank you again."

"Forget it."

"I won't forget it, ever."

Shelter was surprised to see her react with what seemed to be embarrassment. She dropped her head, and he thought he detected a blush on her cheeks. He lowered his eyes too and focused on the silver bangles on her wrist and rings on her hand wrapped around her coffee cup. "I'll always be grateful for what you did for Crystal," she said finally.

"You did quite a bit yourself. You're going to leave the policing to us from now on, right?"

Looking up, she said, "Um. I thought I told you...

"No one tells you what to do. Yeah, I got that." They both laughed.

In that moment he sensed his feelings for her deepen. But he'd already given in to an idea that had been building inside him — their worlds were too far apart ever to be bridged in a relationship. Still, he wanted to leave the door open to seeing her again. An offer of a coffee in a few weeks time, perhaps. But as he tried to formulate the sentence in his mind, he knew it would be crossing a line. It would make it real and force her to make a decision.

He looked into her eyes, noticing once again how large they were and for the first time how long her lashes were. He became aware of her perfume, exotic and intoxicating. Patchouli? Is that what it was called? "Give yourself some time, okay? You've been through a lot."

She nodded and bowed her head, keeping eye contact with him through her bangs with a bashful grin. From her expression, he sensed she'd long since intuited his feelings for her. That didn't surprise him. Women were so much better at reading feelings than men. What he still couldn't tell and wouldn't ask was whether she felt the same for him. "You take care too," she said.

He got up, picked up his jacket, reached for her hand, and held it tight. "You know where to find me."

Shelter and Kelsey walked on the wide crescent of beach in shorts and bare feet, their flip-flops in their hands. The grey lake extended to the horizon, the morning sun glinting off the waves. The view was broken by a single sailboat tacking to the north in a warm, light breeze. That morning, Shelter had awoken groggy in his in-laws' house in Gimli after ten hours of sleep. His mind had cleared after a coffee, and when Kelsey got up, Shelter had invited her for a walk.

He'd driven her up to Gimli the afternoon before and had planned to discuss where she was going to go to school in the fall. He'd read somewhere a car ride was a good time to have a serious talk with a teenager. You had a captive audience and sitting side-by-side was less threatening for the kid than a face-to-face discussion. But he'd been dead tired and sensed she was concerned about seeing her grandparents for the first time since she'd run away with James. She'd jiggled a leg and was unusually quiet. "You don't have to worry about Grandma and Grandpa," he said. "They're just happy you're safe."

"I know that." She'd said it without rancour. She seemed calmer, more reflective. Had the events of the last week matured her, or was she just getting older?

Now, alone on the beach, he was ready to talk to her about the fall.

"Kel, I want you with me in Winnipeg."

"I *am* in Winnipeg."

"Yeah, but you were talking about staying up here."

She gave him a quick glance and smirked, as if to say *how can adults be so dense.* "That's when I wanted to be with James."

"Okay. Right. So you want to go to school in Winnipeg?" Still smiling, she nodded.

He felt a flash of relief. He'd hated the thought of only seeing her on weekends during the long winter, and even after that when the fishing season kicked in again. "I know it won't be easy, but together we can work it out."

"We'll be fine." It was that new, more mature voice again. They'd already talked about what had happened at Taylor's house that night. He'd told her how strong she'd been and how proud of her he was. They climbed onto the long concrete pier that protected the harbour and walked past a couple of old-timers tending fishing rods. They stopped to examine murals painted on the seawall, depicting scenes from the town's history. Screaming gulls circled overhead. When they reached the far end of the pier, they stopped and leaned against the seawall, looking over the lake, where you could just make out the eastern shore.

"I know I wasn't there for you when Mom was sick, and since then," Shelter said. "I'm sorry. I'll do better."

"Don't say you're sorry, Daddy." She hadn't called him that in years. "I haven't been easy on you."

He was overcome with tenderness for her. He took her in his arms and squeezed hard. After a time, they turned back toward town, walking arm-in-arm in silence. Shelter thought about the years to come — Kelsey finishing high school, going to university and hopefully settling down with someone she loved and becoming a parent herself. He'd made mistakes with her, but there was still time to make up for them. He closed his eyes for a second, and when he opened them, he followed the sailboat now heading back to port, lovely in the sunshine and breeze, and thought of nothing else.

# ACKNOWLEDGEMENTS

The writing of *Omand's Creek* has been a long, often rewarding, sometimes maddening journey. I'm indebted to so many people for their kind and generous assistance along the way.

I am grateful to the organizations and talented authors that have supported me in my efforts to learn the craft of fiction and novel writing. At the wonderful Quebec Writers' Federation, I appreciated the guidance of Claire Holden Rothman, Peter Kirby and fellow participants in writing seminars. I am grateful to the Banff Centre for my place in the inaugural Crime Writing Residency, where I learned so much from Michael Robotham and Louise Welsh. I have received continuing and deeply appreciated support from my fellow course participants and now friends, Paddy Hirsch, Kim Murray, Hope Thompson, Sandy Conrad, Marie Fontaine and Tony Berry.

I would not have been able to write this novel without technical guidance from experts in Manitoba who were remarkably kind and patient in answering my questions. An early and ongoing source of information about homicide investigations and the Winnipeg Police Service was James Jewell. David Buck helped me understand the workings of the police service's Forensic Identification Unit. Dr. Peter Markesteyn, Manitoba's former Chief Medical Examiner, was an excellent source of information on forensic autopsies. Bruce Benson answered my questions about commercial fishing on Lake Winnipeg. Shayla Elizabeth brought an intelligent, caring eye to the manuscript.

My thanks to the friends and colleagues who took the time to read and comment on the manuscript at various stages. Thanks to Jamie Orchard and Jean-Luc Boulch for your support and friendship. My poker buddies, Bryan Demchinsky, Joel Yanofsky and Mark Abley were there for me with comments, advice and support. Michelle Lalonde has also been a great source of advice and support. I appreciated the notes, comments and advice I received from Jennifer DeLeskie, Keiran Gibbs, David Lemay and Denis Coupal. Besides his insightful comments and encouragement, Yutaka Dirks told me about the Crime Writers of Canada awards. My thanks to my friend Alina Pahoncia for her support. My thanks to my friends Richard Schultz, Jonathan Cote and Steve Vincent. A special shout-out to Linda Vincent for her care and diligence in reviewing and commenting on the manuscript. Thanks to Alastair Gillespie. Also, my thanks to my friend Jeff O'Malley for reading the manuscript and offering his comments and insights.

Finally, all my thanks and love to my family — Catherine, Julia, Alex and Barbara.

Any errors or oversights are my sole responsibility.

## ABOUT THE AUTHOR

Don Macdonald was born and raised in Winnipeg, Manitoba and now lives in Montreal. He worked for over twenty years as a print journalist. *Omand's Creek*, his first novel, was a finalist for the Crime Writers of Canada's award for Best Unpublished Manuscript. To learn more about Don and *Omand's Creek*, please visit donmacdonald.ca.

Made in the USA
Coppell, TX
29 January 2021